WHEN
SOMEONE
LOVES YOU

WHEN SOMEONE LOVES YOU

Susan Johnson

BRAVA

KENSINGTON PUBLISHING CORP.
http://www.kensingtonbooks.com

BRAVA BOOKS are published by

Kensington Publishing Corp.
850 Third Avenue
New York, NY 10022

All Kensington titles, imprints and distributed lines are available at special quantity discounts for bulk purchases for sales promotion, premi-
ums, fund-raising, educational or institutional use.

Special book excerpts or customized printings can also be created to fit
specific needs. For details, write or phone the office of the Kensington
Special Sales Manager: Kensington Publishing Corp., 850 Third Avenue,
New York, NY 10022. Attn. Special Sales Department. Phone: 1-800-221-
2647.

Brava and the B logo Reg. U.S. Pat. & TM Off.

ISBN 0-7582-0939-8

First Kensington Trade Paperback Printing: August 2006
10 9 8 7 6 5 4 3 2 1

Printed in the United States of America

WHEN SOMEONE LOVES YOU

Chapter

1

London, June 1816

It was the height of the season and the crush at Brooks's Club was to be expected. The hour was late—another reason for the crowd. Those gentlemen who had been obliged to attend society dinners and routs had finally escaped to their masculine sanctum sanctorum where they could indulge in high-stakes gambling and heavy drink without stricture or reproach.

Not that gentlemen who were privileged enough to be members of Brooks's felt the sting of censure to the same degree that others might. And yet, their snug, sheltered male enclave offered them *je ne sais quoi*—an indescribable something.

Exclusivity, certainly.

A free-and-easy bonhomie with one's equals.

Perhaps most prized—deliverance from female company.

Not that females weren't often the topic of conversation in terms of women they wished to bed, those they had, or those considered unattainable. The last category, of course, was always open to debate.

Wives were rarely discussed—actually, never . . . save for brief references to their ability to produce heirs on those occasions when they did. It was an exclusive men's club, after all; everyone understood the reasons for marriage.

And it wasn't love.

Noblemen, married or not, were an independent lot—their interests primarily centered around gambling, horses, and sex—the latter, preferably *not* with their wives.

The woman currently under discussion at the gaming table was equally independent. A woman of great beauty, the object of every male fantasy, Annabelle Foster came by her self-reliance honestly.

She'd earned it.

And in an age that gave women few freedoms and fewer rights, it was an accomplishment of some import.

Miss Foster had first burst onto the scene in her role as Nelly Primrose in *The False Friend* and had become an instant star. Her performances were always sold out, generating such colossal profits for the Drury Lane Theater, she was soon in the position to have her initial contract revised. She wrote plays, you see, and she wished them performed.

Under her new contract they were performed—to universal praise.

Lauded by critics, the darling of society, her face and form depicted by every prominent portrait painter in England— Lawrence's portrayal best capturing her pale, ethereal beauty— she had recently and abruptly disappeared. Not just from the stage and London, but, rumor had it, from England.

"She's dropped off the face of the earth," the Earl of Minto noted with a raised brow. "And that's a fact. Just ask Walingame. He's practically turned the country upside down searching for her."

"She apparently don't wish to be found," young Baron Verney murmured, arranging the large pile of markers before him into neat stacks.

"At least not by Walingame. Not that I blame her. The man's a despot. A woman like the beguiling Belle requires a lighter rein." Lord Bynge lifted his glass. "To the fair lady. May she stay in seclusion until I have the good fortune to sniff her out myself."

A loud guffaw echoed round the table at the double entendre.

"May we all be so lucky." Minto raised his claret glass. "I hear she can make a man forget everything but fornication the moment he crosses the threshold of her boudoir."

"Paget wasn't seen for a week once."

"Nor Whyte."

"While Somerville took to writing bad poetry after she grew bored of him." The man who spoke was near to being designated a Macaroni, with his lavishly tied neck cloth and outrageous display of diamonds and lace.

"Then Walingame returned to London from his father's deathbed and exerted some strange authority over her," Lord Bynge noted with a slight frown.

One of the men looked up from his cards. "I never did understand why she suffered him or his temper. She could have had her pick of suitors."

"Something to do with a contract she'd signed with a money lender when she was very young, I heard." A flash of the erstwhile Macaroni's diamond rings added emphasis to the comment.

"A wily solicitor couldn't handle that for her?" Minto charged.

A diamond-ringed finger touched an arched eyebrow. "Apparently not. Walingame bought the note from the money lender—for a considerable sum, rumor has it. And the lovely Miss Foster became his indentured servant, as it were."

"Surely she's made her own fortune on the stage many times over."

"She has family somewhere that requires support." Another dismissive wave of the be-ringed hand. "Don't all these actresses come from the distant bogs of Ireland?"

"Not our charming Belle," Bynge affirmed. "She's a pure English rose."

"Pure, I doubt. English, possibly, but gentlemen," Baron

Verney said with a smile, "since none of us are going to bed the lovely Miss Foster this evening, I suggest we get on with our game." His smile widened. "Especially since I seem to be winning all your money tonight."

A low groan greeted his cheerful assessment of his good fortune and the men set their minds to more immediate and important matters.

Like winning their money back.

Chapter
2

The next day, the lady who had been under discussion at Brooks was sitting on a blanket in a small cottage garden, a plump baby beside her, the summer sun bathing them both in its warm rays.

"There, there, little one," she crooned, stroking the pumping arms and legs. "Your wet nurse will be out soon. She needs to finish her luncheon, sweetling, so she can keep you fed." And so saying, she picked up the baby, whose little face had puckered up in preparation for a full-blown cry. "Come, darling, let's walk a bit."

Annabelle moved through the colorful garden, rocking the baby gently in her arms, singing to her softly, soothing the fretting child with an expertise acquired by necessity the last few months.

In short order the young wet nurse appeared in the doorway of the cottage, smiling and holding her arms out for the baby. "I heard your fretting, Cricket, and I came a-runnin'. Give her here, my lady, and we'll see that she's got a full tummy right quick."

As Annabelle relinquished the child, she smiled at the young girl they'd been so fortunate to have hired. She was good-natured and cheerful, healthy and robust enough to feed both her own child as well as little Cricket. "Sit by the pear tree if you wish," she offered. "The sun is delightful today."

"Ain't it just, miss. Warm as can be, it is. If'n you'd see that Betty is brung out to me if'n she wakes, I'd be much obliged."

"Of course. Would you like me to bring her out and set her basket next to you?"

"Yes'um, if you please, miss." Molly Whitmore dipped a faint curtsy, in awe of the beautiful Miss Foster who was not only the prettiest lady she'd ever seen, but was paying her so generously that she and her beau, Tom, would soon be able to marry and buy a little farm of their own.

After carrying out Betty, who was sleeping peacefully in her basket, Annabelle brought out Cricket's basket as well and placed it near Molly. "I'll be inside with my mother, but call me if you need anything."

"Don't you worry none, miss. I'm fine with both the bairns. You should rest a bit, mayhap. You were up most of the night."

Annabelle smiled. "Perhaps I will."

But regardless she'd been up late, taking advantage of the quiet to work on her new play, she knew a nap wasn't possible. Her mother required attention as well. The death of her sister, Chloe, had affected her mind.

"Would you like a cup of tea, Mama?" Annabelle asked, as she entered the small cottage.

Her mother looked up from her sewing. "At least we have Cricket," she said, as though she hadn't heard Annabelle.

"Yes, Mama, and she's plump and healthy. We have to be grateful for that."

"I wish we could make those Harrisons pay."

It was a grim, cold statement that had been issued a thousand times over since Annabelle had come home to take care of her mother and Chloe's baby. "We have to think about Chloe's daughter first, Mama. She's more important than the Harrisons right now."

"Promise me you'll get us vengeance some day."

Annabelle answered as she had so many times before. "I promise, Mama."

"On God's eyes, Belle. Promise me."

"Yes, Mama. On God's eyes." Moving toward her mother, she bent down and wiped away the tears streaming down her mother's cheeks. "Let me get you a nice cup of tea, Mama. With a slice of poppy cake. Then you can show me what you're sewing for little Cricket and we'll decide what we need from the greengrocer and butcher today."

Annabelle had come home the instant she'd received news of her sister Chloe's disastrous situation. She'd chosen not to leave word of her whereabouts, knowing her life would be in flux for the immediate future at least. She wished no interference in private family matters. She particularly wished no interference from Walingame, who had become so difficult before she left that she'd broken with him despite his dire threats of retaliation.

And she wasn't without sympathy for her mother's wish for vengeance. She, too, wanted to punish the Harrisons for the brutality and torment they'd inflicted on her sister. They'd made her sister's brief married life a living hell.

With the dream of giving Chloe the respectability she, herself, would never have, through hard work and good fortune, Annabelle had been able to settle a considerable dowry on her sister. Had she been aware of the Harrisons' base and venal motives, she would have stopped the marriage, no matter the scandal or loss of dowry. But she hadn't known, no more than Chloe had, and only too late did she discover that her young sister had been deceived and was being kept in virtual captivity.

She'd immediately gone to her rescue, securing a prominent barrister and Bow Street Runners to free Chloe from her prison and warders. But Chloe's health had been seriously compromised by her cruel incarceration in the Harrisons' attic, and only days after returning home, her sister had gone into premature labor.

Young, sweet Chloe had died without ever seeing her daughter, too weak at the end to open her eyes.

It had been a miracle that little Celia had survived.

And now the child was Annabelle's responsibility.

As was her mother, who had become unbalanced at Chloe's death. Hopefully, her mother's disordered spirits would be restored soon, although Chloe's death could never be forgotten—by either of them. It had been so senseless, such a waste of a glowing young life.

Annabelle had chastised herself a thousand times since, telling herself she should have known better. Having been the sole source of income for her family since her father's death, who better than she understood the cruelty and malice of the world? But Chloe had been so in love, Belle had allowed herself to be drawn into her sister's happy illusions and been momentarily blinded to reality.

But never again.

The lesson of Chloe's unimaginable suffering and death was seared on her soul.

She would never be so credulous again.

But questions of trust or even justice for Chloe were of no interest to her at the moment. She had more pressing, immediate issues to deal with. She had to see that little Cricket continued to thrive. She desperately hoped to see her mother rally and be her old self again. And always—she must remain vigilant against Walingame's pursuit.

She was under no illusions that he would allow her to walk away.

Chapter

3

As the month of June advanced in the small, sequestered hamlet far from the busy thoroughfares of the world, a short distance from Annabelle's cottage, a young man of high station was living an equally reclusive life.

Murray D'Abernon, thirteenth Marquis of Darley, known far and wide as Duff for his dark hair and swarthy complexion, was rusticating at his family's seat.

He'd come back from the Battle of Waterloo more dead than alive.

And profoundly changed by all he'd experienced.

Even after most of his wounds had healed and his health had improved, he'd eschewed his friends and familiar haunts in London. Nor could he be coaxed or cajoled into rejoining the licentious brotherhood of his past, no matter how enticing the offered lures.

After a time, his family and friends had given up trying to convince him to return to his previous pleasures, and he'd taken up residence in a small hunting lodge on the estate with only his batman for company.

Whatever scars he bore from the Peninsula Campaign, and the last, bloody battle between Napoleon and those nations arrayed against the once-most-powerful man in Europe, remained. He seldom smiled. He spoke little. He kept to himself as much as possible.

His parents worried, but held their counsel. His siblings had teased him at first, before realizing no amount of teasing altered the emptiness of his gaze. They all treated him like a wounded animal after that until he'd abruptly said at dinner one night, "You needn't tiptoe around me like I'm an invalid. I'm fine."

No one dared say he wasn't. Everyone tried to behave normally in his presence.

But Duff spent more and more time with his horses; his favorite, Romulus, was only one of a string of ponies he'd carried with him through the campaigns in Spain and Europe. There were times when he even slept in the stables, as though only in the company of those brute creatures, who had seen all that he had, could he find a measure of peace.

And so his monkish hermitage continued until one day, because of his cardinal interest in horses, the marquis met Annabelle Foster.

They were both at a horse fair in a nearby village.

They were both bidding on the same pretty mare out of the legendary Gimcrack's bloodlines.

He recognized her immediately. Who in England wouldn't? She was the leading lady of Drury Lane Theater, as well as a celebrated playwright—and the reigning beauty of the day.

She glanced over and smiled at Duff as he raised her bid. Then she raised hers by a substantial enough amount to bring a gasp from the crowd.

He dipped his head faintly in acknowledgment and doubled her raise.

She dropped out after that; a man like Darley could buy and sell her a thousand times over.

Consider her surprise, then, when the next morning, the mare was delivered to her mother's cottage by a liveried groom. She was handed the reins and a brief note. *My compliments on your good taste. Please accept this small gift as a token of my esteem.* It was signed, simply, *Darley*.

Annabelle's surprise was nothing compared to that of Duff's family, who were apprised of the transaction by the stable master, who was vastly disappointed at the loss of the mare. On the other hand, he explained to the duke, "The marquis done look a bit like he did in the past. You ken—with that light in his eyes anent a purty woman. So it ain't all bad, I reckon, that he didn't get that there mare."

"Indeed not," the Duke of Westerlands replied, immensely gratified. "Thank you for informing us."

"My pleasure, sar. And Miss Foster be right purty, the groom tells me."

"Yes, she is. Very beautiful." Julius had seen Miss Foster on the stage on many occasions, her beauty and poise, not to mention her acting skills, superb. "I shall inform his mother immediately. She's been worried."

"As have we all, Your Grace. The young lord ain't been the same since he come back."

Julius smiled. "A love affair might be just what he needs to bring him around."

"Aye. And the lady kept the mare, me lord." The wiry, middle-aged man winked. "That be a good sign, I'd say."

In the meantime, more realistic about the implications surrounding the expensive present she'd received, Annabelle sat down to write a note to the marquis. She thanked him for his gift but politely refused it. She couldn't keep so valuable a horse, she said, thanking him nevertheless for his thoughtfulness. And then she sent the mare back with Molly's beau, Tom.

Annabelle had no intention of entering into a liaison at the moment—and in her milieu, with a gift of such magnitude, a resulting quid pro quo was taken for granted. Society viewed actresses as little more than courtesans, albeit of a certain more lofty type. And while Annabelle had a very different opinion of herself, she was well aware of the commonly held characterization.

Chapter

4

Duff accepted his congé with mixed feelings. The mare was a beauty. He couldn't in all honesty be displeased to have it back. He even understood that Miss Foster's politely worded rebuff had less to do with him than with the expectations such a gift engendered.

He could have written back and explained to her the mare had been offered without ulterior designs. But they both knew no matter how courteously he defined his motives, she might not believe him. She wasn't a novice in the deceit and guile of the fashionable world.

Nor was he.

He understood her demur.

But that night, his usual nightmares were tempered by pleasing and reoccurring images of the lovely Miss Foster, her pale, blond beauty gliding in and out of the scenes of bloody carnage that normally disturbed his sleep. Her sublime radiance, in fact, largely superseded the grotesque montages of suffering that had so long held him in their grip.

When he woke, the morning sun colored the horizon rosy peach, the birds were singing in joyful chorus, and the smell of coffee and bacon wafted its way upstairs from the kitchen below, tempting his appetite. Stretching lazily, he gazed out on the bright summer day and experienced a feeling of well-being for the first time—since . . . he couldn't remember when. Even his damaged hip didn't ache with its usual intensity. A smile slowly played over his mouth. Perhaps miracles did exist and Eddie's rough field surgery was finally healing. Pushing aside his covers, he rose from his bed with a new sense of purpose.

He even glanced at his wardrobe with more than mere function in mind, selecting a new riding coat his mother had sent over. He smiled again, knowing his mother had hoped this new garment from his tailor would catch his fancy. The coat was an exquisite shade of sage green linen lined with buff striped silk, the buttons inlaid pear wood—a splendid sight, he had to admit. And it fit to perfection, even with his weight loss, thanks to his mother's eye and his tailor's expertise.

His good spirits must have been obvious, for Eddie smiled as Duff entered the kitchen. "Don't you look fine this mornin', sar."

"It's the new coat. Weston did his usual good work." The marquis picked up the coffeepot sitting on the sideboard and moved toward the table in the center of the kitchen. "Breakfast smells good. I'm hungry."

Eddie suppressed his surprise. Darley's appetite had been touchy at best, his breakfast usually consisting of coffee and little else.

Taking a seat at the table, the marquis casually remarked, "I think I actually slept last night."

"I reckon you did. You was damned quiet, at least." Eddie grinned. "Except for the fact you was mutterin' offn' on about the lady Belle."

Duff's brows rose. "You don't say. Hmmm . . . Although, if that was her in my dreams," he added with a grin, "it was a damned improvement over the usual gore."

Eddie hadn't seen his master grin like that for so long, tears sprang to his eyes. Quickly glancing down at the porridge he was stirring to hide his feelings, he said as casually as he could,

"Mebbe you should call on the lady. It must be right boring for her so far from the *Ton*. She might relish a bit o' conversation."

"Don't say you're getting tired of my company," Duff teased, pouring himself a cup of coffee.

"No offense, sar, but you ain't exactly been the talkative type lately. You could use a change of scene, efn' you know what I mean." That the marquis was actually trading jests with him was incredible. "Mayhap we should ride on over to Shoreham today."

Duff shot his batman an amused look. "Since when did you take up pimping, Eddie?"

"Don't know as I have, sar. I was jes' thinkin' the lady might like to go for a ride on that little mare she didn't want. Try it out, like."

"So you were thinking that, were you?" the marquis drawled.

"It's been a while, sar, since we seen any ladies." Duff's celibacy had impinged on Eddie's life as well. And loyal as he was, it had been a major hardship.

The marquis studied his batman with a narrowed gaze. "Don't tell me you've been playing the anchorite for me."

"No, sar," Eddie lied, not wishing to say he'd been afraid to leave the marquis alone with his demons. "What say I saddle up that pretty little mare after breakfast and we take ourselves a ride over Shoreham way?"

Duff glanced out the window, hesitated for a fraction of a second, and then nodded his head. "Why not? It looks like a damned fine day for a ride."

It seemed an age since he'd paid a call on a lady. It seemed even longer since he'd experienced the excitement he was feeling as he rode toward Shoreham with Eddie at his side.

"This has to be one of our better summer days," Duff noted. "The temperature is ideal—a light breeze, not a cloud in the sky. A person couldn't have ordered more perfect weather."

Eddie could have pointed out that the past fortnight had been of equal perfection weather-wise, but he didn't. He said instead, "You got that right, sar. It be a right fine day to be out."

"Miss Foster may not wish to go for a ride." Whether he was warning his batman or himself was unclear.

"It don't matter none, sar," Eddie replied. "It don't hurt to ask."

"I suppose I could explain she could have kept the mare without—" Darley's voice trailed away.

When it appeared that the marquis wasn't going to explain further, Eddie said, "Good idea, sar. I expect she don't get gifts without sumpin' wanted in return, like."

Duff blew out a breath. "Jesus—one forgets all the rudeness and inconsequential rules of the *Ton* out here."

"The *Ton* don't ever forget, though."

"Well, devil take it—and all the harpies at Almack's, too, while we're at it."

Eddie smiled. "Yes, sar. Good idea, sar—seein' how the patronesses kicked you out afor you set out for the Peninsula Campaign anyway."

"Lord, that seems a lifetime ago," Duff murmured.

"Mebbe nine lifetimes ago, sar. You, me, and the cats."

"There were so many who didn't come back, though," he said softly. "Elgin and Graham, Tychson and—"

"When your time's up, it's up, sar. You know that," Eddie interposed, not wanting the marquis to sink into the hell of his memories. Christ, he shouldn't have mentioned the war. What was he thinking? "We was lucky," the batman added, talking fast in the hopes of wiping the frown from his master's brow. "Think of it that way, sar. We was *real* lucky. Not many men would have survived your wounds, sar. Lady Luck's bin on yer shoulder."

"And for what, I sometimes wonder," Duff muttered.

"For this fine day and this pretty mare and the lovely lady we're off to see," Eddie replied with forced cheer.

Duff turned to his batman. "I've been a trial to you, haven't I? How do you keep your temper?"

"Not a problem, sar."

Darley smiled faintly. "Miss Foster *is* very lovely, isn't she?" His smile widened. "And it's a very fine day."

"Yes, sar, on both counts."

"I *am* feeling less bedeviled."

"I can tell, sar." For one thing, he couldn't have coaxed the marquis to call on a lady for love or money a week ago.

"I actually feel as though a weight has suddenly lifted from my shoulders. One hears such phrases bandied about, of course, but who knew they were based in fact? It's very strange."

"Buying that fine little mare might have done the trick, sar. You ain't been shoppin' for no racers in a long time. Mayhap it set you on the right track, so to speak. Mayhap you're feelin' better cuz yer back in the racin' game."

The marquis glanced at his batman. "The season's begun?"

Two months ago, Eddie thought. "There's been a few races, sar," he said, ambiguously. "Your pa took a first at the Spring Meet."

"With Sunstar?"

"None other. By three lengths, too."

"Did you bet?"

" 'Course I did. Won a bit o' blunt on that one."

"Maybe we should gear up again, get my stable up and running. Why don't you see if Harry Landseer is available to ride for me," Duff said briskly, a new energy in his voice. "Tell him I apologize for inquiring at so late a date, but I'll triple whatever he's making with anyone else."

"Yes, *sar*!" Because of a pretty mare and a prettier lady, the marquis had apparently returned from the moribund half-world in which he'd been dwelling for much too long.

Life was good, Eddie thought. First-rate. And his chances of winning some blunt at the races had greatly improved. The marquis's horses came in first more often than not.

Duff was sharing Eddie's belief in the goodness of life. He

felt as though he'd suddenly walked from some dark prison into the sunshine.

And before long he'd be basking in the glow of the lovely Miss Foster's smile as well.

"How much farther?" he asked, as though impatient to get on with his life now that he was once again in possession of it.

"Jes' around that bend, sar, and down into the valley. Ten minutes, mebbe less."

Chapter

5

Thanks to Eddie's foresight, the marquis arrived in Shoreham bearing gifts. A pretty posy of fragrant pinks rested in his batman's saddlebag, along with a dainty set of pearl hair combs that Eddie had come up with from God-knows-where.

Duff found himself smiling as they entered the village, sweet anticipation filling his brain. Strange, how pleasure could suddenly take over one's senses for no apparent reason.

Not that he was averse to the balmy feeling.

Nor was he about to take issue with the piquant excitement gripping him. How long had it been since he'd spoken to a lady—other than those in his family? How long had it been since he'd wanted to?

Three women and two babes were immediately visible as the marquis and Eddie dismounted at the gate. The small group was seated around a tea table set in the shade of the trees.

While the women were in full view across the small garden, so, too, were Darley and Eddie as they walked toward the garden gate.

Annabelle's spine stiffened at the sight of the two men. Quickly coming to her feet, she casually said, "They must have lost their way. I'll be right back." With a nod to her companions, she moved briskly toward their visitors. Apparently, the marquis had not taken her refusal to heart, she reflected. But then, men of his ilk were only familiar with compliance, not rebuke.

The marquis's wishes were irrelevant to her, however. She refused to have her mother upset by visitors. Nor did she wish to answer questions that might arise if Darley joined them for tea. While her mother knew she made her living on the stage, she had no idea about the more risqué aspects of her profession. And so Annabelle preferred it remain.

Some difficult choices had been necessary after her father's death, and she'd willingly taken up the life of an actress so her mother and sister could survive.

She'd not regretted her decision.

But she had taken pains to withhold from her family any notion of what her modish, urbane social life entailed. And while her name was often in the gossip sheets, such papers never reached remote hamlets such as Shoreham, where life went on much as it had for a millennium.

Before Duff had advanced more than a few steps into the garden, she reached him and arrested his progress.

"The Marquis of Darley at your service, Miss Foster." Duff offered her the posy with an exquisite bow.

"Good afternoon, my lord." Her bow was less exquisite by design; she didn't wish to appear in the least friendly. "My mother is ill," she added coolly. "Otherwise, I would invite you to join us for tea." Neither a blush nor a blink gave evidence of the real reason she wished him gone. "I trust you understand," she murmured, playing her role with aplomb.

"I'm sorry to hear it." Duff's expression was solicitous. "I hope your mother's illness isn't serious."

"She recently had a shock to her system." Annabelle wasn't inclined to divulge the details of Chloe's death. "But I believe she's slowly improving."

"Would you like my doctors to stop by? Both Dr. Carr and Dr. Stewart are excellent."

"No, but thank you. Time alone will heal her wounds, I fear."

"Then I wish her a speedy recovery. If I might be so bold, Miss Foster," he went on, all soft-spoken cordiality, "would it be possible your mother could spare you briefly—at some future date, if not now?" The marquis indicated the horses with a nod of his head. "I brought the mare along in hopes you'd go riding with me." As Annabelle opened her mouth to speak, he quickly interposed, "I understand your nursing duties come first. I just thought you might enjoy a ride on such a fine day. I assure you," he added with a smile, "my intentions are benign."

"Allow me to refuse, my lord," she replied with equal graciousness. "Although, in my experience," she added with a deliberately enchanting smile, "men's intentions are never benign."

"What if I were to say I just want to be friends?"

Her brows rose. "Then you'd be the first man I've ever met who did."

"Consider me the exception."

She regarded him thoughtfully for a moment. "As if you don't know you are, Duff."

He looked surprised at being addressed so familiarly.

Her brows lifted again. "You don't remember, do you?"

He smiled faintly. "I admit to being drunk more than sober in my youth."

"We met in the green room after my second performance on the Drury stage. You offered me carte blanche."

"But you eventually took Walingame's offer, I understand," he said, his sisters' gossipy dinnertime conversation suddenly recalled. "How is he, by the way?"

"I wouldn't know."

"Ah."

She could tell he hadn't heard, but then it was common gossip that the marquis had been in seclusion. "We are estranged."

"I should say I'm sorry, but I'm not."

"At least you're honest."

"What's the point in subterfuge?"

"My goodness, Duff, you quite contradict your gender in that regard."

He couldn't blame her, he supposed. A woman of her background was seen only as an object of pleasure. There were rare exceptions to the rule—actresses who married into the nobility—but it was unusual.

At that moment, a piercing baby cry rent the summer air and Annabelle cast a swift glance over her shoulder. "I really have to go," she murmured.

His gaze raked her form. "Is the babe yours?"

"I don't see that it's any of your business," she replied coolly.

"Of course. Forgive me." He should have known better. His tact had been blunted by long disuse.

"Belle, Belle, darling!" Mrs. Foster cried, waving her arms in a come-hither motion. "Bring the nice man over for tea!"

No matter her experience on the stage, this time Annabelle was unable to suppress the blush coloring her cheeks.

"If I promise to behave, might I be allowed?" Darley inquired with a quirked grin, amused by her obvious embarrassment. "I shan't say a word out of turn."

"It looks as though I have no choice," Annabelle muttered with a grimace. Short of shouting back at her mother—an impossible act of disrespect, considering the fact that her mother continued to beckon them with great vigor—she was obliged to capitulate.

"I will be on my best behavior—word of honor."

That charming smile again, familiar not only to her, but to a great number of ladies in the *Ton*. The young marquis had cut a wide swath through the boudoirs of London before he'd left for the Continent. "Just don't stay long," she cautioned. "And I warn you, my mother's mind wanders."

"I am duly warned on both counts," he replied pleasantly, crooking his arm in her direction.

There was nothing to do but place her hand on his arm and follow him down the garden path toward the table set under the shade of the trees. And there was also nothing to do when they reached her mother and Molly but to introduce their illustrious visitor. "Mama, Molly, the Marquis of Darley. Lord Darley, my mother and our wet nurse."

"A pleasure to meet you, Mrs. Foster, Molly." His formal bow was perfection, his smile correspondingly splendid. "Your daughter and I have mutual friends in London, Mrs. Foster. She's a most accomplished actress, as you no doubt know. And that's not just my opinion but one with which every playgoer and critic in the land concurs."

"Belle is perfect in every way, is she not?" Mrs. Foster cheerfully agreed, beaming at Duff's fulsome praise. "Come, come, young man, sit down, partake of our rustic tea and tell us of the doings of the great world."

Annabelle's eyes widened at her mother's sudden animation and polished air, as if she took tea with nobles every day.

Darley immediately understood from whence the lovely Belle had acquired her looks and poise. Ill or not, Mrs. Foster had the bearing of a countess, a lovely smile, and obvious command over her daughter. A point he not only noted, but intended to exploit. Not for nefarious reasons. He simply wished Belle's company this fine summer day. And from all appearances, the mother didn't look seriously ill. Perhaps a ride *wasn't* out of the question.

It was a habit of long standing—wanting what he wanted. But coming from a family of great wealth and title, how could he have escaped those selfish urges? And it *was* a perfect summer day.

Applying the full extent of his charm to the fulfillment of

his wishes, he soon had Mrs. Foster laughing at his jests, teasing him back, conversing with him as though they were old friends. And before long, he had both babies in his lap and was making them giggle, too. "My sister has twins," he noted, gently bouncing the *enfants* on his knees. "I've learned to deal with two babes at once."

That admission induced Mrs. Foster to ask him numerous questions about his family, all of which he answered with complete candor. And after Duff had mentioned that he and Eddie had been living rough at his father's hunting lodge, she insisted Eddie be included in the festivities.

"I don't suppose your valet has had a bit of cake for a long time, then," she declared. "I've yet to meet a man who knows much about baking."

"I can't argue there," Darley replied with a smile, calling over his batman to join them. "Eddie's cooking is of the most rudimentary."

For the next half hour or so, laughter and frivolity became the order of the day. One person no more than pronounced something amusing, than another responded with equal wit. Eddie entertained them with an acceptable ditty or two from his repertoire of camp songs. And whether it was Duff's accomplished baby-minding or because of Eddie's lilting voice, the babies soon fell asleep in the marquis's arms. Without asking, he placed the sleeping babes in their baskets and settled back in his chair with the naturalness of a man who had often cared for children.

Annabelle found his lack of airs unutterably refreshing and far removed from the noblemen she knew who flaunted their consequence. Even his conversation was simple and ordinary, without the bombast and pretense so common in the *Ton*. How enjoyable he was. What a pleasure it was to relax and laugh once again.

As for Duff, he couldn't remember when last he'd been so pleasantly amused. He would have to reward Eddie for having the foresight to suggest this visit.

The others, too, took pleasure in the mummery and high spirits of the afternoon. Mrs. Foster experienced rare moments of joy after having felt only unremitting sadness since the death of her daughter. Eddie understood that the marquis's, and consequently *his* life had taken a solid turn for the better. For her part, Molly relished watching the subtle interaction between her employer and the marquis. It appeared that the nobleman, who preferred being called Duff, was in full courting mode, while Miss Foster had smiled more this afternoon than she had the entire time Molly had been with her.

"If you're going for a ride, you'd best be off before the sun cools," Annabelle's mother suddenly asserted. Silencing her daughter's impending protest with an upraised hand, Mrs. Foster added, "Don't worry about Molly and me. We're just fine. You know how you've always loved horses, darling." She turned to Duff. "Before my dear husband died, we kept a small stable ourselves. Belle was the best rider in the family."

"Are you sure, Mother?" Annabelle's inquiry was replete with caution.

It was obvious who *wasn't* sure, Annabelle's posture ramrod-stiff. But taking advantage of the opportunity given him, Duff immediately came to his feet. "We won't be gone long, Mrs. Foster. I'll have your daughter back before dark."

Belle shot him a heated glance, not sure she cared to be given this Hobson's choice. Even less sure she should go.

Ignoring her fretful gaze, Darley offered her his hand. "My new mare is a darling. Eddie tells me she's faster than blazes." He grinned. "I don't suppose you'd care to race?"

Her expression implied not. Under her mother's smiling gaze, however, Belle's voice was silken. "Perhaps some other time, Darley. I don't have my riding boots with me." She lifted her hem to display blue leather half-boots that matched her simple gown.

"Those will do perfectly well. We'll ride at a sedate pace." He took her hand, pulled her to her feet, and holding Annabelle's hand firmly, Duff bowed to her mother. "Thank you for the tea and cake, Mrs. Foster. I can't remember when I've had a more enjoyable afternoon."

"You're welcome anytime, young man. Laughter is good for the soul, is it not?" Annabelle's mother smiled. "Now be off, you two," she said with a wave of her hand. "Have a most pleasant ride."

Chapter

6

"For your information, Darley," Annabelle muttered as they moved away from the tea table, "I *abhor* authoritarian men."

"Once we're out of sight of your mama, I shall beg your forgiveness in every imaginable fashion," he murmured, holding her hand tightly as she tried to wrestle her fingers free.

"You took advantage!" she charged, mutinously.

"I freely admit it, but if you knew how long its been since I've been in the company of a lovely woman, you'd overlook my incivility. Tell her, Eddie," Darley said, glancing back at his batman. "Tell her how long we've been hermits."

"It's been a right long time, Miss Foster." Eddie caught up to them and met Annabelle's gaze. "It were a blessing we saw you at the horse fair yesterday, miss. It were like the sky lifted, if'n you ken. The marquis ain't been hisself of late, you see."

Annabelle glanced from man to man as though trying to gauge the honesty of Eddie's assertions.

"It's God's own truth," Duff said, making a wry face. "You became a talisman of sorts yesterday. I have no idea why, but there it is." He smiled. "Perhaps you could consider me your charity case today. Not that you're not already involved in charitable obligations to your family. But I would be pleased if you could keep me company for a short time. I just want to go for a ride—that's all."

"A ride and nothing more?"

"Yes."

His reply was so entirely without subterfuge, so bluntly curtailed, she understood that behind the easy smile was something other than ease.

Suffering of a sort.

One didn't have to be a savant to recognize it. Or maybe she knew too much of suffering herself. *Stop!* she silently ordered herself, refusing to acknowledge any affinity with a man like Duff. It would be a ludicrous assumption when they came from such opposite worlds. Worse, it might imply she was succumbing to his charm. And that she *would not do*. She was in Shoreham to care for her family. There was no time for other things, even if she were naive enough to accept his offered friendship at face value.

Not likely that.

Since her contentious break from Walingame, she'd vowed never again to be naive about the motives of noblemen.

"I shall hold you to your word," she said pointedly, pulling her hand free.

Or perhaps he released it. "You have my word."

That blunt simplicity again. She wasn't here to analyze, however. Nor would she attempt such an endeavor with a man like Darley, who, rumor had it, barely spoke to any of his old acquaintances, or sometimes at all, since his return home. "Thank you."

His smile was boyish. "No need to thank me when you've brought me good fortune. Do you have a preference where we ride?"

She was about to say she didn't, or perhaps inquire what he meant by "good fortune." But she did neither, careful not to stray outside the perimeters of the agreed-upon amicable ride. Instead, she said, "If we cross Dunlow Chase we'll come on the monastery ruins at Bedloe. It's a site of great beauty."

"Excellent choice. I used to go there as a boy."

"As did I as a child."

"And yet I never saw you."

Her brows rose faintly. "A matter of no importance."

He grinned. "Speak for yourself. I would have taken great pleasure in seeing you."

She made a moue. "I would prefer you not flirt with me."

"I shall try not to. Eddie will keep me in line. You hear, Eddie? You are to be our duenna."

He'd played many roles of late in the marquis's life, but duenna was not among them, Eddie thought. Nor did he feel he would be effective should Duff set his mind to seduction. But he answered dutifully. "Yes, sar. You be in me sights, sar."

Duff grinned at Annabelle. "Consider yourself doubly safe from my advances."

Annabelle found herself thinking with utter absurdity what might have happened if she'd taken Darley up on his offer of carte blanche all those years ago. Other than his stark slenderness, he'd changed little. How many years had it been? How old was he now? "How old are you?" she asked, as though her thoughts proceeded uncensored to her tongue.

He met her gaze, a sudden look of surprise in his eyes. But when he spoke, his voice was without inflection. "Twenty-seven. I shan't ask you how old you are," he said with a grin. When he knew very well she was exactly five years younger; the night he'd met her in the green room was clear as though it were yesterday, now that she'd recalled it to his memory. She'd just recently turned eighteen, she'd told him that night. He was twenty-three and admittedly very drunk, but he remembered her dazzling beauty. And the crowd of men demanding her attention. Suddenly bending low, he put his mouth near her ear and asked a pertinent question himself. "Tell me. Is Cricket yours?"

"No." She had no idea why she'd answered honestly. She knew less why she didn't want him to think Chloe's child was hers. After all these years in the demimonde, surely it couldn't matter what people thought.

"I didn't think she was."

"And yet you asked." She spoke quietly like he, their voices low so Eddie wouldn't hear.

He shrugged. "I don't know why I did—actually . . . I do. I didn't want you to have Walingame's child. And I have no idea why it would matter."

"Things like that matter to men," she replied bluntly.

He shook his head. "Not to me. I've been living in a black hole these many long months since Waterloo." He smiled tightly. "Very little matters to me anymore, my sweet."

"I'm not your sweet, Lord Darley," she replied crisply. "Although I'm truly sorry for your distress," she added in a different tone of voice. She understood misery. Her entire family had been sunk into despair since Chloe's death.

"Allow me to apologize again—for addressing you so informally. And truth be told, I'm actually exhilarated today—thanks to you. No, don't protest . . . you are under no obligation for my moods or anything else concerning my life. I do promise to refrain from taking any further liberties in address, though. No improper phrases shall pass my lips." He grinned and pantomimed a locking motion across his lips.

She laughed. She hadn't intended to. She really wished she hadn't when she was trying very hard to maintain her distance.

His grin widened. "There—you see? It's not so difficult to laugh. And consider, your mama likes me. That should make me at least marginally acceptable."

"As if anyone wouldn't like you when you focus your charm on them."

"Perhaps you as well?"

She laughed and punched him lightly on the arm. "Enough. Today, we're going on a ride. And that's all we're doing."

Chapter

7

Darley swung Annabelle up into the lady's sidesaddle, adjusted her stirrups, handed her the mare's reins, and stepped back to admire her seat. "Your mama was right. You're a natural in the saddle. Consider keeping the mare. She fits you perfectly."

"She's too expensive, as you well know, but thank you. Perhaps at another time I might have taken you up on your offer. But not at this juncture in my life."

"That sounds like a declaration of great portent."

She flashed him an easy smile. "Not in the least, my lord. I only meant my life is very busy at the moment."

"Duff, please."

"As you wish."

"Don't say you're becoming docile of a sudden," he said with a smile, swinging up onto Romulus's back.

"I am never docile, *Duff*."

She uttered his name in a sultry contralto that registered in a portion of his anatomy that had been long dormant. Shifting in his saddle, he suppressed the spiking jolt of pleasure, conscious of both his promise to her and himself. This afternoon visit wasn't about seduction. He wasn't so dissolute. Nor had he ever been, even in his more prodigal youth. Sex wasn't about records or numbers. It was about mutual pleasure. At the moment he was content to feel the warmth of the sun on his back, the supple power of prime bloodstock beneath him, and with the lovely Miss Foster at his side, he intended to take in the full beauty of a world he'd been absent from too long.

Annabelle, too, had been away from the world, although for different reasons. But about to see one of her favorite childhood places, she was feeling a modicum of exhilaration herself. Perhaps after weeks of taking care of her mother and Celia, the opportunity to ride to Bedloe was reason enough for her high spirits. That she was in the company of the handsomest man in England—as defined by the *Ton*, not necessarily herself, she carefully noted—couldn't be discounted, either. She cast a surreptitious glance his way as though to confirm that assessment.

Duff smiled. "Ready?"

Maybe she *had* been away from the world too long. Discomposed by his direct gaze and the fact that *she'd* been caught out looking at him, she stammered, "Yes, yes . . . certainly— anytime." Chagrined that her faltering reply made her sound like a wet-behind-the-ears schoolgirl, resolved that Darley's good looks were *not* going to turn her head, she abruptly said, "Ten quid says I can beat you to Dunlow Chase."

Her mare leaped forward at the flick of her whip.

Duff grinned and gave Romulus his head.

Eddie knew better than to give chase. Kicking his mount into a sedate trot, he followed at an easy pace. With the marquis having so recently emerged from his morbid despondency, he wasn't about to superintend what could turn out to be a pleasant afternoon ride. The resplendent Miss Foster seemingly held the key to the marquis's renewed good spirits. What better way to restore his master's well-being than to allow him privacy with the lady?

Eddie had been with Darley from his youth, the men having grown up together. His father had served the former marquis as valet, his father's father having filled the same role for the old Duke of Westerlands until his death. A Harley knew how to melt into the background at the appropriate time or he wasn't worthy of the name.

And now was the appropriate time.

Annabelle's mare reached the Chase first with a two-length lead. Reining in her mount, she smiled at Duff as he pulled up beside her. "You owe me ten quid," she noted cheerfully.

"Didn't I tell you the mare was fast?" Not as fast as Romulus, but he was always a gentleman.

"She's an absolute darling."

"She's yours if you wish, you know."

"I don't wish."

He smiled faintly. "I seem to be overly optimistic about my powers of persuasion."

She gave him a narrowed glance, although a twinkle gleamed behind the fringe of her lashes. "You have your way too much, I suspect."

He shrugged, not about to say if he had had his way these many months past, he would have erased the grim memories that haunted him and kept him awake at night. "Perhaps I do," he said, and quickly changing the subject before being caught up in the grip of those memories, added, "We should have brought a picnic. I'm hungry already."

Curiously, Annabelle also was—although she'd eaten a considerable amount at tea. "The inn at Bedloe serves excellent fare," she offered.

"Perfect. Food first or the views at Bedloe first?"

"It's up to you." It was politesse only, for she was actually feeling peckish. Molly would be pleased, she thought, Cricket's wet nurse continually chastising her for her lack of appetite.

"In that case, food." Those close to Duff since his return home would have been as surprised as Molly.

"Will your batman know where to find you?"

If Eddie could find him lying on a battlefield in the dark

and fog, Darley thought, he could find him in broad daylight on a country road. "I don't expect a problem."

She grinned. "Are you up to losing another five quid, then?"

He winked. "Maybe you'll lose."

"We'll soon find out," she replied gaily, feeling so light-hearted she might have considered some sorcery was at play if she wasn't focused instead on beating Darley. "First one to the inn wins!"

He was thinking he was a winner already. "Done."

She rode like she'd been born to the saddle, and he pressed her this time to see what the mare could do. Gimcrack's blood-lines proved credible indeed; Romulus was running hard at the end.

As Annabelle's mount careened into the inn yard, she reined the mare to a stop with finesse, and tossing a glance over her shoulder as Darley brought Romulus to a halt behind her, playfully said, "In consideration of your losses, perhaps I should buy *you* lunch."

Duff could have bought the inn or the entire county if he wished. "I would be delighted," he replied, bowing slightly from the saddle. "Seeing as you're a woman of means." Dismounting, he handed his reins to a stable boy.

"I am indeed." She might not be able to buy the county, but the inn wouldn't be beyond her means. Her fame and no-toriety had had its compensations. Handing her reins to an-other young lad who had come up, she slipped her feet from the stirrups and smiled at Duff, who was reaching up to lift her down.

They stood close for a moment as he set her on her feet, his hands still on her waist. He took a small breath as his senses quickened.

She felt a sudden nervousness, as though she'd not stood this close to a man before.

Then his hands slipped away and he stepped back.

"You don't wear riding gloves." Like some missish young maid, she uttered the first thing that came to mind.

"I never have, although," he added, turning his hands palm up, "I probably should. Calluses." He smiled easily as though he was ready to discuss whatever she wished. "They're not acceptable in the *Ton*."

"Apparently it hasn't mattered." The fact that Darley stood apart from the crowd had never been in question.

"I admit lily-white hands have never been high on my list of priorities." Crooking his arm, he nodded toward the inn. "Are you as hungry as I?"

How unconstrained he was. Relaxed and relaxing in turn. "Perhaps more," she said with a smile.

He shot her a swift look. "And yet you're slender as a willow"—he grinned—"except for those areas where you're not."

"You're overstepping the rules of the day, Duff." But she returned his grin as she placed her hand on his arm. "Now, I'm in the mood for pudding. How about you?"

For the first time in months he was in the mood for something else entirely, but ever courteous, he said instead as they moved toward the inn, "I believe a good baron of beef is more to my liking."

Her brows rose faintly. "How terribly male."

He looked amused. "I confess to the—what . . . infraction?" He smiled. "Shall we?" Having reached the door to the inn, he held it open for her.

The moment they entered the small parlor, conversation ceased and all eyes followed them as they moved toward the only unoccupied table in the busy tavern. The exclusively male crowd was blatantly openmouthed on seeing Annabelle, while the two barmaids' covetous gazes were trained on Duff.

The fashionable couple's grace and beauty aside, it wasn't often that Bedloe Inn had customers of quality. Off the beaten path, far from even a village of any size, its primary trade was local farmers.

Pulling out a chair for Annabelle that gave her a view out the window, Darley took a seat opposite her. With her back to the room, she wouldn't be as conscious of the gawking stares as they ate. And whether his decision was meant to assuage himself or her, he chose not to regard.

Even before Duff was fully seated, two smiling barmaids were at his elbows. "What might we do for you, me lord?" the older one said as her young compatriot giggled and openly stared. That the services they were offering were not exclusively food and drink was plain.

Annabelle watched with amusement as Darley ignored their adoring gazes and asked whether they had some good beef and hock.

The spokeswoman answered in the affirmative on both counts and added silkily, "If'n his lordship be interested in resting after his meal, we have some right fine rooms upstairs."

The implication in the word *rest* was so abundantly clear, Annabelle suppressed an urge to laugh.

Darley noticed. "It's entirely up to the lady," he said casually, as though unaware of the barmaid's inference. "Would you like to rest, my dear?"

"I would prefer eating," Annabelle replied sweetly.

Duff looked up and offered the maids a bland smile. "We require only food and drink at the moment."

As the maids retreated with sullen looks, Annabelle met Duff's gaze. "You could have enjoyed yourself, my lord, with a pair of willing serving girls."

"I'm already enjoying myself. Why would I look afield?"

"How polite you are."

He shook his head. "Just discriminating. You're a gem of the first water, Miss Foster, although I'm sure you know that. And you delight me."

"I may not want to delight you."

"Nevertheless, you do." He smiled faintly. "I have no intention of doing more than enjoying the view. Rest assured, you're safe."

Somehow she knew she could take him at his word. "I appreciate your understanding."

"There was nothing to misunderstand."

"Most men are not so agreeable."

"Perhaps most men haven't seen what I've seen. To indulge in a pleasant ride and a rustic luncheon with a beautiful woman is the pinnacle of content."

She forced herself not to overscrutinize his assessment. Although, in her experience, only guile and cunning would be behind such a description of *content*. But such ambiguities were better left unexamined. "We forgot to ask for pudding," she said instead, opting for an innocuous topic of conversation.

"If you don't mind, I'll wait to ask for it when our serving maids return."

She smiled. "Don't tell me you shrink from their adulation? Surely you're used to it."

"I find it awkward."

"You astonish me," she said with genuine surprise. "You've been the object of female pursuit for years."

He slid into a lounging pose and gazed at her from under his lashes. "Nevertheless, I dislike it."

"Most men would be gratified by a female's worshipful glance."

"Surely, if anyone understands adoration and worship, you must. Do *you* find it satisfying?"

She made a moue.

"Exactly." He tipped his head ever so slightly. "Now— enough of such inanities. Tell me how you happen to be in the country, or, if you prefer, I shall tell you how I have come to be here and we'll have a nice coze while we wait for our food."

"You tell me first." Whether she was simply postponing an explanation or whether she would deny him one, she wasn't sure.

He spoke then in a general way of his loss of interest in the fashionable world, telling her a little of his daily routine, of his family and stable. "Eddie is pleased that I've decided to race my thoroughbreds again. He's been suffering more than I in my hermitage. I don't suppose your mother might forgo your company for a day if I asked you to the races."

"Perhaps," she said, surprising herself with her answer.

"We could go just for the afternoon races if it would help."

"That might be better."

"You should consider taking my offer of the mare. You could race her."

"You know why I don't."

"The gift is free of any liability. I mean it." The price of the mare was a mere bagatelle for him, although he wasn't so gauche as to say so. "She might win a few purses for you."

"I don't need money."

"I didn't mean you did. I only meant there's pleasure in winning. You used to have a race stable. Have you given it up?"

"I did recently."

"Ah."

"I don't have to explain."

"Of course not."

"Don't look at me like that, Darley." She smiled. "You quite unnerve me."

"Duff," he corrected with a grin. "And I wager there isn't much that unnerves you, me included."

He may or may not be right, although she wasn't about to admit to any indecision. The man had an inordinate natural charm—quite outrageous in its impact. In fact, for the first time in years, she found herself on the verge of feeling a distinct frisson of attraction.

She must have been rusticating too long, she decided.

Or she'd been in the company of so many selfish, calculating men of late that Duff was like a breath of fresh air.

Or maybe she was simply another in a long line of women who had succumbed to his enchantment, and her feelings had nothing to do with her life, past or present. "Ah—here's your man," she said with such obvious relief he took notice. Turning around, he looked out and saw Eddie dismounting in the yard.

Duff immediately came to his feet. "I'll be right back. Will you be comfortable alone?"

Looking up, she smiled. "I doubt these bluff yeomen will harm me."

He grinned. "I'm sure they won't. I just didn't want you to think me discourteous, leaving you by yourself."

"Good God, Duff, I'm not made of swansdown. I'm of sturdy stock." She waved her hand. "Go."

Chapter

8

A few moments later, Annabelle watched Duff walk up to
Eddie in the inn yard and apparently give him some instructions. Eddie only nodded from time to time, not speaking
until the marquis turned to go.

Whatever Eddie said, Darley didn't like. He shook his
head.

Apparently undeterred, as family retainers were often wont
to be, Eddie pulled a slim leather box from his saddlebag and
thrust it at the marquis.

Darley took a step backward.

With a smile and a brief comment, Eddie closed the small
distance between them and slipped the box into the marquis's
coat pocket.

Darley instantly swung around and strode back toward the
inn, a frown creasing his brow.

Annabelle had seen those pretty red boxes from Grey's
often enough, her admirers sending her jewelry from the pres-
tigious shop in hopes of gaining her favor. So the marquis had
come bearing gifts—the posy and now this.

She smiled faintly.

Or at least his batman had come bearing gifts.

Darley's expression had softened by the time he approached her, but his mood had not. Scanning the empty table as he dropped into his chair, he growled, "The service here is wanting."

If Annabelle hadn't been so absorbed in the scene outside in the yard, she might have noticed no one had so much as set a jug of water on the table. But before she could respond, both barmaids came their way bearing wine, glasses, and dinnerware.

Annabelle smiled. "There, you see—they were waiting for you."

"Please, don't start." But his smile was cordial, the churlishness gone from his voice. "We agreed to speak of more interesting things."

"Your batman found you, I see." She knew how to take a cue, or, more aptly, how to please a gentleman. That she was inclined to do so caused her a moment of trepidation—quickly erased. She was past the point of having her head turned by a handsome man.

"Eddie could track me through the desert," Darley replied. "And on occasion he has," he added.

"And where would that desert be?"

"In Morocco. We took the caravan route to Timbuktu once in search of bloodstock and became separated in a sandstorm."

"The most exotic location I've ever seen was Venice during Carnivale."

His brows rose. "Definitely strange, and outlandish as well."

"Nothing to compare to Morocco, I suspect."

"Come with me sometime," he said, as though they were long-standing friends, as though he frequently offered ladies invitations to travel abroad with him, as though he ever did.

"How generous you are."

He smiled. "It depends on my company."

At Darley's warm smile, the older barmaid who had reached

the table first shot a resentful glance at Annabelle and plunked down the wine jug with such force, wine splashed over the front of Annabelle's gown.

"So sorry, mum," the maid murmured, her voice sweet with malice. "Mayhap you should go out back to the pump and wash that there wine off your gown."

"It's of no concern," Annabelle replied calmly. "The frock is old."

"Are you sure?" Duff asked, eyeing the stains on her gown, his gaze resting on her bodice perhaps a moment too long. He cleared his throat, not quite sure how to offer his assistance without appearing forward. Forcing his voice to a bland neutrality, he said, "If you need help rinsing—"

"No, no, really, this gown is absolutely out of fashion," Annabelle quickly interjected, not sure why the thought of him touching her in even so innocuous a manner unnerved her, but it did. Purposely speaking in as neutral a voice as he, she added, "I was planning on discarding this frock anyway."

"Then all is well." He grinned. "Perhaps you'd like some wine in your *glass*?"

How smooth he was, how polished. "Yes, please," she said, smiling back with equal affability.

And for the next few moments, they both sipped on their wine and allowed their unsettled sensibilities to return to normal while the two barmaids served them their rustic fare: roast beef; coarse bread; creamy butter; the inevitable boiled potatoes.

Annabelle noticed that the marquis was being granted expansive views of the serving girls' plump breasts as they bent low to set each dish before him. She reminded herself that she wasn't in competition with serving maids; more to the point, she was without amorous intentions apropos the marquis. That she was even deliberating about female competition, she chose not to acknowledge.

Duff maintained a bland expression throughout the flaunting of female flesh. And only when all the food was in place did he ask, "Might you have some pudding?" knowing better than to mention that the lady wished it.

"Cherries are in season, me lord," the younger girl replied. "Cook done herself proud with a right nice cherry puddin'."

"Excellent. I should like some," the marquis observed. "With clotted cream."

With a last low-dipping curtsy, the two maids retreated.

"My, my," Annabelle murmured, unable to restrain herself after such an overt exhibition. "You are obviously in great demand."

Duff leaned over and poured her more wine. "If I were in great demand with you, I would be considerably more gratified."

Lifting her glass, she fluttered her lashes prettily. "If I weren't rusticating in the country to avoid such things, I might be *tempted* to flatter you."

Offering sincerity to her arch flirtation, he said, "What if I tried to change your mind?"

"Not today, Darley. We're out for a ride and no more. Remember?"

He smiled faintly. "You can't fault a man for trying."

Her gaze was cool. "I can, actually."

"Then I beg your forgiveness." As though his apology reminded him of the box in his pocket, he drew it out and set it on the table before her. "Accept this as a small token of my honorable intentions."

"The gift your batman insisted you take."

He shrugged. "Not necessarily."

"Come, Duff, you didn't want to."

"Actually, I didn't know if *you'd* want it." He blew out a small breath, slid lower in his chair, and held her gaze. "Look—Eddie is persuaded you'll like me more if I curry your favor with gifts. He *really* wants you to like me. My dark moods are making him nervous. So, take it for Eddie's sake," he said with a small smile. "He'd be most pleased."

"You've been worrying him?"

Duff's brows arched faintly. "An understatement of vast proportions."

"So if I take this, I would be allaying some of Eddie's concern."

"Definitely." Duff grinned. "And the news of my recovery will spread to my parents' house at lightning speed—servants' gossip being what it is."

Her lashes fell slightly. "Not that gossip is the exclusive prerogative of servants."

"Touché. You've been the subject of gossip often enough, haven't you?"

She smiled. "Once or twice."

"Is that why you're rusticating in the country?"

"It's part of the reason."

"Tell me the other part." Sliding up in his chair, he leaned forward and, resting his elbows on the table, offered her an open, unclouded gaze.

She made a moue. "I don't know if I wish to."

His shoulder lifted in an infinitesimal shrug. "How can it matter? I go nowhere. I see no one. I don't even answer my mail."

"You tell me first why you're a hermit. I may need another glass of wine or so before I'm willing to divulge my reasons."

"In that case, drink up," he said, his smile boyish and warm.

She laughed. "I have no idea why I'd want to tell you anything."

"Then again, after a glass or two you might not mind, and consider, I might not remember what you say if *I* drink enough."

She gave him an assessing look. "Do you drink a good deal now?"

He shook his head. "Hardly at all. I'm not looking for more nightmares. Although, thanks to you, they seem distant at the moment."

"Perhaps it's not me—perhaps any distraction would do as well."

He dark gaze was direct. "Allow me to disagree."

"Very well," she noted briskly, his glance much too provocative, or perhaps only her reaction to it was. "I'm so glad they have cherry pudding," she added brightly. "It happens to be my favorite."

She reminded him less of a woman of the world at that moment, and more like some uncertain ingenue fresh from the schoolroom. Not that he was in any position to question whether or not she was fully in control of her emotions when he'd been struggling to balance his own since Waterloo. And as she'd reiterated often enough, this afternoon was about a ride in the country and nothing more. Brushing aside all the more complicated issues of why he and she were here, he instead set about putting her at ease and enjoying himself in the bargain.

They drank and ate and spoke idly about the races and the local countryside, about the weather and crops, about the coming horse fairs as though they were simple farmers like the others in the room. They particularly found common ground in their passion for racing bloodstock and the turf.

"Not that I've had time lately to indulge those interests," Annabelle noted. "It takes enormous time and resources to keep a stable, neither of which I have at the moment."

"Because of your family situation."

"Yes." She met his gaze, glanced down and exhaled softly. Looking up again, she quietly said, "I suppose there's no point in being obtuse. Everything comes out sooner or later, I've found."

"Whatever you say goes no farther. My word on it."

She hesitated a moment longer, then said in a rush as though needing to speak headlong or not at all, "You must understand—one of my top priorities is to avoid Walingame for a great many reasons I choose not to enumerate. You must give me your *assurance* you will speak of this to no one."

"I assure you, whatever you say will be kept in the strictest confidence." He'd never liked Walingame—a bully of a man—and whether it was fear or repulsion he saw in her eyes, he proceeded to offer her his protection. "If you need a deterrent to Walingame, please allow me to be of assistance."

"Thank you, but I'll manage." Like she had in the past.

For a man who had defended English interests throughout the campaigns in Europe, helping a woman was a minor affair. "In any case, the offer holds should you change your mind."

"You're very kind." Perhaps the wine had loosened her tongue, or maybe it was comforting to confide in someone after so long. She couldn't discuss her concerns with her mother in her current state—no more than she could have in the past, she conceded. For the sake of her family's reputation, Annabelle had always sanitized her life in London.

But Darley knew who she was and what she was and took exception to neither. That he'd been suffering his own demons gave him a vulnerability she found appealing. There was a benevolence in him as well—an understanding of adversity and hardship unusual in men of his class.

"You may regret asking for an account of my visit to Shoreham," she said with a rueful smile. "It's not a pretty picture."

"Nor is my nightmarish life of late. In any case, I am beyond shock at this point if ever I was."

"Very well." She took a breath, exhaled, and began. "Several months ago, I learned my sister was being kept prisoner by her husband and immediately came to Shoreham armed with barristers—you know George Martin's firm—and several Bow Street Runners. My sister was in a nearby village, and with the aid of my small army, I was able to free her from her abusive situation. But she didn't long survive, dying only days later after giving birth to Cricket. I've been in Shoreham ever since. Walingame is looking for me, I'm sure; we didn't part on good terms. And there it is. Not a happy story."

"I'm sorry for the loss of your sister. It must have been terrible to find her so abused. If I can help in any way, you need but ask. We have family barristers who could exact retribution on her husband if you like."

"I want nothing more to do with any of them. If I were inclined to take action against them, I fear they may retaliate by taking Cricket away. Legally, they have every right. Fortunately, they only wanted Chloe's dowry and have no interest in her child."

"At least you have comfort in that."

"Yes. And thank you for your offer, but we are managing willy-nilly. Molly has been a virtual godsend, and in time I'm hoping Mother will recover. Losing Chloe unhinged her completely."

"I'm aware of what trauma can do to the mind. Perhaps too much aware."

She held his gaze. "I've bared my soul; it's your turn. Tell me about your seclusion."

He explained, in an edited fashion similar to hers, how Eddie had literally brought him back from the dead after finding him in the mass of slain bodies at Waterloo. "He nursed me with the help of a local peasant family, and after a very bad week, he tells me, he began to have hope that I might survive. My family was frantic, of course; they'd come over to Belgium looking for me. Eventually, we were reunited, I was carried home, and I've been here ever since. Recuperating but not recuperated." He smiled tightly. "Your mother and I could no doubt share accounts of our mental travails."

"So we are all struggling to find our way."

"Constantly. Although recently, you've brought a great deal of pleasure into my life." He held up his hand at the sudden closed look coming over her face. "I make no demands of you. None at all. Now, enough of this grimness on a pleasant summer day. Open that box from Grey's and tell me if you like what you see."

"I shouldn't," she said, understanding it would be prudent to reject all overtures from a man of such formidable charm.

"It's the merest bagatelle," Duff returned with a casual wave of his hand. "A curate's wife could accept it without a qualm."

She gave him an amused look. "Are you in the habit of giving gifts to curates' wives?"

He grinned. "Not lately."

"But you have."

"I hope we're not going to share tales of our amorous adventures."

"Yours, perhaps, were more adventuresome than mine."

"If you like, we could discuss the topic when we know each other better."

"What makes you think we're going to know each other better?" she replied flippantly, even while she found herself taking curious pleasure in the prospect.

He grinned. "Call it a good feeling."

She should chastise him for openly flirting; she should make it clear she wasn't in the mood for seduction. If she wasn't enjoying herself so, she might have. If her life hadn't been wrapped in gloom for so long, she might have been more inclined to offer him rebuke. Instead, she said, "How pleasant it is to actually smile and feel good."

"Amen to that—and ten hallelujahs." He gestured at the box again. "Open it."

When she lifted the lid, a set of mother-of-pearl combs handsomely decorated with small sapphires glistened up at her. "They're gorgeous," she breathed, lifting one out and turning it to catch the light from the window. "Any curate's wife would be enchanted," she said with a smile, knowing full well a curate's wife would never have anything so expensive. Unless, of course, Darley was bedding her.

"They match your dress," he observed. "It must be fate."

She had to agree the color was very close to the shade of blue lutestring she wore. Her brows arched upward. "So—you believe in fate?"

"More than the goodness of man," he retorted with a raised brow.

She grimaced faintly. "I shan't argue with you there."

"I fought in Wellington's campaign against Napoleon for three years and saw enough inhumanity to man to last me ten lifetimes. It makes one inclined to embrace the life of a hermit," he muttered, a scowl drawing his dark brows together. Visibly shaking himself a second later, he forced a smile. "Humor a jaundiced soul and take the combs. Put them in your hair for me—if you think they'll stay," he added, surveying her curls. Her pale hair was clipped short in the *dernier cri* of fashion, only those women in the vanguard of the *beau mode* capable of carrying off the revolutionary style.

She hesitated briefly, the comb in her hand; and then, with a nod, obliged him, pulling back her curls at her temple and securing them.

"Perfectly lovely," he murmured, not necessarily alluding to the comb.

"I thank you," she replied with a faint dip of her head, and lifting the second comb from the box, she clasped back the curls on her opposite temple.

"I thank you more," he said, an odd note of wistfulness in his voice. "I hadn't realized how much I've missed the company of a beautiful woman."

"Perhaps we've both been hermits too long." It was a spontaneous utterance, but undeniably true.

"In regard to our overlong hermitages, may I say I'm very much looking forward to the views from Monastery Hill," Duff observed, deliberately keeping his tone light. "I think I shall see them with fresh eyes."

"I agree. I can't recall when last I've been sightseeing."

"Forgive me in advance, for I'm already taking advantage of your friendship, but do check with your mother when we get back and see if she'll give you leave to attend the races." Not wishing to frighten her off, he refrained from saying he would actually look forward to tomorrow if she were to say yes.

"I'd like that." She chose not to parse her feelings or worry about what she should or should not say. She could blame the wine if she wished, although she knew better. Her good spirits had more to do with Duff's charm than alcohol.

The cherry pudding suddenly arrived, reminding them to eat, and putting aside unhappy topics, they enjoyed a hearty meal, a jug of wine, and convivial conversation.

If it had been possible to define contentment, both parties would have agreed their meal at Bedloe Inn offered them an explicit précis of that feeling. Duff couldn't remember when he'd last laughed so often or felt so joyful, while Annabelle relished their time together as though it were forbidden fruit.

It couldn't last.

But while it did, she would take delight in every moment.

Chapter
9

The views from Monastery Hill were more spectacular than either had remembered, the valley below spreading out lush green and fertile as far as the eye could see, the patchwork of fields bucolically dotted with grazing livestock, the river flowing through the flat as blue as the summer sky.

They sat on a horse blanket Duff had spread on the ground and talked of other times they'd sat thusly and seen the exact scene through a child's eyes.

"Life was simpler then," Duff murmured.

"Unarguably simpler," Annabelle said with a sigh.

"Things will get better." Eddie was too far away to hear, but had he heard, he would have danced a jig.

"I hope you're right." There were times she wasn't so sure.

"Let me help you and your family." As she opened her mouth to respond, he quickly added, "You'd be doing me a favor."

"Come, Duff, don't gull me. If ever a man had everything life could offer, it's you."

"Wealth alone isn't enough."

She snorted. "Don't say that to those who struggle every day to put food in their mouths."

"I understand. But it would give me pleasure to offer your family assistance."

"I am capable of taking care of my family."

"I know you are. But we have servants by the score and there must be times when you could use an extra pair of hands to ease the burden for Molly and yourself."

"Don't do this, Duff." She pursed her lips.

"But I want to."

She shot him a heated glance. "While the last thing *I* want is to be beholden to you."

"You wouldn't be."

"Of course I would. Do you take me for a grass-green girl? Men invariably want something for their favors."

"I don't."

"Have you been emasculated by your wounds?" she said with deliberate rudeness.

He didn't rise to the bait. Instead he said with a smile, "Would you like to find out?"

"There, you see? You're acting exactly like every other man who pretends not to want what he clearly wants."

"You're very defensive."

She gave him a flinty look. "And I shouldn't be?"

"Not with me."

"So I can accept all you offer with no fear of you importuning me for more."

"Why don't you say it? Importuning you for sex."

"Very well. You *don't* want sex with me?"

"I didn't say that. I'm only saying I won't ask for it."

"Of course you will."

"No, I won't."

Her gaze was mocking. "I don't suppose you'd care to make a wager on that?"

"You'd lose."

"I doubt it."

He smiled. "It's up to you, but I wouldn't bet more than you can afford to lose."

Duff's utter calm annoyed or insulted her—she wasn't sure which. But the upshot was she found herself challenging that calm by posing the question, "What would you say to five hundred pounds?" That most of the noblemen she knew could no more control their sexual urges than they could hold back the tides no doubt made her bold.

"What I'd say is, don't bet so much. Your family could use it more than I."

"I don't intend to lose."

"You're sure?"

"Absolutely."

"Five hundred pounds it is. Do we have some time frame?"

"Forever?" she queried flippantly.

"I'd prefer a more practical limit."

"Because you have ulterior motives?"

He laughed. "No, because I'd like to collect my winnings."

"Such arrogance."

"Not really. I just know what I can and cannot do. And while we're deciding on the rules, I would like if you would let me help your family in the interim. Why don't we say— what . . . two months? Is that enough time to assure you my motives are honorable?"

She didn't answer for a very long time, not sure she wished to become involved on any level with the Marquis of Darley— scarred by the wounds of war or not. On the other hand, he was offering a type of assistance that would be welcome. And she couldn't discount the possibility he might be useful to have around should Walingame discover her whereabouts. Lastly, five hundred pounds was five hundred pounds. "Two months?"

"Yes." He didn't say *unless you ask me before that*—a thought that took him so much by surprise, he quickly added, "You decide, of course."

"Very well. I can always use five hundred pounds."

He smiled. "Done." He put out his hand.

She clasped it.

And the bargain was made.

He immediately spoke of other things then, as though their wager was incidental. As though he gave no more mind to it than he did the light breeze fluttering the leaves overhead. He spoke of how he used to come to the ruins as a child and play at knightly battle games with his friends. He showed her where he'd tumbled from the highest point on the partially collapsed nave wall and had frightened his playmates half to death by lying there comatose for several minutes. "My parents forbid me to climb that high after that," he said with a smile, reaching out to touch the moss-covered wall as though recalling those times long ago.

"And did you mind them?" Annabelle asked, as capable as he of bland social intercourse. "I expect not."

"I tried." He grinned. "And failed, of course. It was too much to expect from a young boy, in any event. But I was more cautious at least. I don't expect you played battle games up here?"

It suddenly seemed as though he was standing too close; his male scent, his cologne fragrant in her nostrils, his sheer size stirring provocative feelings she'd rather not feel. She took a step back. "As a matter of fact, I came up here to paint." It took an extra modicum of self-control to speak in a normal tone of voice, although she'd been an actress too long to let her agitation show. "The ruins were an ideal subject for an impressionable young girl, conjuring up all kinds of romantic fantasies. In fact," she said with a lifted brow, "I wrote a medieval tale with Bedloe as backdrop."

"How old were you when you came here?" Her hair was like spun gold in the sunlight, he thought, flexing his fingers against the sudden urge to touch it. Perhaps cued by those golden curls, a sudden image of another blond head sunk into the mud at Waterloo leaped into his brain—Merriman's death a gruesome, bloody sight. Duff went rigid, every muscle taut and unyielding as he struggled to deal with the harrowing memory.

"Eight or ten. Are you all right?" Duff appeared as though cast in stone, his gaze tormented. "Is there something I can do?" Belle murmured, reaching out to take his hand.

He jerked back.

She cried out.

Whether her shocked cry or her expression of fear restored his sanity, he instantly became conscious of his surroundings. "Forgive me," he said with as much casualness as he could muster. "I didn't mean to frighten you. Unfortunately, some of my battle memories appear at the most inconvenient times. I apologize if I alarmed you."

"You needn't apologize. I sympathize with your plight." Knowing what agony Chloe's death had caused, she could only imagine how greatly Duff suffered. War was always brutal and the casualties at Waterloo had been horrendous. "Would you like to leave?"

He wished to say *I won't harm you* or *Eddie is near so don't be afraid*. But neither would calm her if his recent moment of delirium had been disquieting for her. "We probably should," he said politely. "I've kept you away too long."

"No, not at all. I only meant to be helpful if you weren't feeling well."

How polite she was. But then, she was an actress of note. She was capable of affecting an effortless urbanity, even under stress. "I'm fine, but thank you. However, if you wish to be helpful," he said with a small smile, inclined by both birth and personality to be willful, "if you'd go to the races with me tomorrow, I'd be most grateful. Say yes and we'll leave now."

She looked startled for a moment, his choices oddly constraining.

He laughed. "You misunderstand. You're free to go regardless your answer. It's just that I would like to escort you to the races tomorrow—with your mother's consent, of course."

"Your moods are highly changeable, my lord," she said with just a hint of wariness in her voice.

"I admit they are at times. But in your company, the worst

of my demons are held at bay. Not that you're obligated in any way to be solicitous on that account. I state a fact only." He shrugged, the light in his eyes playful once again. "So what do you say? If you're concerned with my mental state, you'll be quite safe in the midst of the race crowd. And consider, you could win a sizeable sum if you bet with me."

She smiled, reassured by his honesty, liking the fact that he could openly acknowledge his demons. Most men couldn't. "Are you saying you know horseflesh better than I?"

He grinned. "I might. Why don't we see?"

She laughed. "Not another wager, Duff. One is enough."

"In any case, the racing should be excellent. And if the weather holds, how can we lose?"

"How indeed." She felt a piquant excitement, something uncommon of late, the thought of the races tomorrow altogether pleasing. "Why don't I see how Mother is doing in the morning and I'll let you know."

"I'll send Eddie over."

"Rather than have Eddie ride over, perhaps needlessly, if you don't hear from me by noon plan on stopping by, say, at one?"

A faint smile played about his fine mouth. "I shall pray for your mother's continuing recuperation."

She dipped her head. "I shall as well."

"Good," he murmured, taking her hand in his.

She didn't pull away, although she should have.

A small silence fell.

Bending low, he dropped a light kiss on her forehead. "Thank you for your pleasant company," he murmured.

She hadn't been kissed so platonically in years. It was a lovely, beguiling gesture. She smiled up at him. "Thank *you*," she said.

"Until tomorrow, then."

"Provided all the stars are aligned," she noted.

"I'll see what I can do." A roguish certitude infused his words.

"Even you aren't so arrogant, Duff, as to think you can command the stars."

"You don't know me very well."

She should have said she had no intention of getting to know him well, but she said, instead, soft and low, "Nor you me."

He grinned. "Don't say you're flirting with me?"

"I most certainly am not," she protested, lying to herself as well as him, feeling an unalloyed joy even as she perjured herself.

"Whatever you say, Miss Foster."

"Belle," she offered.

"Belle," he repeated, a delectable enticement in his silken tone.

What was she doing, she thought with alarm. Why was she succumbing to his practiced charm? Who better than she should know better? Pulling her hand from his, she moved swiftly toward their horses. "Do you think your mount has any chance at all of beating my little mare on the ride home?" she asked as though nothing had passed between them, as though she didn't feel the need to pretend indifference to his allure.

"It depends how well you ride," he replied drolly, quick to pick up on her altered mood.

She swivelled around. "I can ride as well as you."

"Ten quid says you can't." He understood her need to put more distance between them. He was grateful she was sensible for them both.

She began running toward the mare. "You're going to lose!" she cried.

If he wasn't afraid of losing badly, he would have stood there enjoying the view. Her feet were flying over the grass, her skirts billowing out around her, her curls bobbing, her slender form a delight to the eye. He particularly liked that she was wearing his hair combs, the sapphires sparkling in the sun as she ran. He'd have to bring her something more tomorrow—something to make her smile.

Then he broke into a run and shouted, "I'm gaining on you," just to hear her laugh.

She did.

Somehow he'd known she would.

As though they shared some common bond.

In his new joyous mood, he refused to acknowledge that bond as shared misery.

He much preferred the notion of a spiritual renewal.

Or say, optimism.

And maybe two months from now, it could be something else entirely.

Chapter

10

Duff surprised his family by appearing just as they were sitting down to dinner.

"Come in, darling," his mother exclaimed, waving him in as he stood in the doorway. "How nice you look."

"Eddie convinced me it was time to dress for dinner again," Duff said, moving into the room. Recently, he'd been disinclined to honor the formality. On the occasions when he'd come for dinner he'd been casually attired. "You must have seen to the alterations on my evening clothes," he said, smiling at his mother as he strode across the large room that was bathed in the saffron glow of a midsummer twilight. "This fits."

"Weston sent a man up. He's always so very accommodating. You look quite elegant, my dear. Sit here . . . by me," the duchess added, signaling that a footman set another plate beside her. "Our big excitement today was little Liza's pony ride. She rode her pony for the first time and we all cheered her on. What have you been up to?"

"Not much. Eddie and I rode to the monastery ruins at Bedloe. The view was astonishing as always." No one gave any indication they'd already heard of his activities. But taking note of everyone's smiles as he approached the table and understanding the swiftness of servants' gossip, he added, "As you no doubt have already heard, Miss Foster accompanied me."

"Did she?" his mother remarked blandly. "How lovely. Julius, did you hear?" she said to her husband seated at the other end of the table. "Duff had company this afternoon."

The Duke of Westerlands smiled. "And very pleasant company, I warrant. What is Miss Foster doing in the country this time of year?" The season was in full swing and Annabelle, on friendly terms with all the great hostesses, was always invited to the best parties.

Debating how to answer, Duff stood for a moment behind his chair, his fingers curved over the polished mahogany back. "Miss Foster is spending some time with her family," he said, choosing a neutral reply. "If her schedule allows, she's agreed to go to the races with me tomorrow." They'd know soon enough, he thought; he might as well tell them. "Also, I only frightened her once with one of my trances, so all and all, things went well."

"Well, you're to be commended," his mother noted with a smile. "Or perhaps Miss Foster is to be commended for her tact. Sit, darling," the duchess murmured, playing the perfect hostess and not querying him further. "Have a glass of wine. Your papa had a few of his special bottles brought up tonight."

They all knew, Duff thought. They knew he'd be coming to dinner. Were they apprised of Annabelle's family situation as well? Not that he was about to ask. He'd given Annabelle his word he wouldn't discuss it.

But his entire family had watched over him with varying degrees of apprehension since his return from Waterloo. News of his outing would have been gratifying to them.

In fact, his parents and siblings had all, on one thin pretext or another, foregone the season and chosen to spend the summer at Westerlands Park in order to be near him. His two married sisters and their children, as well as his younger brother, were in residence. Not that Giles was averse to avoiding all the maneuvering mamas in London with daughters to marry off. But Georgina and Lydia were sacrificing their pleasures; they adored the whirl of parties. They missed their husbands as well, who had estates from which they couldn't be absent for long periods of time.

"You're looking remarkably well, Duff. Truly you are," Georgie said with a smile. The youngest of his siblings, she shared their mother's fair coloring and blue eyes. "How delightful to see you out and about again like your old self."

Duff wondered what the hell Eddie had said—his "old self" prone to a decidedly intemperate life. But he chose to reply in a different vein. "Eddie thinks the new mare I bought became a talisman for my recovery." He smiled. "Perhaps he's right. God knows, he's put up with my black moods long enough to recognize an improvement."

"Are you thinking about racing your stable again, then?" His sister Lydia had been horse-mad since childhood, her thoroughbreds consistent winners. "Everyone's missed your flashy bloodstock on the track," she said with a lift of her dark brows. "Your jockey, Harry, could always be counted on for a dazzling show."

"I *am* considering putting my prime'uns out again. Eddie's going to talk to Harry and see if he can be cajoled into riding for me."

"He's working for Armitage. You might make an enemy," his sister warned.

"It's Harry's decision," Duff said with a shrug. "As for Armitage"—he smiled—"the old coot should pay his jockeys better and they might not stray."

"He pays well and you know it." Giles gazed at his brother over the rim of his wineglass.

Duff grinned. "But not as well as I."

"And Harry dearly loves you." The duchess smiled at her son. "I don't know how many times he was over before the race season, hoping you were well enough to speak to him. He'll ride for you. You needn't worry."

"I appreciate the vote of confidence." Duff shot a glance at the rest of his family. "I suppose everyone has a racer on the course tomorrow."

"But of course, darling," his mother replied. "Papa has won three races this year and my new little mare is doing well. Giles has a brute of a horse that has a bit of training yet to accomplish, but Georgie and Lydia"—she glanced at her daughters. "Tell Duff about your wins."

At that point, horses and racing took over the conversation, a not uncommon occurrence at the Westerlands' table. And for the first time since his return to England, Duff felt a sense of normalcy. Not that his former life would have been characterized as normal by the more staid circles of society. But it had been typical of a wealthy young buck about town.

Gambling, racing, and women had consumed his days and nights, his name a byword for high play, prime horseflesh, and carnal pleasure. While the legions of women in pursuit had been the envy of his male colleagues, he'd accepted female adulation with a casual imperturbability that only added to his allure. Although his reputation for delivering sexual pleasure with a deft and flattering attention to detail couldn't be discounted. Nor his superior physical endowments and stamina.

Not that he'd been doing anything that required stamina in bed of late.

However, if his recuperation continued apace . . .

A thought well apart from the heated discussion of horses and jockeys transpired at the moment.

Much later, though, over dessert, when the candles had been lit and the duke's excellent wine had loosened tongues, Georgie said, "You must bring Miss Foster to our box at the track tomorrow. I haven't seen her for ages. She simply disappeared from society."

"She may prefer her seclusion." Duff's voice was reserved. "I'll extend your invitation, but I can't promise anything."

"How mysterious you sound, although she vanished from town just as mysteriously." Georgie held her brother's gaze for a pertinent moment. "You know Walingame is searching for her high and low."

"I know."

"No one has seen Annabelle for months."

"I saw her at the horse fair in plain sight of everyone," Duff pointed out. "She wasn't exactly hiding."

"Whatever she chooses to do, I'm sure it's none of our business," the duchess asserted, giving her daughter a warning glance. "Miss Foster has had her share of fame. Perhaps the country offers her a much-needed respite."

"I believe she's enjoying her quiet," Duff agreed.

"That's quite enough said on the topic," the duke interposed, attempting to put an end to the catechism. "Whether we see Miss Foster tomorrow or not is of no consequence. We'll visit with her some other time." Annabelle was much feted by society—not unusual, considering her plays were all the rage.

"Why not invite her to dinner," Giles said with a grin. "We're secluded enough here at Westerlands Park."

"Giles," the duke said repressively.

Duff smiled. "Never mind, Papa. I can't fault Giles for trying. Miss Foster is enchanting. If she wishes to come to dinner, I'll let you know, Giles," he added with a grin.

"You needn't keep her all to yourself," his brother muttered.

"We're just going to the races. I'm hardly keeping her to myself."

"Boys, for heaven's sake. Julius, tell them to stop," the duchess insisted, looking to her husband to referee the brothers.

"You heard your mother. The subject is closed. I think it's time for port." The duke nodded at a footman as he came to his feet. "We'll have tea and port in the drawing room." He moved down the table to his wife, Elspeth, who looked radiant in aquamarine tissue silk, her beauty undiminished at fifty-four.

While older, the duke was still fit and handsome, although his dark hair had grayed at the temples.

Perhaps their love kept them youthful. Their marriage was filled with joy, their affection for each other deep and abiding.

Taking Elspeth's hand, the duke helped her to her feet, then turned to his children and deliberately shifted the conversation back to racing. "Why don't we make our day at the track tomorrow a little more interesting. What say I give five-to-one odds on my black? Although he's going to win, so perhaps there aren't any takers."

"I don't know about that, Papa," Lydia quickly retorted. "My bay has a good chance of winning. He came in only seconds behind your black during the practice run this morning."

"Not to mention Lord Greyson's ringer from the North is running tomorrow," Giles noted, rising from his chair. "Your black may not win."

The duke's gaze narrowed. "How do you know it's a ringer?"

"So gossips attest. Or more to the point, a reliable bookmaker said as much."

The duke softly swore, then quirked his mouth in a faint smile. "We'll have to find out the truth before the race tomorrow, now won't we?"

"Excellent idea, darling," Elspeth said. "You know how I hate to lose."

Over port and very little tea, the next day's race card was dissected and discussed, everyone placing their bets on the morrow's race as was their habit.

It was late when Duff finally rose from his chair and bid his family good night.

Had he stayed to listen at the door he would have heard his family's consensus strongly favoring his new friendship with Miss Foster. Everyone agreed she was the best thing that had happened to him since his return from Waterloo. His family agreed as well that should events progress sufficiently, Miss Foster should indeed be invited to dinner.

"But I shall do the inviting," the duchess stated firmly.

"And you are ordered to behave, Giles. We want nothing to disturb your brother's improved situation."

"I was only teasing, Mama," Giles protested.

"Your mother is aware of both your susceptibility to beautiful women and Miss Foster's splendid good looks, however," the duke noted. "Miss Foster can be very dazzling, so mind your manners."

"Dazzling?" The duchess sent an amused look her husband's way. "Do you mean to say you've noticed?"

"I only have eyes for you, darling," he replied with a grin. "That does not mean, however, that I'm blind."

"I understand, sweetheart," the duchess noted gently. "We all agree that Miss Foster is a diamond of the first water. Now if only she will be kind to our dear Duff."

The issue of kindness to the marquis was hardly under debate at the Foster cottage that evening. Annabelle's mother and Molly were loud and persistent in their praise of the marquis. And while Annabelle was perhaps a tad less enthusiastic in her response, she had to agree in principle that Duff was indeed charming.

And, she decided, it wouldn't be a question so much of being pleasant to him, but rather of taking care not to be *too* pleasant.

"By all means you must go to the races tomorrow with that nice young man," her mother insisted. "Molly and I can care for Cricket very well without you."

"Mama, please don't read anything more than casual friendship in Darley's interest," Annabelle warned, not wishing her mother to harbor false hopes about their relationship. "You know as well as I that nobles keep to their own kind. We are well below his station."

"It doesn't hurt to enjoy yourself at the races," Mrs. Foster retorted. "Does it, Molly?" she added with a wink at the wet nurse. The two women had discussed the marquis at length while Annabelle was gone.

"Not one bit it don't hurt," Molly agreed cheerfully. "A little fun would be good for you, Miss Belle."

"You must wear something pretty tomorrow, my dear," her mother declared, her good humor in sharp contrast to her recent despairing moods. "Perhaps that lovely pink sprigged muslin with the ruffled hem and lace collar."

Belle made a small moue. "I'm not sure I wish to wear something so colorful with Chloe so recently gone."

"Nonsense. Nothing will bring Chloe back no matter if you wear the blackest black forever," Mrs. Foster asserted steadfastly. "And your dear sister would want you to be happy. Since Papa died we've been sadly lacking in anything resembling that emotion. Do you know the marquis made me laugh today," her mother said, softly, "when I thought I'd forgotten how. And it felt ever so good, darling," she added with a brisk nod. "So be a dear and wear something nice for me tomorrow."

How could she refuse when her mother had been lost to her inner world of misery for months? How could she possibly refuse such a simple request. "If you wish me to wear the pink sprigged muslin, Mama, I shall," Annabelle said, smiling at her mother.

"What a good girl you are," her mother said cheerfully, as she had so many times during Annabelle's childhood. "Now, you'll need a bonnet for the sun, what with the racetrack out in the open. Do we have anything pretty?"

"I have that small leghorn bonnet, Mama." It had been left behind on one of her previous visits.

"Yes, yes." Her mother clapped her hands. "The little straw with the pink ribbons and silk roses. Perfect. Now, you must make sure to be ready by one so the marquis isn't kept waiting."

If going to the races with Duff and wearing pink could make her mother this happy, she would gladly comply, Annabelle decided. "Don't worry, Mama, I'll be ready beforetimes."

And in truth, perhaps she might even be looking forward to

a festive afternoon at the races in the company of the charming marquis.

Duff was very different from the men she'd known.

Less covetous and predatory, touched with a kind of grace.

And he was willing to be a friend, he'd said.

Although time would tell about that.

In her experience, friendships between men and women didn't exist.

Chapter
11

The next morning, Eddie walked into Duff's bedroom, bringing him his morning coffee and a small leather box from his father.

"The duke's steward brung it over," Eddie said, depositing the box on the bedside table and handing Duff his coffee. "I figured it wer serious business to get old Norton out this far."

"Was there a note with it?" Duff recognized Grey's signature red box.

Eddie dug in his waistcoat pocket and pulled out a folded card.

Taking the card from his batman, Duff flipped it open with one finger as he drank down his coffee in a single draught. "Christ," he muttered a moment later, tossing the card aside, shoving his empty cup at Eddie and leaning over to grab the red box. "Apparently I've been an invalid too bloody long." He opened the lid to find a small jeweled pin in the shape of a rose resting on crushed white satin. "Pink diamonds for Miss Foster," he drawled. "My father doesn't think I have brains enough to court her properly."

"There be a few more items downstairs, too, sar," Eddie noted sheepishly. "I didn't know if'n—"

"I'd toss you back downstairs if you brought them all up?"

"Yes, sar," his batman murmured, keeping his distance.

"Good thinking," Duff growled.

"They all mean well, sar."

Duff grimaced. "I know they do." He sighed softly. "So what the hell else is Miss Foster getting today?"

"I don't rightly know, sar. But every single one in your family sent somethin' over."

"*Everyone?*"

"Including the dowager duchess, sar."

The marquis's eyes widened. "Even Grandmama is making plans for me, it seems," he said with a faint smile. "Well, bring the bloody things up, I suppose, and we'll see what we have." Throwing back the bedclothes, he rose from the bed. "Better yet, I'll come down. There's hot water on the stove, right?"

"Yes, sar."

"You can douse me with it outside. It's a fine, warm day and if I'm reading my family's concern right, I'd better see that I'm spotlessly bathed, dressed to the nines, and on my best behavior with Miss Foster. Good Lord, I must have been a worry to them all," he noted, striding over to the window and leaning on the sill. "Although the sun does seem to be shining with an added glow these days, Eddie. Damned if it doesn't."

"I'm pleased to hear it, sar. Would you be wearing somethin' new today?"

Duff swung around. "Has my mother replenished my entire wardrobe?"

"A right good part of it, sar. What with your weight loss and all, she been keeping Weston busy."

Duff chuckled. "Pick out something. I don't care. Although, keep in mind my family's censure will fall on your shoulders should I not be outfitted to perfection," he added drolly.

"I'll do me best, sar."

While the marquis was dressed by his batman, Annabelle was attended to with the same degree of attention. Molly had ironed every little wrinkle from the pink muslin and the bonnet ribbons, Mrs. Foster had insisted on helping Annabelle with her hair, and even Cricket and little Betty had been propped up to oversee Annabelle's toilette. As Annabelle twirled around at the last to show off her ensemble, the babies cooed their approval and smiled, as if even they understood the importance of the occasion.

"This is just a race meet, Mama," Annabelle said, feeling the need to point out the obvious in the midst of such giddy expectation.

"Of course it is, sweetheart. We know that, don't we, Molly?"

At which point the women both giggled and grinned, and Annabelle's apprehensions grew in direct proportion to her companions' all-atwitter moods. But it was pointless to belabor the issue, Annabelle decided, when neither woman was willing to accede to reality. And to see her mother in such high spirits was truly a miracle. So she kept her counsel and let her mother and Molly buzz around her, both of them fussing till the last with a tweak to her hair or a smoothing of her skirt or some exhortation of one kind or another warning her to be polite and smile.

As if she didn't know how to deal with a gentleman.

As if she wasn't the consummate companion if she wished to be.

The real question was whether she did or not.

Or to what degree she wished to please the marquis.

Although she couldn't help but smile as Duff brought his smart black phaeton to a halt at her garden gate shortly before one, secured the reins, leaped down, and strode up her garden path, whistling.

There was something about Darley that made one want to smile, she thought, watching him approach—as though he were capable of transferring his good cheer to you with ease. She didn't quite know what to make of it. She wasn't giddy by nature. Or frivolous.

She'd never had the opportunity.

Her father had been ill for several years before he'd died,

and she'd helped him with his silversmithing as a child. As his illness progressed, she'd taken on more and more of the burdens of his business. She half smiled. She still could turn a pretty bowl or candlestick if she'd been so inclined. And if her father's creditors hadn't taken advantage of her mother after he died, she might have been a silversmith today. They'd been left with nothing but the small shop, empty of merchandise and mortgaged to the hilt.

At Duff's knock on the door, she shook away the melancholy memories, put a smile on her face—she was an actress, after all—and went to open the door.

Her mother rushed forward and opened the door instead, greeting the marquis like a long-lost friend. "Do come in, Lord Darley. What a lovely day we have, don't you think? Perfect for the track."

As her mother and Duff exchanged pleasantries, Annabelle stood in the passage from the parlor listening and watching, like she might have in the wings at one of her plays.

Darley was more handsome than any principal actor of the day, his manner completely unstudied and natural, as though he wasn't a peer of the realm visiting a modest cottage, but rather a neighbor of lesser rank—an old friend.

"There you are, darling," her mother called out, catching sight of Annabelle in the shadows. "Do you have your reticule with you? She always forgets it, the dear—since she was a child. Don't scowl at me, sweetheart. I'm sure the marquis doesn't mind that you're a bit forgetful," her mother added with a warm smile. "She always has more important things on her mind, you see. Her plays and politics and such. She reads the papers she has sent out from London every day and books—my goodness . . . so many books—"

"I'm sure the marquis doesn't care about my books, Mama," Annabelle interposed, touching her mother's arm. "I'm quite ready," she noted, smiling up at Duff. "Reticule and all."

"You two have a marvelous time!" her mother exclaimed. "And bet a few shillings for me on any little gray mare," she added, handing some coins to Duff. "They're always lucky for me."

"Consider it done, Mrs. Foster." He offered his arm to Annabelle.

As they strolled down the path to the phaeton, Mrs. Foster and Molly stood in the open doorway radiating good cheer.

"He's sweet on her," Molly whispered. "It's plain as the nose on my face."

"He is sure enough, but Belle's right not to expect anything more than friendship," her mother murmured. "She'll enjoy herself today, though, and for that we should all be grateful."

"Amen to that, ma'am," Molly agreed. "We all be right pleased that somethin' fun be a-happenin' for Miss Belle."

And indeed the afternoon was highly entertaining.

Duff was on his best behavior, taking care to be charming and amusing in equal measure, never stepping over the bounds of the most casual of friendships.

Annabelle, in turn, responded with wit and disarmingly candid replies, perhaps even mildly flirtatious comments at times.

They agreed the weather was perfection, the crowd a lively crush, the lemonade more tasty than usual.

They found they were inclined to bet on the same horses and they favored the same jockeys as well.

It was an afternoon of congenial accord.

They even won a sizeable sum on two of the Westerlands' racers.

"I told you," Duff said with a grin as the duke's thorough-bred finished by an easy five lengths.

"I would have bet on him anyway," Annabelle replied, smiling. "That horse is absolutely glorious from nose to tail. He looked as though he could have raced another ten miles without effort."

"He can," Duff affirmed. "The desert breeds are known for their stamina. If you like, you could ride him sometime."

"Thank you. I may take you up on your offer," she remarked courteously, when she had no intention of going anywhere near his family. She'd already politely declined his offer to take a glass of champagne with them at their box in the stands. While she was enjoying Duff's company, she knew better than to allow herself to go beyond simple enjoyment. In fact, what most appealed about their friendship was its platonic nature. He'd promised not to ask her for more and he'd kept his word.

It was very liberating to find him charming and leave it at that.

Or so the rational part of her brain attested.

The less rational part of her brain was finding him increasingly attractive.

But she sensibly repressed those feelings and as a result, the afternoon at the races was excessively agreeable.

They counted their winnings and recapped the better races on their drive home, the few miles between the racetrack and Shoreham flying by as they discussed the events of the afternoon with the ease and affability of old acquaintances.

Just before the village of Shoreham would have come into view, however, Duff drew the phaeton to a stop in a small copse bordering the road.

Annabelle felt a predictable apprehension, importuning men a constant in her life. And now she would have to give him his congé as politely as possible.

Twining the reins around the whip stand, Duff turned to her with a grimace and a sigh. "I've been trying to find a discreet way to approach you on this subject," he said, "but to no avail. So I shall simply soldier on and hand these over to you," he added, swiveling around and pulling a small linen sack from a luggage compartment behind the seat and placing it in her lap. "This is all from my family. Apparently, I've become so pathetic, they felt the need to woo you for me. Not that I intend to go back on my word," he quickly amended at her frown. "Not in the least. If you please, though, do me a favor and take these small gifts in the spirit in which they were given. In friendship."

He was so obviously disconcerted, Annabelle couldn't but feel sympathy for him. "Your *family* sent these?"

"Yes. I've been in the grip of the blue megrims for too long, it seems. I didn't notice, but everyone else did and when you entered my life—they noticed that as well." He grinned. "I've been smiling more—or actually . . . again. So, please, consider these as offerings of gratitude from my very worried family."

She hadn't realized the extent of his prostration. "You've been *hors de combat* the entire time since Waterloo?"

"More or less. I've forgotten what normal is."

"You must be plagued by morbid memories."

"Always. Nights are worse."

"Are you able to sleep?"

"Not much—correction . . . better now, thanks to you," he said with a smile.

"To me?"

"My dreams of blood and gore have been tempered by occasional images of your lovely face. For that, I'd willingly buy out Grey's myself, but I haven't been to town for almost a year. So these are gifts from Grey's by association," he lightly added, not comfortable discussing his collapse. "And since my family expects me to bestir myself in this regard, please look at them and tell me you like them."

"Are they expecting a written report?" she teased.

"I wouldn't doubt it. They're treating me like a child."

"You, too? My mother and Molly practically told me what to say in order to engage your interest."

"Tell them not to worry." He grinned. "I'm thoroughly engaged. In fact, if I wasn't afraid of offending you, I might press you to amend our wager to something less than two months." His brows lifted marginally. "Don't say no right off. Say you'll think about it."

"Very well, I'll think about it and then say no," she playfully retorted.

Clasping his hands over his chest, he fell back with a groan. "You're breaking my heart," he murmured, coming upright again with a smile.

"I didn't know you had a heart, Duff. Or at least so gossip contended all those years when you left a series of repining ladies in your wake."

"Maybe I've discovered my previously errant heart," he said, grinning broadly.

"And maybe I wasn't born yesterday, my lord."

"You wound me grievously," he said with a dramatic sigh.

Annabelle laughed. "If I look at these gifts, will I alleviate your torment?"

"Vastly," he immediately replied. "And my family's concerns as well." He wanted her to have the jewelry. Even more than his family, perhaps. He was grateful for her friendship, and their wager aside, he wanted her to feel comfortable accepting the gifts.

There were six boxes in all—from his grandmother, mother, father, two sisters, and brother. Giles's offering, in fact, was decidedly splendid, and Duff wondered which of his brother's light o' loves would go without until the ruby bracelet could be replaced.

"It's too much, of course," Annabelle said several moments later, the jewelry twinkling in her lap.

"Rather, it's not enough by half," Duff remonstrated. "You've brought me back into the world. And if you don't take them, I'll sink back into my gloom."

"No, you won't."

"I might."

She gave him an assessing look, understanding how difficult it was to both accept and reject these offerings from his family. She didn't wish to offend the Westerlands. On the other hand, it would be difficult to bring so much expensive jewelry home. "If I were to accept these, it could cause problems with my mother. She's unaware of my life in the city—other than my stage work."

"I understand. But they'll fit in your reticule."

"I don't know," she murmured. "While it was very kind of your family to do this, taking these is a bit awkward."

"My family meant only to please you for all you've done for me. And they hope our friendship will prosper, of course."

Her gaze narrowed. "Why would they want that?"

"You misunderstand," he quickly said. "They mean for it to prosper in the most benign way. You're invited to dinner anytime you wish to come. My mother is intent on sending you an invitation in gratitude for my recovery."

"I'm indecisive, as you can see." Annabelle hesitated a moment more before saying, "In fact, I'm not sure I wish to extend our friendship to"—her nostrils flared—"very well, I'll say it—to your family."

"Dinner could be extremely informal. It's not as though you don't dine with any number of the *Ton*," Duff maintained. "At least think about it. Why don't I tell Maman it depends on *your* mother's health."

"So you *are* recovered?" she queried, in lieu of responding to his dinner invitation.

"Let's say, I'm well on my way"—his brows rose—"after nearly a year. So think what you will, but you are very much an angel of mercy to my family and me."

"I don't know what to say to such a fulsome compliment, other than thank you."

"You're very welcome." He grinned. "You've made the entire D'Abernon family ecstatic."

She smiled. "And how easy it was." Indeed, she should be thanking him for bringing joy into her family, her mother's spirits thoroughly revived. But more cautious in her position, she remained silent.

"So, then, I'll bundle these into your reticule"—he began placing the bits of jewelry into the purse hanging from her wrist—"and I'll bring you home."

She felt an odd remorse at the thought of him leaving. But ever pragmatic, she shook it away. "Thank you so much for a lovely afternoon. I mean it sincerely. I can't remember laughing so much." She made a small moue. "It's been some bit of time . . ."

"Would you like to come and see my stable and racers tomorrow? We could bring your mother and the baby if you don't wish to leave them again so soon. I could drive over in a larger carriage."

"How many horses do you have?" She should have said no; if she were truly pragmatic, she would have.

"Just ten at the moment. But four of them followed me through the campaigns in Europe. You saw Romulus yesterday; his mates are equally fine. Eddie could make tea for your mother if you like."

She laughed. "I'm sure he'd be pleased about that."

"Believe me, he's pleased about anything that takes me out into the world again. Say you'll come. We'll have a picnic."

"I shouldn't."

"Why ever not?"

She couldn't think of a good reason. It wasn't as though he was asking for anything out of the ordinary. "Very well, I'll ask Mother."

"Perfect. And why don't I ask her if she'd like to join us?"

But when he did, Mrs. Foster graciously refused, citing her invalid status as an excuse. "There's no reason why Annabelle can't see your racers, though," she quickly added. "It's lovely to see that rosy glow on her cheeks again. She's been inside too much and working so hard lately. You have, darling—don't look at me like that. It's the truth." Mrs. Foster turned to Duff. "What time will you be coming to fetch Annabelle?"

"Would ten be too early?" He only stopped himself from saying eight by sheer will.

"Not in the least. We all rise with the sun."

"You're sure you and Molly wouldn't like to come along and bring the babies too?" he offered politely, extending the invitation in all sincerity.

"Heavens no, but thank you. And thank you as well for my winnings." Mrs. Foster patted her skirt pocket where she'd placed the bills Duff had given her. "Gray mares always win for me. And I'll see that Annabelle is ready at ten, Lord Darley. There, see what she's learned on Drury stage?" Annabelle's mother said with a smile. "She can make the oddest faces. Now, darling," she added, patting Annabelle's arm, "a little sunshine and fresh air will do you wonders. Just you wait and see. And thank Lord Darley for the invitation, sweetheart. Hmpf, as if that mumbled thank-you is sufficient. Well, we thank you, my lord, even if my daughter has forgotten her manners."

"You're very welcome, Mrs. Foster. It's my pleasure, believe me." He caught Annabelle's eye and smiled. "Until tomorrow," he murmured and with an exquisite bow, he turned and left.

"Mama, for heaven's sake," Annabelle hissed as Duff walked back to his phaeton. "Would you please desist from practically shoving me into the marquis's pocket? It's humiliating!"

"Nonsense, darling. The man is as pleased as punch that you'll keep him company tomorrow. Isn't that so, Molly?" Mrs. Foster turned to her co-conspirator with a smile. "Wasn't he just as sweet as can be, asking us to come along?"

"That were the nicest thing I ever heard. An invitation from a man of his station. Can you imagine!" Molly exclaimed, wide-eyed.

"Now we must consider your ensemble for tomorrow," Mrs. Foster said, as though she were dresser for the queen.

"If you don't mind, Mama, I can very well dress myself," Annabelle retorted heatedly.

"My, my—my darling is in a right fine pet. One might almost think Lord Darley has struck some nerve when thou dost protest so much," she intoned archly.

Unable to refute her mother's pointed appraisal when her feelings were more involved than she would have liked,

Annabelle announced in what even she recognized was a thoroughly childish tone, "I'm tired. I'm going to my room." And she flounced off with the dramatic consequence of the premier actress of Drury Theater.

In contrast, Duff sang softly under his breath all the way home.

Chapter

12

Lord Innes entered White's gaming room, surveyed the crowd, and found the man he'd come to see. Walking up behind Walingame, he watched the play for only a few seconds before tapping him on the shoulder.

Glancing back, Walingame grunted, "Later, Dougal. Can't you see I'm winning?"

"I saw her."

Walingame spun around in his chair and held his friend's gaze. "Are you sure?"

"Yesterday at Whiting Hill track. With Duff."

Walingame tossed his cards on the table, muttered, "I'm out," and without a backward glance at his sizeable stack of markers, came to his feet and propelled his friend from the room.

"Tell me everything," Walingame growled as the two men stood in the quiet corridor outside. "I want to know what she looked like, what she said—did you speak to her? Was she really there with *that fucking cunthound*? I want to know every detail," he snarled.

"She looked gorgeous as usual, and—"

Walingame grabbed Dougal's arm. "Did you talk to her?"

"I wasn't able to get close enough." Innes shrugged off

Walingame's grip. "She and Duff were standing at the rail for some reason, and you know what the hoi polloi mob is like. They wouldn't budge for the king himself. Although she also had her share of swains around her. She's absolutely stunning, of course, so there was reason enough for that sort of crowd. But she had her bonnet off, too, and you know what her flaxen hair is like when it catches the light—that glorious shade of—"

"Yes, yes," Walingame growled. "We've all seen her hair." Cut short, it was even more striking.

"Some more than others when it comes to that," Dougal noted with a smirk.

With the possibility of finding Annabelle after so long, Walingame ignored his friends' leering comment and brusquely inquired, "Were you close enough to see how friendly she was with"—he spat out the word—"*Darley?*"

"As far as I could see—I went up into the stands to get a better look—they appeared *quite* friendly."

"Fucker," Walingame ground out. Competition from the likes of Darley, who could have any woman he wanted, wasn't conducive to his peace of mind. Not that his mind had been in the least peaceful since Annabelle had decamped. "If that rutting prick Darley thinks he's going to cut me out, he's fucking mistaken!"

"If Annabelle's left you, Darley wouldn't exactly be cutting you out."

"She hasn't left me." It made no difference that Annabelle had paid him back every shilling of the moneylender's note he held. He refused to give her up. "She's just taken a short hiatus from the theater to write," Walingame lied.

"If you say so." Dougal knew rumor suggested otherwise. Annabelle's house was closed, and at the height of the season, too. None of her friends knew her whereabouts. The owner of Drury Theater was tearing his hair out, hoping each day she'd return.

"Damn right, I say so." Walingame shrugged as though dismissing his doubts. "Now, where the hell is Whiting Hill?"

"It's an hour or so west of Newmarket. That's why no one knows it."

"And you were there for what purpose, pray tell?"

"I have an uncle who lives in the vicinity."

"An uncle with money, I warrant."

"Of course." Dougal smiled. "Would I venture to such an outland otherwise?"

"Would you care to ride back there with me?"

"Why not? I can lose my money here anytime."

"Bring your pistols."

"Are you expecting problems?" Not that Dougal wasn't always ready for a dust-up.

"I just want to make sure Belle understands I'm serious. And if a display of firearms is necessary, so be it."

"You know what everyone's saying, don't you?" In the event Walingame was oblivious to the gossip, Dougal felt it necessary to warn his friend that he was being regarded as simply another of the men Miss Foster had found wanting.

"Of course I know," Walingame snapped. "And I don't give a damn. She's coming back with me, she's *staying* with me— and all the gossipmongers can go screw themselves!"

"Well, that's clear," Dougal said with a flicker of his brows.

"Bloody right, it is." Walingame had always been a ruthless man, but after coming into the earldom and its considerable fortune on the death of his father, his despotic qualities had increased proportionately. "And the sooner I find her, the sooner she'll be apprised of my feelings on the subject," he growled. "And this time my headstrong Miss Belle will be kept on a short, tight leash."

"The lady might protest," Dougal drawled softly.

"Ask me if I care," Walingame muttered. "She's a god-damned actress. She has no rights." Then, with a jerk of his head, he headed toward the staircase. "I want to be on the road within the hour," he said as Dougal ran to keep up with him. "So step lively."

Chapter
13

Duff had come awake with the sun. But having passed a night of uninterrupted sleep, early rising was no hardship. He felt completely rested, and so much like his old self that even Eddie noticed his altered state.

"Yer a changed man, sar, if I do say so meself. I reckon yer back to business again with that smile on yer face."

"It certainly feels that way. Consider your nursemaid duties over," Duff replied cheerfully, leaning back in his chair like he'd been wont to do in the past, precariously balancing on two legs. "Whatever gloom and doom was filling my head has retreated. I slept through the night. I didn't dream once. I woke up starved and"—he grinned—"not exclusively for food. Although, that's for your ears only. The lady and I have come to an agreement—a wager of sorts—and I intend to honor it."

"Good luck with that, sar," Eddie murmured sardonically, spooning some buttered eggs on Duff's plate. "And you'd best eat up, jes' in case that there agreement of yers is altered one way or t'other. Jes' askin'—but what do you lose if you lose yer wager?"

"Five hundred pounds."

Eddie snorted. "Then it ain't the money yer doin' it for.

I've seen you bet ten times that amount on the turn of a card. I'd say you be sweet on the lady."

"I wouldn't go so far as that," Duff replied, smiling faintly, bringing his chair back down on four legs. "You know I'm not inclined to be sweet on anyone."

"Well, whether you are or not, if yer considering the lady's feelings for five hundred pounds, it sure ain't about the money."

"Hmmm . . ."

"Think on it, sar—that's all I'm sayin'."

Duff looked up, a piece of toast in hand. "She's very beautiful, you must agree. Anyone would be attracted."

"As if you ain't had a hundred or more o' those kind o' ladies, sar."

"She makes me laugh, too." He took a bite of the toast.

"Good for her."

Duff chewed and swallowed before grinning at his batman. "Do I detect a bit of sarcasm, Eddie?"

"All I'm sayin' is don't make light of what yer feeling. She ain't the same, that's all. Whatever way she's different, she's different for you. Ye ken?"

"Could we not talk about this?" Duff said with a faint frown. "I don't care to think this hard about enjoying myself."

"More coffee, sar?" Eddie knew how to take a cue.

"You're worth every shilling I pay you," Duff said with an amused look, indicating his cup with a nod.

"Since you pay me enough to make me banker happy," Eddie noted, filling Duff's coffee cup, "I can mind my tongue with the best o' them."

Duff's brows lifted. "Your banker?"

" 'Course, sar. I got me money in Bank o' England notes."

"Is that so?" Duff spooned sugar into his coffee. "So what are your plans for all this wealth?"

"Someday, sar, when I'm in the mood I'm going to propose to some sweet young thing and buy me a farm."

Duff stopped stirring the sugar in his cup. "You don't know anything about farming."

"Don't need to, sar. I thought I'd get meself a farm manager with yer money."

Duff laughed, liking both the sound and thought of laughter on so lovely a day. "Well, at least give me some warning should you decide to take a wife and leave me."

"Don't worry, sar. I ain't in no rush. I reckon when you get leg-shackled is time enough for me."

"In that case, we're both safe for a great while," Duff replied with a grin.

"That's what I figure, sar. And that's right fine with me, now that we're entertaining ourselves with the ladies again."

"Speak for yourself. I have no immediate plans."

"I ain't sayin' I don't believe you, but I'm guessin' yer thinkin' on it at least."

Duff waggled his hand. "Perhaps."

"Perhaps—nothin'. It's only five hundred pounds, sar. Jes' pocket money fer you."

"I'm not sure the lady's ready," Duff observed affably. "But as for yourself, feel free to spend your evenings elsewhere. I'll be fine here by myself."

"I'll see."

"I mean it, Eddie—your continual presence is no longer required."

"Yes, sar. Whatever you say, sar," Eddie noted, complying while not actually complying as any good retainer would. "Now, are you bringin' the lady a posy this mornin'?"

"Why do I get the impression I am?" Duff said, gazing at his batman from under his lashes, a half smile on his face.

"Yer ma sent over a pretty posy o' violets, sar."

"How did I ever manage to interest a lady before without prompting from so many of you?"

"I reckon you jes' muddled through, sar," Eddie replied with a perfectly straight face. "Although, I hear tell a great many ladies liked yer muddling jes' fine."

Duff suddenly felt as though all the previous women he'd bedded were mere prelude for his relationship with Annabelle—

platonic as it was at the moment. Although, perhaps that might change, he consciously admitted for the first time. "Maybe you're right," he murmured. "Miss Foster isn't like all the rest," he added, struck by the vast differences between then and now, his earnest solicitude for Annabelle's feelings a distinct break from his past when he'd made a habit of overlooking such subtleties.

"I got that impression, sar."

"I don't know exactly how or why, though," he said, exhaling softly, trying to get a grip on the novelty of their friendship. Or was it the abnormality of it?

"I reckon you'll find out soon enough."

"Maybe I will," Duff replied, beginning to think Eddie was right about the five hundred pounds not being a factor. As for the rest—the lady's wishes and desires in particular—he would just have to see . . .

As he walked up the path to Annabelle's cottage door a few hours later, he still wasn't sure whether he'd act on his feelings or not. Whether the ramifications of reneging on his wager would be detrimental to his interests.

If he knew what those interests were.

Was this just about sex and seduction as in the past, or did he wish to enjoy Annabelle's company for however long she remained in the country?

A dilemma he could have answered with ease prior to his illness.

It wouldn't have been a dilemma then. Sex was sex was sex.

But now . . . he wasn't so sure.

Merde, did that mean he was becoming a moralist?

Had all his mental trauma turned him into a pattern card of high-minded rectitude?

Then the door opened as he approached and Annabelle appeared, smiling at him, and hot-blooded desire jolted him to the core.

With skintight breeches in fashion, any hint of arousal

would have been obvious, so he immediately tried to think of something else—anything else—like, say, the price of tea, as if he'd know . . . better yet, his father's way of scowling when he was angry. That fortuitous memory turned out to be an instant curb against lust and by the time he reached the door, he was once again in control of his emotions. "Good morning." His tone of voice was completely normal. "Did you sleep well?"

Damn and bloody hell. Not a good choice of words—an image of Annabelle in dishabille immediately leaping to mind.

"I did. And you?"

Her voice was cool as her dove-gray gown, the ultimate in tranquility; he was grateful for her composure. "I slept extremely well," he was able to reply in an equally dispassionate tone, replacing mental images of Annabelle in dishabille with more sensible depictions of racehorses. "I hope you're hungry." Christ, was every word he uttered today going to resonate with double entendre? "That is, I meant to say, Eddie is preparing a picnic for us."

"I knew what you meant." Her smile was reassuring, as though at least one of them had their wits about them. "Are those flowers for me?"

Apparently well acquainted with flustered men, she was prompting him like a schoolboy, he thought resentfully. "My mother thought you'd like violets," he muttered, holding out the flowers, wondering if his novel virtue was contributing to his awkwardness.

Annabelle smiled. "How nice of her."

Her fingers brushed his slightly as the posy was exchanged; their eyes met for the briefest of moments, and he suddenly saw something he'd seen countless times before.

His resentment instantly dissolved.

He was back on familiar ground.

She was not only partial to him, but willing.

He'd bet his title on it.

"Do you think your mother might change her mind about accompanying us?" he inquired pleasantly, as though he hadn't seen that small heated desire in her eyes, as though he had nothing more on his mind than their excursion this fine summer day.

Annabelle shook her head. "I'm afraid Mother's intent on matchmaking," she replied, as capable as he of mummery. "She wishes us alone."

His smile was roguish. "Should I be concerned?"

"That's for you to decide, of course," she said with an answering smile. "I couldn't possibly comment."

"Matchmaking, eh?" His heavy-lidded gaze was insolent.

"You're excused, my lord, should you wish to flee." Her gaze in contrast was straightforwardly direct.

"That's the devil's own choice," he murmured.

"Or a warning."

He grinned. "On the other hand, it can't be any worse than Waterloo."

She laughed. "I don't believe I've ever been so romantically wooed."

"If you're serious about being wooed," he said, "consider me at your disposal. You entice the hell out of me, as you no doubt know. Plain words, but there it is."

Her gray eyes held a degree of gravity quite apart from her faint smile. "Why don't we see what transpires, my lord."

"What if I preferred not playing games?" Duff said, his months of celibacy perhaps impetus for his impatience. Or maybe the female scent of her was triggering his lack of reserve.

"But I'm never done playing games, my Lord Darley." Along with the heat in her eyes was a flinty determination. "You should know that. My whole life is a series of roles. Come now, make your bows to my mother," she said as if they'd been discussing nothing more untoward than the weather, "and then we'll go on that picnic Eddie is arranging."

She'd pronounced the word *arranging* as though she suspected some ulterior motive behind the activity. "Rest easy,

Miss Foster, I have no nefarious plans." His voice was blunt, umbrage in his gaze. "I find scheming pointless."

"There, now I've made you angry," she murmured, lifting the violets to her nose and gazing at him with such blatant submission she reminded him of one of Greuze's paintings of docile females.

"Keep it up and you really *will* make me angry," he said with a grin, suddenly realizing she had no way of knowing he wasn't like the other men she'd known. "And pray, relax. I have no designs on you even though you interest me vastly. I'm quite capable of controlling myself."

"How reassuring," she said, letting the posy drop and holding his dark gaze for a telling moment. "If you mean it."

"Of course I mean it. Keep me company and I'm content."

"You amaze me, Darley. I say it in all honesty."

"While I'm amazed how much I relish your company. And speaking of enjoyment, do you have some breeches you could bring along? I thought we might go riding."

"But not sedate riding?"

He grinned. "That's why you need breeches."

"I might be able to find some." He offered a level of comfort she'd never felt before, particularly with a man.

"Perfect. Should I wait here?"

She lifted her brows. "No, of course not, although take note of how Mother is staying out of sight in order not to interfere with our *tête-à-tête*. Unlike you and I, Duff, she's a romantic. Mother, Molly!" Annabelle cried out, turning back into the house. "You may show yourself. We're coming in." She smiled at Duff and held out her hand. "You may charm Mother and Molly while I find those breeches."

In short order, Annabelle and Duff were driving back to Westerlands Park, the pair of bays in the traces flying along at a spanking pace.

Duff held Annabelle to steady her on the turns, the high-perched phaeton seat tippy at tearing speeds. She held on to the seat as well, although she didn't mind in the least when the marquis put his arm around her. It felt good. Safe. A novel feeling—that of safety with a man. Not that she was even remotely in the market for a protector. But she couldn't discount the pleasure of his company.

Duff was in a superior mood. He and Annabelle had the entire day together and she wasn't indifferent to him. Not that any woman had ever been, but as discussed earlier with Eddie, Annabelle Foster was different.

Or perhaps he was, after his illness.

Or maybe the world he'd come back to was where the difference lay.

Chapter

14

"A ride first, our race stables, or a picnic! You decide!" His voice was raised to be heard over the sound of the wind as the horses raced down the road.

"Riding!" she shouted back. It was too soon after breakfast to eat, and she was avoiding the Westerlands property. Although riding had been her first choice since Duff had mentioned he kept his string of campaign ponies at the hunting lodge. Any horse that could survive the risks and hazards of combat was sure to be a superior mount.

As they approached a large Jacobean brick structure surrounded by old yews, Annabelle tapped the satchel at her feet. "Why don't I change in the stables?" She'd chosen to bring her breeches with her rather than wear them in the event they met someone on the road who would look askance at a female in pants. The locals were prone enough to gossip without deliberately soliciting their attention.

"Nonsense, change in the house. Eddie might be in the stables," the marquis noted, pulling the horses to a stop. "He doesn't seem to be around." Although he suspected his batman was making himself scarce for the same matchmaking reasons as Mrs. Foster.

"Are you sure you didn't plan for your valet to be absent?"

Annabelle inquired, gathering up the small bag as Duff jumped to the ground and secured the horses' reins.

But her tone was sportive, so he answered honestly. "God only knows what Eddie's motives are. I've been an invalid so long, he's probably more anxious than anyone that I return to what he perceives as my normal life."

"And that includes women, no doubt."

"To be perfectly honest," Duff replied, lifting her down, "I don't know what *normal* entails anymore." He guided her toward the house. "It's been a year."

And he still favored his right leg, she noticed, his stride shifting slightly from time to time as though to ease some aggravation. "Your friends missed you, I understand," she said politely, in lieu of voicing her thoughts.

"They stopped coming out after a time, but their letters continued to arrive. Or so Eddie says. I haven't seen them."

"Surely you intend to read them now that you're feeling better."

He'd heard that tone in a woman too many times not to take notice. "Pray, let's not argue about my letters," he said with utmost diplomacy. "You read them if you like."

"I hardly think that would serve the purpose."

"You need but tell me what you deem purposeful," he murmured, a touch of amusement in his eyes, "and I shall immediately comply."

"Now if only I were young and naive, my lord," she said with a mocking glance, "such flummery *might* be believable."

"And you and I are long past naivete, aren't we?" he murmured.

"I'm not sure naivete is a virtue."

"I wouldn't mind a glimpse of it from time to time after all I've seen," he said, frowning faintly.

"I'm afraid I can't help you in that regard." A mild sarcasm resonated in her words.

"You mistake me. I meant I'd like to see a less bloodthirsty world—one not completely bereft of human kindness."

"How can we possibly alter the larger world of affairs, my lord? I've long since given up such pretensions."

"So pragmatic, my lady," he said with a smile.

"I find it very unwise not to be."

"Ah."

"Indeed. While you may indulge in your dreams of innocence, I cannot. Now, come, Duff," she murmured. "It's too nice a day to dwell on things that can never be. I would much prefer living in the moment on such a glorious day," she added with a smile. "And consider, if we race, I might let you win this time."

Her smile was magical—her rosy, upturned mouth lush and sweet, and she was right, of course. Neither one of them would change the world today. "Perhaps I only *let* you win last time," he replied roguishly.

"Oh, ho, do I detect a challenge?" she said with a playful wink, pleased to have shifted the conversation to something more pleasant. She was the least likely person to have any influence over the social order. "Let me change and we'll find out who's the better rider."

He grinned. "How can I refuse such sport?"

"How indeed? Do I have a choice of horses?"

Every one but Romulus, he wished to say, but remembering his manners, said instead, "Yes, of course. You choose." Opening the entrance door a moment later, he ushered her into a vaulted hall cluttered with riding equipment. "Sorry about the mess," he said, suddenly aware of disorder he'd never noticed before. "I'm afraid Eddie isn't the best housekeeper."

"You needn't apologize. It looks very much like any bachelor establishment."

He shouldn't have taken issue with her familiarity with bachelor apartments, but he did. He wasn't, however, stupid enough to vocalize his feelings; she wasn't beholden to him in the least. He gestured at an L-shaped staircase, the ornate balustrade embellished with bas reliefs of hunting scenes.

"Feel free to use any of the rooms upstairs. In the meantime, I'll see if Eddie left us our picnic."

"I'll be down in a thrice," Annabelle said, and moved toward the stairway. Just before reaching the landing, feeling as though Duff's gaze might be on her, she glanced back.

She'd been right.

He smiled.

She smiled back, but her heart suddenly began beating like a drum, and a spiking rush of desire spiraled downward, warming every sensitive nerve and cell in her body until it came to rest with a lustful jolt in her newly aroused, gently throbbing vagina.

His slow, lazy smile was much practiced, she didn't doubt. Not that such a judgement in any way reduced its efficacy or its danger.

Shaken by her intense response, she didn't dare look back again. And only when she reached safe haven in the second floor corridor did she allow herself to stop and take stock of her skittish, fevered feelings. Heavens, she was trembling. This would never do, she decided, drawing in a deep, hopefully calming breath in an attempt to mitigate her agitation. This was most unusual. She had never been prone to such *unwanted* emotion before. Nor had she been the kind of woman to lose control.

What was perhaps even more galling was the fact that a man like Duff was overly familiar with female acquiescence—and adulation.

She refused to join that sisterhood.

She absolutely *would not*.

How many years had she spent nurturing her independence—Walingame's recent blackmail aside. Even then she'd managed to keep him in check until she'd been able to pay him off and regain her freedom.

And free she would remain—in every sense of the word.

Having satisfactorily, or at least intellectually, resolved the issues of her physical response to Duff, she pressed on down the corridor. The lengthy hall was intersected with numerous smaller hallways and lined as well with a rabbit warren of rooms in the style of the time.

Having marginally regained her composure, she allowed herself to yield to perhaps a female's curiosity about Duff's lair or refuge or whatever one wished to call the place he'd chosen to reside in while licking his wounds. She briefly surveyed the interior of each room as she passed. That she might be interested in gaining some insight into the marquis she chose not to acknowledge. That the marquis even interested her in any but the most superficial way, she resisted admitting. She settled instead on the fiction that she might make use of one of the rooms as a future stage set.

Ah, denial.

It turned out that Duff's bedroom was located at the far end of the corridor. He must like the morning sun, she thought, standing in the doorway, surveying the bank of east-facing windows. Since this wasn't the largest room—several others had been larger—he'd chosen this room for a reason. Was it the large bed or had that been brought in? The other rooms were furnished in Jacobean relics—the population much shorter centuries ago. He must have wanted a bed he could stretch out in.

She half-smiled.

Duff certainly had been right about the mess. The bed was unmade, the quilted coverlet dragging on the floor, the sheets rumpled. Clothes were draped over chairs and tossed on tables, two pairs of his riding boots had been left in a heap by the door. A number of crumpled neck cloths had been discarded on the dressing table, testament to fashionable custom. A perfectly tied cravat was *de rigueur.*

Moving into the room, she dropped her bag on the bed and wandered around the room, intrigued by the opportunity to glimpse the man behind the legend.

Books were scattered everywhere. His taste ran to treatises on horses, naturally; the family's breeding program was the best in England. Although a smattering of fiction lay amongst the discarded books, a copy of Kleist's *Michael Kohlhaas* open on his bedside table, a book not designed to raise the spirits. But she liked Duff's taste. Kleist was also one of her favorite playwrights.

The sage-green coat he'd worn the day they'd gone to the monastery ruins had been tossed on a chair near the bed, as though he'd taken it off and fallen into bed. Picking it up, she put it to her nose, inhaling his fragrance. The coat smelled of musk with undertones of leather. Thoroughly male, like him, she thought, moving to a nearby desk. Placing the coat in her lap, she sat down on his desk chair to study a small portrait propped against the cubbyholes at the back. The painting was of Duff and his siblings as youngsters. As the eldest, Duff stood with one hand resting on the back of a settee where his sisters and brother all sat like little birds in a row.

My lord, how old was he there? Ten, perhaps? So tall and straight and serious. One sister couldn't have been more than two or three, a golden-haired little girl with a winning smile. The rest were all dark like Duff, although he was the only one who looked grave.

Somehow she'd never thought of him as somber, his entire adult life in London given over to amusements. (Although certainly the year since Waterloo had been devoid of pleasure.) But he'd been notorious before leaving for the Peninsula, his reputation scandalous, his high play at the clubs still setting records for profligacy and excess.

The man himself had always remained illusive, however, his persona as consummate lover and libertine the only one offered for public consumption.

She remembered that night long ago in the green room at Drury Lane. When she'd refused him, he'd smiled, offered her an exquisite bow, and moved on to one of the other young actresses in the room.

How much had happened to them both since then.

Some good and much that was not.

But they were both mending now, and there was no point in holding oneself hostage to the past. Not on such a thoroughly beautiful day. She intended to enjoy it. And on that more positive note, she rose, dropped his coat on the desk chair, and moved to the bed to open her valise.

She adored riding and Duff's mounts were sure to be first-rate.

Unbuttoning her black lawn jacket with hussar-style braid and pompom trim, she slipped it off and set it aside before pulling her gray gown over her head. Her petticoat and shift came off next. Stepping into her nankeen breeches a moment later, she buttoned them at the waist and knee, put on her short jacket once again, buttoned it up, and glanced about the room, looking for a mirror.

None. Surely this was a man indifferent to the world.

Her ensemble was adequate enough, though, she knew, her black half-boots and white stockings typical dress for a youth. Which was in fact her role when she'd last worn these breeches on the stage many years ago. Fortuitously, they'd been left at her mother's, for with her recent trip home made in haste, her packing had been the most superficial.

"SHOULD I COME UP OR ARE YOU COMING DOWN?"

Duff's voice echoed up the staircase. Annabelle hesitated for an irrational fraction of a second before taking two steps toward the open door and calling out, "I'LL COME DOWN!" She refused to even consider her moment of hesitation; it was an aberration. That she would want Duff to come up to his bedroom was inconceivable.

As though to suppress any possible future folly, she bundled up her clothes, stuffed them into her valise and carried them with her. If Eddie wasn't around on their return, she could change back into her dress in the stables. She wasn't about to leave herself open to temptation.

As she reached the top of the stairs a few moments later, she heard Duff's quick indrawn breath. But when she looked down, she thought she may have imagined the sound, for he was gazing up at her with a bland smile.

At the sight of Annabelle's shapely form in tight breeches, the marquis had given in to a rare gaucherie—quickly suppressed—and his voice was composed now as he spoke. "The last time I saw you like that was in the role of Jacintha. I still remember the roar of the crowd when you first walked on stage."

"Women in men's breeches invariably draw that kind of reaction," Annabelle noted, starting down the stairs. "Although, my costume today is for purely functional purposes. I'm looking forward to our ride."

"As am I," he replied affably. But his eyes were less affable and more covetous.

"Did you find a picnic basket?" She was trying with some difficulty to speak casually. He'd changed his coat and now wore a chamois jacket that fit like a second skin, the fashions of the time purposefully accentuating the male physique— not a flattering style for the portly Prince Regent who had to resort to corsets. But corsets weren't a necessity for the marquis's tautly honed body. Both his short jacket and his buff leather riding pants could have been painted on. He was decidedly lean, yet curiously powerful as well, his hard, muscled arms and shoulders, his lean hips and strong thighs an irresistible sight. As was his rising erection limned against the soft, buff leather of his riding pants.

She shouldn't have been looking, of course.

Or perhaps she should blame him for not better curbing his appetites.

A barely perceptible frisson raced up her spine.

Or it would have been imperceptible had the atmosphere been less fraught with desire.

"You're not cold, are you?" He shouldn't have spoken. He should have pretended he hadn't noticed.

"No—a little touch of a breeze, I think," she lied.

And then she reached the bottom of the stairs.

Where he stood—waiting . . .

Only the sound of their breathing was audible—his rough, hers less than steady as the silence lengthened.

"I'm not asking," he said at last, his voice hushed. "But I'd like to."

Her mouth quivered slightly, as though she debated speaking at all, and then she said, "As would I."

As though given license by her words, he smiled. "I willingly forfeit our wager." He lifted his hand, but let it fall to his side at the sudden apprehension in her eyes.

"This . . . is . . . so sudden," she said in a small, suffocated voice. And whether she was lying to herself or him wasn't entirely clear. "Give me . . . a moment . . . to think." Her eyes suddenly flared wide. "Don't touch me!"

His hand dropped back to his side, but his dark gaze was flame-hot. "What if I said no?" Patience wasn't one of his strong virtues, nor obedience.

"Just don't." Her voice shook.

He took a step back. She reminded him incongruously—for a woman of her background—of a quivering, young ingenue. Holding his hands out, palms up, he slowly enunciated, "I-won't-touch-you."

She glanced around as though trying to find her bearings, then exhaled softly and offered him a tentative smile. "I always forget who you are," she said with a kind of artless simplicity.

"Is that good or bad?" he inquired cautiously.

"At the moment, good."

"And in the next moment?"

"We'll just have to see."

Reassured—she'd said *good*, not bad, nor had she fled—he smiled. "You tell me when you're ready. It's up to you."

She looked at him for a protracted moment—the sound of the birds outside suddenly like an anvil chorus in the quiet entrance hall.

They could both feel their hearts beating in their chests.

Apparently coming to some decision a moment later, she rose on tiptoe and kissed him lightly while he remained motionless, his hands clenched at his sides. It was a butterfly caress, fleeting and sweet, and as she dropped back on her heels, she whispered, "I'm ready now."

"May I touch you?" He didn't want her to bolt.

She nodded, eyes downcast.

Was she playing a role or sincere? Playing, he decided a second later; Annabelle Foster was too experienced for such modesty. But he placed his hands on her shoulders cautiously and drew her near with circumspect deliberation, as though he were wooing a virginal young miss. He had to improvise, having never actually come in contact with a virginal miss, but simple courtesy certainly couldn't go amiss.

They stood very close, their bodies almost touching. Crooking a finger under her chin, he gently lifted her face to his and bending low, kissed her like he might have when he'd been a well-mannered adolescent. But politeness notwithstanding, his senses were on full alert and with the expertise of considerable dalliance, he began to gauge her reactions with a minute regard.

Her lips were sweet; she tasted of peppermint and smelled of roses, an altogether lush combination of gratifying sensations. Having brought his hands to rest at the base of her spine, he held her with the gentlest of pressure as he delicately kissed her.

"So well behaved, Duff," Belle murmured, after several moments of mannered kisses. Twining her arms around his neck, she adjusted her body slightly, as though better accommodating her ripe curves to his hard length and opening her mouth to his, kissed him with a degree more passion.

Taking his cue, he eased her back against the wall and leaned into her, their bodies pressed hard against each other for the first time, his erection rigid between them. "I'm not in a hurry; we have all day," he whispered, exploring the minty sweetness of her mouth more fully but slowly, yet offering her pleasure in small, safe increments. Or perhaps teasing her. Or after a year of celibacy, more likely savoring what was to come.

She found his courtesy arousing, but even more, the tantalizing imprint of his hard, rigid length stirred her desires. But regardless his formidable strength and power, he neither forced himself on her nor wielded his authority and for that she was grateful.

She'd fought too long for independence to suffer tyranny.

He seemed to understand. Or perhaps, susceptible to doubt and pain since Waterloo, he'd gained a sensitivity to the vulnerabilities of others. But when her hips brushed against his in invitation or what he took as invitation, he eased away marginally and said on a softly indrawn breath, "Playing the gentleman has its limits. We should go upstairs in the event Eddie returns."

"Upstairs?" A distinct uncertainty rang through the word.

"It's entirely up to you," he murmured urbanely.

She half-smiled. "Are you always so polite?"

"There haven't been any alwayses of late. I have no comparison."

"So we are both venturing out of our celibacy today?"

He tried not to let his shock register and only marginally succeeded.

"It's been a very long time for me," she said as though in explanation to his modulated surprise. "A very long time indeed." Her smile was suddenly sunny with cheer, her indecision in full retreat for reasons unknown. Perhaps for reasons having to do with Duff's grace and civility. "Are you sure you're ready to accommodate my amorous cravings?"

"I'm certainly willing to try," he drawled softly. "Although I have a small warning of my own. After a year, I'm probably more ravenous than you."

She laughed, the silvery trill one of gay delight. "That almost sounds like another wager?"

"This one you'd lose."

"So sure, my dear Duff?"

He wanted to say, don't allude to your past; I don't want to hear about it. But he understood he was the last person in the world to make accusations about sexual excess. He'd spent too many years indulging his vices. "Very well," he said, in compromise to both his feelings and the past. "Why don't we say a token wager of ten pounds?"

"Or no wager at all," she murmured, reading the constraint in his voice.

"Better yet. Now come," he said, taking her hand. "Let me entertain you."

This time she was the one unable to conceal her surprise.

He laughed. "Don't say you don't like to be indulged?"

She had been in so many ways, but from a man like Duff—perhaps not. "I look forward to the experience."

"Not as much as I." And bending down, he lifted her into his arms and carried her up the stairs.

Chapter

15

He stood in the doorway to his bedroom holding her, a faint frown creasing his forehead. "This room could use a maid. Perhaps we should find another."

"This is fine. It smells of you," she said, smiling up at him. "And I mean it most kindly. Who makes your scent?"

"A little shop in Mayfair."

"It's tantalizing."

"Speaking of tantalizing," Duff murmured, not inclined to discuss scents when he had other things on his mind, "how do you feel about"—he grinned—"a certain haste in this endeavor?"

She laughed. "Thank heaven. That's how I feel. And speaking for myself, *instant* is the operative word."

"I'm not usually so impatient."

"Nor am I usually so needy."

He grinned again. "So you won't mind an unmade bed. I could find some clean sheets, perhaps, although I'm not altogether certain where they're kept. And Eddie does change them every day—just not yet today."

"As if I care about that. Put me down."

His brows rose.

"I'll undress," she explained.

"I'm not in that much of a hurry," he said with a smile, walking to the bed and seating her on the edge. "Especially since I've been thinking about undressing you most of my waking moments."

"Let me help." She was ravenous when she was never ravenous. When she couldn't remember if she'd ever considered the word in conjunction with sex. "You're much too handsome, Duff. I'm all a-quiver." She reached for the braid-covered buttons on her jacket.

"Humor me," he murmured, taking her hands in his, slowly lowering them to the bed. "I'll do it." His voice held a hint of gruffness. She was much too familiar with undressing for a man. That it suddenly mattered to him when he'd enjoyed the company of any number of actresses in the past, he chose not to contemplate.

"You must alter your tone of voice." She, too, had her bug-bears.

"Must?" he said, a sudden coolness in his gaze.

"There. You see? That's why I shouldn't have come." She was certain now of her mistake; she was too well-versed with that look in Duff's eyes—that presumption that the world must yield to a nobleman's will. "If you'll excuse me," she said brusquely, beginning to slide off the bed.

He stopped her, lifted her back in place, and spoke in what he hoped was a more amenable tone of voice. "Could we discuss this?"

She shook her head.

"I apologize, naturally. And most humbly."

She shook her head again. "In truth, I never should have come." She held his gaze as though in emphasis. "I don't know what I was expecting, or rather I knew what to expect and came anyway. I don't care to repeat patterns from my past that don't bear repeating." She smiled faintly, understanding he had nothing to do with the life she'd lived. "The thing is, I've turned over a new leaf. And then you came along and charmed me from my resolve. It's a testament to your masterful abilities, although," she added with another smile, "I don't discount your handsome good looks either. You've heard that before, I suspect, but nevertheless, I quite fell under your spell. In fact, I can't remember when I've wanted someone more."

"Certainly you don't expect me to let you go after hearing that," he said, his smile dazzling and very close. "And while I've never subscribed to the notion of spiritual connections, I confess, darling Belle, that you have struck some chord deep within me. I have succumbed to *your* spell."

Her gaze narrowed in cynical rebuke. "Please. Your impulses have nothing to do with spells or spiritual connections. You simply haven't had sex for a year."

"I wish it were that simple," he disputed. "I'm the last person in the world to acknowledge strong emotion of any kind"—he grinned—"other than lust, perhaps."

"And your passion for horses."

He shrugged in acceptance. "And my family, I suppose. Very well, I concede to those passions. But in terms of more tender passions, you alone have moved me. I'm not altogether certain of why or how, other than I know I don't wish you to go. So stay. I'm more than willing to forgo sex if you wish. Keep me company for other reasons. We'll go riding as we'd planned and have our picnic."

She wrinkled her nose and grumpily said, "You are becoming most troublesome to me."

He was instantly encouraged, but then he'd had considerable practice reading the baffling moods of females. And the delightful way in which she'd wrinkled her nose was so damnably alluring he was quite taken with her all over again. "On my word, I promise *never* to use any but the most courteous tone with you, nor will I make demands. Just stay. You make me very, very happy." He looked stricken for a moment. "You see, I've quite lost my senses to openly avow such feelings—"

"To a woman?" she murmured.

"Very well, I confess to a lifetime of utter selfishness," he said, denying the casualness of his previous amours impossible with the *Ton's* ear for gossip. "But," he added, pausing for a moment as though conscious of the significance of what he was about to say, "consider me reformed."

She couldn't help but laugh. "If only I were fifteen and not an actress myself, I might almost believe such penitence from a man of your repute."

He was inclined to object to her mockery, but knew it wouldn't serve. Novice he might be in feelings of tenderness toward women, but in all else he was highly accomplished. "Pray believe me," he said with both sincerity and the most beguiling smile, "I am reformed—at least in regard to you."

"Am I special, then?" she inquired waggishly, not entirely gullible, but enjoying herself nonetheless.

He grinned. "As if you don't know after years of adulation from every man who's come within your sphere. But should it matter, you're very special to me and I don't wish you to leave. Tell me what I must do to make you stay and I'll do it willingly."

"Make love to me." She shouldn't have said it, of course. She should have left long ago.

He scowled. "Don't make sport of me."

"I wish I were. On the contrary, I'm quite sincere." Although hesitancy resonated in every syllable and inflection, and the pursed set of her mouth suggested more than a modicum of cavil.

He couldn't help but smile. "You have reservations."

"So many you might want to think twice about this."

"Not likely that."

"At least one of us is sure," she said with a disgruntled sigh.

"Why don't I be sure for both of us?" His voice was smooth as silk.

"How gallant," she replied sardonically. Then she didn't speak for a moment, some internal debate clearly going on in her mind.

He waited, if not calmly, visibly composed.

"I have one request," she finally said.

"Only one? My gratitude would allow many more."

"I ask that you refrain from ordering me about. Ever."

"Rest assured, I won't."

She softly exhaled, her remaining qualms mollified by his certainty. Although, even without his assurances, would she have been able to walk away from the joy she felt in his presence? Probably not, or she wouldn't have been seated where she was with Darley very near, smiling at her. "Forgive me for being so indecisive," she said, smiling back. "You've been most gracious with my wavering resolve. Shall we move on now?"

"Perhaps you should write down your directions, so I don't put a foot awry." His dark gaze was disarming in its candor, his smile only half teasing. "I wouldn't want to offend you. And truthfully, I'm not sufficiently in control of my feelings yet to offer any guarantees of politesse. Once things have reached"—he paused, searching for a suitable word—"say, a point of no return, you might not be able to—"

"Stop you?"

"Yes—I mean, no, you wouldn't. Eddie tells me there are times when I'm not fully aware of the world around me. And at that stage—"

"If I could say no to any of this, Duff, I certainly would," she said, interrupting him. "You're not the only one who isn't fully in control."

The innocence of his smile could have charmed the birds from the trees. "We are an odd pair, are we not?"

"With apparently an ungovernable appetite for each other." Having given in to Darley's bewitchment, she spoke of her feelings with pleasure.

"An *unslaked* appetite," he pointed out, softly.

"*Frenzied*, too. And for your information, *frenzied* has never been in my vocabulary."

"In that case, I am your obedient servant, Miss Foster,"

Duff murmured, the conventional courtesy taking on an entirely new meaning.

"You needn't be so docile."

He grinned. "Make up your mind."

"That's my problem, Duff. I can't make up my mind about you. About what I want from you. What I wish to give you. And how long I wish to be in this ravenous state of indecision and lust."

For a man of his experience, her admissions amounted to a carte blanche invitation. "While you're trying to decide," he murmured, his plans decidedly back on track, what was precarious now certain, "let me set this bed in order."

She looked at him as though he'd gone mad.

"It'll just take a minute," he said, lifting her onto a nearby chair. "I don't plan on leaving it any time soon."

"I have to be home by dinner," she noted firmly.

He glanced back at her as he pulled up the sheet. "I'll have you home in time."

"You quite unnerve me, Duff, with your domesticity."

Her small smile warmed him out of all proportion to its brevity and scale. "Give me a minute and I'll unnerve you with something much better," he said, husky and low.

"In that case, I should save time and undress. May I?" For some reason, it no longer bothered her to ask.

"No—if you please," he quickly amended, polite to a fault in this capricious dance. "I'd like to undress you." Sweeping the quilt up from the floor, he tossed it over the foot of the bed. "Now then, that didn't take long, did it?"

"Long enough," she said with a delicious little pout.

He laughed. "Now tell me who wants their own way?"

"I'm allowed."

"And I'm not?"

She grinned. "We can talk about it."

Moving to where she sat, he pulled her to her feet. "Maybe we'll talk later," he murmured, with an answering smile as he reached for the buttons on her jacket. "After a degree of shall we say—satisfaction?"

"Mine first, if you please."

He stood, his hand arrested, her tone while not precisely imperious, enough so that it gave him pause.

She giggled. "You're scowling."

He quickly altered his expression. This near to orgasm, it wouldn't serve to lose his temper. "My apologies." He began unbuttoning her jacket.

"You don't really mean it, but I apologize as well. That was very rude of me. I expect you don't need instructions."

He smiled faintly. "It's been a while since I did."

"So I should probably stop trying to give orders."

"I'm not saying you can't try," he said, a roguish gleam in his eyes. "But I'm not sure I need them. I'm pretty good at this."

"Even after a year?"

"Particularly after a year." He lightly touched her bottom lip. "So just relax now and let me take care of things."

His casual authority was highly provocative, as was his reputation for signal feats in the boudoir, not to mention the smoldering heat in his eyes that effectively kindled an answering heat deep inside her. She stood very still at that point, absorbing the glorious sensations—a rush of arousal pinking her cheeks, racing through her blood, alerting all her senses to the certainty of future pleasures.

"Your hair is shorter than mine," he murmured, ruffling her curls.

"Should I say I'm sorry?" Her tone was lightly sardonic, although in her current heated mood she might not mind apologizing.

He smiled. "Would you if I asked?"

They'd both heard the stories of each other. They were both accomplished at this game.

"It depends," she purred.

"On?" He freed another fabric-covered button.

"On whether I was properly compensated."

"That could be arranged."

"Such confidence, my lord."

A flash of humor shone in his eyes. "Years of practice. One learns."

A little heated ripple streaked through her vagina at the lush implications in his drawling reply. "So the broadsheets have always asserted. You were their darling for years."

"I'm glad we finally met—under the right circumstances," he murmured, too polite to mention that she, too, had been featured with great regularity in the broadsheets.

"Thanks to the horse fair." Maybe even then, she'd understood the inevitability of this. Or perhaps, she was simply no different from any woman who came within the marquis's magnetic field.

"You wore the brooch." Duff lightly touched the pink diamond rose on her lapel before sliding her jacket off.

"I like it very much—although I like you even more," she added, when she shouldn't have, when she knew better than to be earnest with men like Duff.

"I'll buy you a bouquet of these roses," he offered, as though heedless of her comment, "in every color. For the sweetness of your company today." His voice was low and dulcet as he slipped his fingers under the lacy neckline of her chemise. "And for the pleasure you bring me," he whispered, languidly caressing the swell of her breasts.

His callused fingers were rough on her skin, his dark gaze unruffled as though he'd been here a thousand times before. Shivering under that clement gaze, she wasn't sure she wished to give herself up to a man who relinquished nothing. "I don't know . . ." she breathed, suddenly wavering. She had distinctly wished to avoid such a calculated, impersonal encounter. "I'm not sure I wish to stay."

But she hadn't said *don't touch me* or *stop*, he noted, and perhaps he even understood her reluctance. He knew the stories as well as anyone, how she played at love on her terms. So he didn't argue or challenge her. Instead, he gently moved his hands upward, holding her lightly by the shoulders. "Just stay a little longer. You might change your mind."

"And if I don't?"

His smile was cheeky. "All my years of practice would go to waste."

"Insolent libertine."

He assumed it was a slur, although her inflection was equivocal so he wasn't entirely sure. "Should I apologize for all my past iniquities?" he queried, his smile wicked.

"Yes." Although the warming desire in his eyes effectively subverted all her best intentions. Her nipples swelled, grew taut, the pulsing between her legs accelerated and she actually found herself speculating on whether any of his past iniquities would be of interest to her.

He could see her jewel-hard nipples pressing against the sheer fabric of her chemise, and while he wasn't privy to the throbbing between her legs, he suspected as much when she shifted her stance. "Naturally, I apologize." His brows rose. "I don't believe I've ever apologized so often to any one person. Are we friends again?" he said, his smile boyish, perhaps even winsome.

Without waiting for an answer—he had, after all, considerable experience with women not saying exactly what they meant, he drew her closer. Their bodies touched, breast to breast, thigh to thigh, his chamois jacket and breeches rough against the lighter fabric of her chemise and nankeen breeches. "You must tell me what you want."

He was offering her everything. "No matter what?" she whispered, as though she had improbable expectations. Although with Duff, perhaps she did.

His smile was benevolent. "No matter what."

Nothing intimidated him. And whether she was seduced by

his benevolence or by her own desires, impulse trumped reason. "Then I'll stay and play," she purred, like a well-trained sultana, or an actress of note.

He disliked that lush provocation in her tone. "I'm not looking to play," he said, cool and precise, his words surprising him even as he uttered them.

"Oh?"

Another conscious act of drama—that wide-eyed look. "Don't do that," he muttered, as though he had the right.

"What do you want from me?" Pushing him away, she stared at him. "Tell me, because I'm not sure. All I've seen so far is the Darley of popular repute—seductive, assured, conspicuously nonchalant. And even then," she said with a grimace, "I stayed."

"I owe you another apology—a record, I'm sure," he murmured ruefully. "The thing is"—he hesitated, and then with a sigh went on—"I want more than dalliance. I don't know why." He smiled finally. "I don't care why—I just do."

She'd either been offered the most silken mendacity or she was the recipient of the most satisfying indulgence. "You've been away from the world too long." She had to at least attempt to put his comments into some reasonable perspective.

"Haven't you?"

"You're not helping. I would prefer being sensible."

He snorted. "I'm the last person to help you there, I'm afraid. Just say you'll think about it. I'm not asking you to sign a contract today."

"Very well. I'll think about it. Whatever *more than dalliance* entails," she said with a smile.

He shrugged. "We are both novices outside of amour, are we not?"

She could have said something flirtatious, but somehow the truth seemed more appropriate—as though this entire situation required some exaggerated authenticity. "I confess—and I'm the least likely person to do so—I am enamored of you when I never am enamored of anyone. There, I've said it. You may run."

"I don't wish to."

"There may be no tomorrow for us," she warned softly, her life having taught her that lesson.

He smiled wryly. "I've learned not to plan of late."

"Then we will gather rosebuds while we may." Giving herself up to a rare, unhampered delight—as though she'd suddenly been given license to live an unexamined life—she impetuously threw herself at Duff, wrapped her arms around his waist and flushed with happiness and joy, clung to him with all her strength.

He went rigid.

She instantly loosened her hold. "I'm sorry," she breathed, stepping back, her cheeks bright red with embarrassment. Having lived so long in the world of brittle insincerity, she should have known better.

"It's nothing to do with you."

The words were so softly uttered, she had to strain to hear.

"I had a friend die in my arms—like that. He wouldn't let go."

"Oh, dear." She didn't know what to say. Crossing her arms over her breasts, as though her half-undressed state was suddenly inappropriate, she watched Duff struggle for control.

A heavy silence fell.

He was unapproachable, his gaze remote.

Having only seen Duff's malady once before, she stood helpless and inarticulate as he took himself away from her and went to some afflicted place. The hush was oppressive, taut, punitive. Even the glowing sunshine abruptly dimmed in the room as a cloud passed over. "I should go," she said finally.

As though some survival mechanism came into play with her mention of leaving, he seemed to come out of his stupor. "No," he said flatly. "Don't go. I couldn't bear it." Jerking himself to attention, he blew out a breath, ran his fingers through his overlong hair, and after dropping his hands to his sides, smiled the most practiced and dazzling of smiles. "I'm fine. My apologies. Did I frighten you?"

She shook her head, afraid to speak for fear of setting him off again.

"Good," he said, as though he'd not been stricken dumb short moments ago. "Where were we?" Raising his hands, he ran his palms over her breasts in a brief, impersonal gesture, before moving to untie the bow at the neckline of her chemise. He bent to his task as though no disruption had intervened, as though he was back on some track of his own design.

The intensity of his focus was frightening or wildly arousing; Annabelle wasn't certain which. But a tiny frisson shivered up her spine as he manipulated the blue silk ribbon and she suddenly felt like he appeared—wildly impatient.

The bow fell open and he quickly set about opening the buttons on her chemise, his fingers nimble, his motions economical from top to bottom and within seconds all the pearl buttons were undone. Swiftly slipping off the garment, he let it fall to the floor.

He was incredibly intent.

Perhaps not entirely in a reasonable frame of mind.

Nor was she, if truth be told. She wouldn't have come here today if she was even mildly reasonable.

Nor would she have stayed.

He undressed her without speaking, quickly, efficiently, as though he was under some time constraint. Her half-boots were swiftly removed as he kneeled at her feet, her silk stockings and garters followed. Still on his knees, he unbuttoned her breeches, jerked them down over her hips and legs, nudged her to lift first one foot then the other and in brief moments she was stripped of her clothing.

It was not a scene meant for the stage.

There was no dialogue.

But maybe they'd talked enough or too much and it was

time instead for the main act to begin. Standing nude in Duff's bedroom—sunny once again with the cloud having passed, she watched him rip off his clothes while she trembled like a leaf in a gale. When she never trembled. When sex had never been about hysteria or even sentiment.

If she wasn't caught up in some fantastic, intemperate madness of her own, she might have recognized that her life was coming undone. That she was succumbing to a dangerous, unprecedented craving.

Duff, on the other hand, was immune to all but the driving need for consummation pounding in his brain and in his aching cock and in every functioning nerve in his body. Sex would be his remedy for brutal memory, fornication the relief for his tortured mind and hotspur and volatile, he charged head long toward that compelling goal. He was vaguely aware of Annabelle's large, lush breasts and slender form, her flushed cheeks and fevered gaze as he wrenched buttons open and tore his clothing from his body. But that she was his oblivion and salvation, his carnal focus and ultimate release was as real as the frantic beat of his heart. What was even more real was the certainty that he would soon lose himself in her sweet, welcoming body.

Seconds later, scooping her up in his arms, he silently carried her to the bed and deposited her on the rumpled sheets. Gazing down at her, he suddenly went motionless again, his eyes unfocused, his hard, austere body immobile save for the twitching of his huge, upthrust erection.

As he hesitated, his attention centered on some strange internal scene, unaware of his surroundings or her, Annabelle chided herself for so tamely waiting for him to mount her. He was clearly oblivious to her. She could have been anyone lying in his bed.

If only she wasn't fascinated and enticed by Duff's compelling beauty and sexual allure—the full extent of that allure expanding before her eyes, his engorged penis rising higher, the turgid veins inflated and pulsing—she might have been able to deal with this logically. And if she didn't so desperately want what he was about to give her, she could have taken issue with his indifference. Or offered him sympathy in his delirium. Or tender accommodation. Or done the sensible thing and left his bed, his house and him.

Instead, as bereft of reason as he, she ignominiously yielded to her cravings. Jettisoning every shred of dignity and autonomy, becoming someone she didn't recognize, Annabelle reached out and touched Duff's arm. "Please, Duff, don't make me wait," she whispered. "I can't—please, I beg of you . . . make love to me."

He glanced over, saw and heard a woman begging for sex— a common, even habitual scene from his past—as was the scent of female arousal fragrant in his nostrils. The familiar sight, the riveting aroma, the pleading tone, triggered associations and reflexes as automatic as breathing itself.

With a businesslike nod, as though casually acknowledging her need and his function, he moved the two steps to the bed and settled over her with a lithe grace. Gently spreading her thighs to better accommodate his size, he rose slightly on his knees, swiftly guided the head of his penis between the soft folds of her labia, said with a mechanical courtesy, "Forgive my brusqueness," and precipitously plunged forward.

Annabelle's high-pitched, breathy scream echoed through the room as the full measure of Duff's erection plumbed her sleek passage in a single rough, punching downstroke.

He seemed unaware of her cry, nor did he hear her frenzied whimpers commence a short time later when he'd settled into a powerful rhythm of thrust and withdrawal, a considered, highly competent oscillation, perfectly gauged to deliver maximum sensation. He was operating on instinct, his much-vaunted career as a libertine coming to the fore, neither comprehension nor judgement required when he was following a well-beaten path, as it were.

As Annabelle's delirium heightened, he remained oblivious to her breathless pants as well, his ears attuned to the more familiar, haunting cries he'd been hearing day and night since Waterloo.

His eyes shut, braced on his palms, his biceps bulging with the strain, Duff plunged in and out, insensible, yet hypersensitive, his lower body pumping, ramming, driving hard. He was sheened with sweat as he restlessly hammered, withdrew, thrust in again, groaned and growled, straining to reach that place of forgetfulness where the keening cries would be silenced, the bloody images purged, where he might find peace at last.

In search of her own oblivion, albeit frenzy of another kind—Annabelle gave herself up to Duff's explosive rhythm, gasping as inexplicable pleasure jolted her to the quick with each downstroke, absorbing the full, heart-stirring ecstasy with a kind of breathless gratitude. She'd never felt so heated and greedy, so ripe for sensation, so alive.

It was all because of Duff; there was no question. She didn't know what was happening or why, although all the women before her would no doubt testify to his expertise. But it was more than sex. She understood the refinements of physical sensation; this was a whole new world—splendid, sublime, spangled, and festooned with luxurious pleasure.

A virtual paradise in which one could willingly lose oneself.

Perhaps she might even do so.

A thoroughly audacious thought, but at the moment compelling.

Cushioned by her warm, scented cloud bank of bliss, her heart filled with tenderness, awash in a rare magnanimity of passion, she looked afield from her own selfish desires. Duff had been right, she concluded—about sorcery being at play, for she found herself in charity with the word, the concept, the actual existence of *love*.

A heretic thought she didn't long allow to persist.

But her benevolence toward the man who had opened her eyes to paradise remained. Raising her hands, she softly touched Duff's brow slick with perspiration, smoothed away his distress, consoled him in his anguish, murmured words of comfort as he lavishly ministered to her passions.

Caressing his eyelids and temples, his hard-set jaw and taut throat, she gentled his pain. Pushing away the sweep of dark hair falling over his forehead, she whispered his name—as much for herself as for him—taking inexpressible delight in the sound on her lips. "Duff, Duff, Duff," she breathed softly, feeling both wistful and impatient, inexplicably possessive as well, as though she owned him for those few brief seconds of each plunging downstroke when he paused, submerged within her body. An aberrant sensation quite unlike any she'd ever experienced. But unspeakably fine. Stroking his face, she whispered his name, as though in this blissful paradise, however fleeting, he was hers.

Sluggishly, his senses began to stir, come to life. Slowly, he left his nightmares behind, became aware of her touch on his face, heard the sweetness of her voice. Heard as well as he returned to the surrounding scene, a minute impatience underlying her words.

"Here—Duff, look at me," Annabelle whispered as his eyelids fluttered up and down and the rhythm of his lower body began to slow. "Can you hear me? Please, please." A fevered intonation animated her words now, a moody, demanding inflection. She was hovering on the brink or perhaps she had been for a very long time and had abruptly reached her point of no return. "Did you hear me, Duff?" A sharper note in her voice, the most celebrated prima donna of the English stage wanting what she wanted. "Open your eyes."

He opened them and actually saw her.

"I'm very near orgasm, if you don't mind," Annabelle said ever so sweetly, as though in compensation for her recent sharp tone.

"So you'd like a little help." Duff's voice was normal—and amused.

"Yes, something less fevered, if you don't mind." A hon-eyed, frictionless intonation.

He almost said, *Is there some diagram you'd like me to follow?* but she'd been obliging to him in his delirium, so he smiled instead and said, "How can I refuse such a sweet-tempered lady?"

"Don't tease, Duff. I don't have much time."

"Your servant, ma'am," he murmured suavely, immediately shifting into a rhythm of exquisite delicacy and finesse. "And if I hurt you, I profoundly apologize . . ."

"I'm much too wet to be hurt."

"Good." He smiled. "You like me, then."

"Rather a lot, as you can tell."

"Perhaps I can make you like me even better." He grasped her hips, his fingers splayed wide. "Tell me what you think of this?" Driving forward, he held the crest of his erection against her womb with the quintessential degree of pressure—that knowledge acquired from his French governess who had not only taught him French but a great number of ways to please a woman.

In this case, another woman profited by Mademoiselle Belloc's teachings. Awash in glorious sensation, Annabelle was momentarily speechless, unless one considered a long, low moan a creditable utterance.

Not that Duff was necessarily expecting a reply, although her feverish little moans signaled a degree of success. And when he withdrew marginally before plunging in again, her squeal of dismay caused him to smile. A very brief time later, when the lady had been whimpering as though she were being deprived of something she desperately wanted, Duff casually said, "I'm going to come in you now."

"Thank you," she breathed, as though she had been trans-formed into some covetous wanton without constraint and her body was fueled by lust—not to mention a lurid partiality for a disreputable marquis she should know better than to fancy. "Thank you so very, very much," she purred, ignoring niceties of judgement for more gratifying pleasures. "How splendid of you . . ."

He should have taken alarm. Particularly for his own shocking assertion; he never climaxed in women. Not that Annabelle's blanket submission shouldn't have been equally unnerving.

But neither were fully cognizant of the rules today.

"Ready?" he facilely inquired, shifting slightly against the warm resiliency of her soft flesh.

"Hmmm . . ."

It was the most seductive murmur he'd ever had the good fortune to hear. Dipping his head, he dropped a kiss on her luscious pink mouth. "You set the pace, sweet puss."

Had he not been completely enamored for reasons unknown, he might have taken issue with her virtuoso technical accomplishments. He was accorded the full indulgence of her nimble vaginal muscles, the captivating witchery so intense he could feel the rapturous sensations jolt his brain when she flexed around his cock in a particularly subtle way. And she knew an ingenious method of moving her hips that was stunning. He literally stopped breathing each time she artfully stirred her pelvis in that piquant fashion.

As for the marquis, he apparently had the ability to stay rock-hard indefinitely. If she wasn't currently the recipient of that tantalizing aptitude, Annabelle might have allowed her jealousy to surface. As it was, she was not so foolish.

But they were both so thoroughly enthralled and irrepressibly in heat that what would have been annoyances became instead the merest bagatelles.

They were both operating—or fucking, as it were—outside the normal perimeters of their lives.

They both understood it.

They were functioning beyond the pale.

When they finally came in a glorious, sublime flush of rapture, Duff found the nirvana that had always eluded him.

Annabelle might have said something thoroughly unacceptable in terms of love before she lost consciousness.

Actually, she did.

Chapter
16

When she came awake she was in Duff's arms.

He was seated, holding her in his lap, and as her eyes fluttered open, he smiled. "You said it's been a while. Welcome back."

He was lounging against the headboard, looking cool and insouciant, and for a small, heated moment, she resented his imperturbability. Unable to curb her pique, she said pettishly, "Apparently you suffered no ill effects from your year's celibacy."

"As a matter of fact, I've never felt better. And by the way," he said with a grin, "I love you, too."

"I never said that!"

"*Au contraire*," he said, looking amused.

"Well, if I did," she caviled,"I meant sex-love, not love-love."

"It didn't sound like it to me," he murmured in a cheerful singsong.

She was blushing cherry-red at her gaucherie. "Then I certainly apologize. I must have been much enamored with your sexual expertise—and him." She touched his barely diminished erection that lay between her hip and his stomach.

"Then we both thank you," Duff replied with a dip of his head. "But I'm not averse to love-love, either."

"Don't tease. You are the last person in the world to utter such nonsense and I am the last person in the world to believe it."

He grinned. "I don't know about you—although I daresay your swoon may have been an indication of some powerful feelings—but personally, I saw nirvana. So don't discard love-love out of hand, darling."

If she weren't who she was, and if Duff wasn't who *he* was, *and* if she wasn't once more in a cooler frame of mind, she might have been inclined to consider the possibility. Under the circumstances, however, any question of love was ludicrous and impossible. "Very well, I shan't," she replied, rather than argue about something so ridiculous.

"Does this mean we're betrothed?" he inquired blithely.

"It means you may give me another orgasm when you feel up to it again."

"Better yet," he noted sportively. "Although," Duff added, running a fingertip lightly down her wet cleft. "We should wipe you up." Grabbing a handful of sheet, he began swabbing at the fusion of semen and her pearly dew.

She clutched his wrist. "Wait!" Taking a shallow breath, she exhaled before giving him leave to continue with a nod. "Carefully, if you please," she murmured.

"I *did* hurt you, didn't I?" he said, looking distressed. "I'm *so* sorry—I was afraid something like that might—"

"I'm fine," she interrupted. "More than fine," she added with a smile.

He looked puzzled. "You're not hurt?"

"On the contrary. I am, shall we say, *hypersensitive*, in a very nice but rather overcharged way."

His mouth slowly lifted into a smile.

She put up her hand. "We should wait just a moment, if you please."

"Are you sure?" He bent low so his eyes were at a level with hers. "It's always better the second time and you needn't worry, I'll be ever so careful."

"If you don't mind," she said, when it was clear from her tone that *she* did. "I don't care to be instructed any more than you do." Whatever his methodology for second times, she didn't care to hear about it when she was desperately jealous already—a sensation so outré for her, she couldn't quite grasp the notion.

"I understand," he said with excessive tact, responding to the pique in her tone.

"You needn't be so conciliatory, either," she replied testily.

He'd obviously said something wrong. "We'll just wait, then."

"I don't suppose you have any wine. I'd like some." Sulky and peevish, she was not above the pettiness of exerting her authority. As if by casting him in the mold of the biddable men she knew, she would be free of her outrageous jealousy.

"Will this do?" Obliging, he plucked a decanter from the bedside table.

She should have known. Why was she only gullible with Darley? "You planned all this today, didn't you?" she said, her voice acerbic. "Wine at the ready. Eddie strangely absent. That little doubtful pose downstairs."

"No, I didn't." This time his voice was sulky. "The decanter is always there."

"Oh," she said in a very tiny voice.

"Would you like some wine?" Insulted by her accusation when his feelings for her were intemperate, perhaps even extreme, his voice was very close to a growl.

She nodded, unable to conjure up a smooth apology with him scowling at her, when she was obviously in the wrong, when her brain was in tumult. She wanted him, knew she shouldn't, but wanted him anyway, the unresolved litany obstinately looping through her mind. How could she be so foolish? she chided herself. Everyone knew Duff was notorious for the brevity of his affairs.

Setting the decanter on the bed, Duff picked up a glass from the table, handed it to her, and taking out the stopper from the decanter, commenced to pour the glass full. "I'll drink some, too," he muttered to her questioning look.

They shared the glass of wine in silence as though neither was quite capable of reasonableness, and in lieu of saying something objectionable, they chose not to speak.

When the glass was empty, he didn't ask her if she wished more wine, apparently immune to her venture as autocrat. Setting aside the glass, he glanced back, and said with punctilious restraint, "You're dripping on my leg. Would you mind if I wiped it away?"

She would have preferred throwing her arms around his neck and telling him how he captivated her beyond reason and prudence and maybe love-love wasn't out of the question after all. "No, I don't mind," she said instead, as dispassionately as he.

He grimaced, blew out a breath, then smiled tightly—or perhaps it was another grimace. "You are an annoying little vixen," he muttered, speaking with discernable reluctance. "But I still want you beyond all comprehension."

"You are a hellishly troublesome man," she answered, her reply equally tentative. "But, regardless, I find you tempting beyond all belief."

He swore softly.

It was not the sound of high favor or endorsement. "I should go home," Annabelle murmured.

When presented with that option, Duff's answer was swift. "No."

"You can't say that to me."

Who could do what to whom was not a reasonable debate, he thought, when she was in his home and his bed and he not only outweighed her, but perhaps had fewer scruples. Well-mannered, however, he said instead, "Please don't go."

She sighed. "I don't like feeling this way."

Her tone gave him hope, nor had she tried to leave. "Nor do

I—yet I am bewitched by you, and am"—he almost said *half in love*, but caught himself in time—"going mad for want of you. So please stay and I will be gallant to a fault."

She smiled. "And you know exactly how, I expect."

"Consider me at your disposal, ma'am," he murmured silkily, further encouraged by her smile.

"In all things?" A seductive whisper of a query.

"Without question," he replied unequivocally.

"Very well."

Neither was capable of giving up the pleasure. He understood. And to that purpose, he didn't question her further, he merely nodded downward, wanting to move past this hindered conversation. "You're still dripping. May I take care of that now?"

"Yes, I would greatly appreciate it," she said, overpolite, like she might have been at a royal reception.

He tried to suppress his smile. "Such unctuousness, darling."

"It's merely courtesy," she retorted primly, her feelings still in flux.

"Do let's not fight again."

She looked at him from under her lashes. "I am simply agreeing with you and being accommodating."

There was something too sweetly obliging in her tone, a practiced appeasement that grated on his nerves. "And you know how to accommodate men," he drawled.

"What do you mean by that?" Her voice remained neutral only with effort.

"Nothing."

"Don't say you're jealous," she murmured archly.

"Fuck, no."

Her brows rose. "Then I fail to see what's at issue."

"Perhaps what's at issue," he said, his resentment flaring despite his attempt to curb it, "is that this hot little cunt"—his hand swept over her cleft—"has been accommodating to far too many men." And as though pointedly taking possession of that particular part of her anatomy, he precipitously shoved two fingers palm-deep up her vagina.

She tensed against the harsh pressure of his fingers. "You didn't even know who you were with a few moments ago," she said on a suffocated breath. "Don't berate me about exclusivity. You could have been in bed with anyone. It wouldn't have mattered one whit to you."

"But it wasn't anyone, was it? It was the beautiful Miss Foster who has every man in London panting after her. What the fuck is this?" Jerking out his fingers, he held up a piece of sponge.

"You're no novice. What does it look like?"

"So you were planning for this little rendezvous," he growled, tossing away the sponge.

"No, I was simply protecting myself against your advances, which, as you see, occurred," she said, haughty and righteous, lifting her chin contentiously. "I was correct in not trusting you."

"I didn't hear you saying no," he returned brutally, blind with jealousy, begrudging her every suitor she'd ever had.

"I doubt you were listening—like all men."

"For God's sake, don't put me in the same category as fucking Walingame."

"I wish you good day," she said coolly, beginning to slide off his lap. She wasn't about to argue the inarguable or debate the age-old question of double standards apropos male and female sexual amusements.

"Not yet," he retorted sourly, his fingers leaving marks on her arms.

"Yes, now," she said, heated and low, trying to shake him off. "You've taken out my sponge and I have no intention of getting pregnant."

"For your information, I never climax in a woman."

"Except me," she retorted with testy sarcasm. "How fortunate I am." Her gaze suddenly narrowed and she looked at him askance. "What do you mean, you never climax in a woman?"

"I just never do. I'm disinclined to have children of mine scattered about the world."

"But you came in me." Her voice had gone quiet, and even she wasn't sure why she was asking the question.

He shrugged. "I have no explanation."

"How typically nonchalant," she said with withering contempt. "I could have been left pregnant because of your casual disregard."

"Don't say this has never happened to you before," he said, clipped and cool.

"I set the rules, Duff."

"Don't tell me about your rules." His voice was sharp.

"I have had no rules for a very long time, until," she added caustically, "you came along and disrupted my life."

His smile was instant; it was as if the sun had come out after a storm. "And you succumbed to my charms."

"Maybe I just wanted sex, like you," she said, thin-skinned and touchy.

"I'll settle for that. I'll settle for anything, so long as you stay. I don't care what your reasons are—just don't go." He spoke without hesitation or doubt, unlike the man who had left London for the Peninsula—the man who had perfected suave flattery to a fine art.

Annabelle hesitated, or tried to, while a little voice inside her head screamed, *Yes, yes, yes, yes, stay!* Attempting to ignore the strident, wholly impractical voice *and* her own heady longings, she managed to withstand their inducements for perhaps ten seconds at most. "You cannot come in me," she said then, as though that simple dictate would absolve her of responsibility. "I mean it absolutely or I'll leave this instant."

"You could *try* and leave, you mean." The marquis was not beset by the weighty issues of responsibility. His cheerful grin indicated as much.

"Duff, don't make jest of this. I will not become pregnant on someone's whim."

"There must be some sponges in the kitchen. Is that better?" He shifted her slightly in his arms, so he could meet her serious gaze squarely. "I will be your remedy in all things. Don't worry." He patted her arm in assurance. "And at the risk of possibly angering you again, I shall also mention that I intend to pay my forfeit on our wager. No, don't protest. I was the one who asked. There was no question. And if you don't want the money, give it to Molly and Tom." As she opened her mouth to speak, he put up his hand. "One more thing. If I ever go crazy, like I recently did"—he folded her fingers into a fist—"just hit me hard." He brought her hand to his mouth and rapped it. "Like that."

She felt tears brimming in her eyes. He was so serious. "I don't want to hit you when you're already miserable." She touched the sabre scar on his shoulder and the one on his chest and the terrible wound on his hip where Eddie had done rough field surgery and dug out the musket ball.

Duff moved her hand from his hip and clasped it gently. "I'm getting better. Wait and see." He smiled. "Because of you. Because of us. Because of this." Leaning over, he kissed her, sweetly and then not so sweetly. And when his mouth finally lifted from hers, he said, "I'd better go and find some sponges."

He came up after a time with sponges and a picnic basket. "I'll feed you afterward," he said with a grin, tossing two large sponges on the bed.

Annabelle glanced at the sponges and smiled. "You must have outrageous expectations."

He looked back from setting the basket on a table. "Why run out?"

"That won't be possible in the time we have," she countered drolly, the two sponges enough for countless sexual engagements. "And I hope you have scissors."

"In the desk." Two strides later, he'd pulled them from the

drawer. "There now," he said, bringing them over to her. "I am at your command, Miss Foster."

And he was, but no more than she was for him.

It turned out to be a day of such inexpressible pleasure that both of them knew such joyous rapture could not be duplicated beyond the vulnerable purlieu of their warm embrace. Deeply touched as they were by both the desperation of their desire and the boundless delight in yielding to it, they were not so lost to reason that either expected this fever pitch of rapture and sweet surfeit to last.

But for now—for these summer days—they had breathlessly agreed, between fond kisses and explosive orgasms, between amorous words and soft laughter, that they would explore these newfound, gladsome shores of love.

Chapter
17

Late that afternoon, as Duff turned his phaeton into the lane bordering Annabelle's cottage, she gasped.

Duff shot her a glance. "Walingame?" A black traveling chaise was at the gate.

She nodded, her worst fears suddenly realized.

"I'll come in with you. You needn't concern yourself."

"I'm not sure that would be wise."

"Nevertheless, I shall. You're frightened."

"I'm afraid of what he may have said to Mother—of my life in London." She'd long dreaded this moment—rather, she'd hoped it would never come.

"Whatever he might have said can be refuted. His word isn't believed, even by his closest acquaintances. Nor has it ever been. And I'll tell your mother as much. Once I see him on his way," Duff added, his voice chill.

"Please, Duff. I don't wish an altercation." But even as she spoke, a small flutter of hope stirred inside her. Could Walingame be sent away peacefully?

"Rest assured, I shall be civil," he promised, pulling his team to a halt behind the chaise.

"Oh, dear," Annabelle murmured softly, beginning to tremble. "Just when everything was . . . so pleasant . . . and agree-able."

Quickly tying the reins to the brake, he took her hands in his, and dipping his head enough to meet her gaze, said, "Everything will be agreeable once again, just as soon as I send Walingame back to London."

Her mouth quivered. "He won't go," she whispered.

Lifting her hands to his mouth, he lightly kissed her fingers. "Darling, you fret unnecessarily," he murmured, placing her hands back in her lap. "He'll go. I guarantee it."

There was something unequivocal in his tone that bol-stered her flagging spirits. "I do apologize for putting you in the middle of this contretemps. Do you actually think he might be civil?"

"I'm certain of it. He only wishes to woo you back," Duff replied, his aspect and address completely unruffled, as though Walingame's presence was of no consequence. "I ex-pect he'll say his piece and then be on his way," he added, perjuring himself without a qualm.

Annabelle's expression brightened, even while she knew she was grasping at straws. "I hope you're right. I hope he hasn't alarmed Mother. I dearly hope he hasn't seen Cricket or frightened Molly." She half smiled. "I might as well hope for an end to poverty as well while I'm engaged in such wistful fantasies."

"Come, now, no fantasies are required to solve this dilemma," he said with the assurance great wealth and privi-lege had conveyed on him. "We'll go inside, see that your mother is faring well, make our bows to Walingame, and then send him on his way." He grinned. "Politely, of course."

"How chivalrous you are," she murmured. "If only Walin-game had even a fraction of your graciousness, I wouldn't be in such a stew."

"Nor should you be because of him," Duff murmured brusquely. "If nothing else, he understands force, although—don't worry," he amended at her sudden alarm. "I shan't embarrass you in front of your mother. I shall be all tact and diplomacy."

"Much as I dislike falling into the role of female in distress, I confess I'm vastly pleased that you're here," Annabelle said with feeling.

"As am I. You shouldn't have to deal with him." Nor did he want Walingame anywhere near Annabelle for any number of reasons, jealousy most prominent. "Smile now," he said, focusing on the task at hand rather than on more difficult issues. "We are about to walk on stage."

As they entered the parlor short moments later, Mrs. Foster offered Annabelle a bewildered look, Innes casually raised his hand in greeting from a chair in the corner, and Walingame immediately came to his feet and bowed punctiliously. "Your mother informed us you were riding with Darley," he said with a silky, unctuous smile. "Did you enjoy your ride?"

If it were possible to feel relief with Walingame in her home, she did briefly on hearing his greeting. Was it possible he would be well mannered?

"It was a lovely day for a ride," Duff answered, although he hadn't been addressed. "What brings you to Shoreham?"

Walingame visibly bristled at Duff interjecting himself into the conversation, but his reply was couched in the same patently false amiability. "We found ourselves in the neighborhood. Innes has a family connection not far from here." He gave Annabelle a sly glance. "Since I hadn't seen Miss Foster for some time," he murmured, innuendo in every word, "I thought, why not stop by?"

His predatory gaze sent a small shiver up her spine. How often had she seen that loathsome glance? "You look fatigued, Mother," Annabelle suddenly said, keeping her voice calm with effort as she moved across the room toward her mother's chair. "Let me help you to your room." She wanted her mother away, and to that end, she would press the issue whether Walingame wished it or not.

Fortunately, her mother's presence seemed to be of no concern to him. Walingame merely addressed a pleasantry to Mrs. Foster as she and Annabelle walked past him.

But the moment Annabelle and her mother passed out of earshot, her mother hissed, "Who is that terrible man? He wouldn't leave, even though I told him in no uncertain terms that you were away from home and I didn't know when you'd return."

"He's just an acquaintance from London. I hope he hasn't bothered you too long."

"No, thank heaven—he only just arrived in the past hour. But he wouldn't be deterred from sitting down," she noted disapprovingly. "Even when I said I'd rather he return when you were at home. And the ill-mannered wretch kept asking any number of questions about you," she added pettishly. "None of which I answered with any clarity because I didn't wish to oblige him. I do hope he will leave soon. He's not at all the sort of acquaintance I would wish for you."

"I'm sure he'll leave forthwith," Annabelle replied, when she wasn't at all sure *what* Walingame might do. "And thank you, Mama, for being so astute as to circumvent his questions. He is not a connection I wish to keep. By the way," she inquired with a casualness she was far from feeling, "did the babies bother him with their cries?"

"They've both been sleeping like lambs, the dears. And luckily, too, for I'm sure he would have frightened them out of their wits. His curt, brusque tone and scowl are most uninviting."

Annabelle was both grateful and relieved it wouldn't be necessary to explain Chloe's daughter. That her sister's tragic story might have become a morbid tale for public consumption would have been distressing. "Why don't I get you a nice cup of tea, Mama," she offered as they entered the small breakfast room at the back of the cottage. "And once our visitors have left, I'll come and tell you of my pleasant day."

Chapter
18

"**I** heard you were dancing attendance on my mistress," Walingame said with a sneer the moment Annabelle and her mother left the room. "So I thought I'd best come and fetch her back."

"Strange," Duff drawled lazily, "I understand she broke with you and left no word of her whereabouts. Which, no doubt, is why you haven't previously troubled her."

"She's lying," Walingame growled. "Women like her always lie."

"We disagree," Duff murmured. "And rather than cause the lady any further distress, I suggest you hie yourselves back to London."

"Lady?" Walingame snorted. "She's hardly that."

"She's very much a lady and *under my protection*." Duff's brows rose faintly, a half smile playing about his mouth. "I hope that's perfectly clear."

Dougal rose from his chair. "I told you as much," he said to Walingame. "Come, it's time to go." He didn't like the chill in Darley's voice, nor the hard look in his eyes. The marquis's temper was well known. He'd killed a man in a duel before leaving for the Peninsula. Not that the scoundrel didn't deserve to die, but Langley's demise had been the proverbial straw, as it were. Dueling was illegal—Duff had taken part in too many. And this last duel—a royal duke's mistress had been involved—brought with it the possibility of prosecution. Duff had been forced to flee England until the scandal died down.

"I'm not afraid of you," Walingame snarled, standing his ground.

"You should be." Soft menace underlay the words.

Walingame took a threatening step forward.

Duff didn't move; he didn't so much as blink. "Name the place and time, Walingame," he said, his voice no more than a whisper.

"Don't be a fool," Dougal hissed, grabbing his friend's arm.

Walingame shook off Dougal's grasp, but he was sweating and his color had risen. "Is she worth dying for?" he blustered.

"I have no intention of dying," Duff replied calmly. "You, on the other hand, have to decide if you wish to leave this mortal coil."

The bastard was cool as ice, Walingame thought resentfully. Not that he intended to meet Darley on the dueling field. Principles of honor were for other men—stupid men. "I'll be back," he muttered, "and we'll see who's left alive."

Duff smiled tightly. "Anytime. Although, I won't be careless like Harmon." Walingame had hired thugs to viciously beat the viscount rather than face him at twenty paces like a man.

"Fuck you," Walingame growled.

"I think not—if it's all the same to you," Duff mockingly replied.

Frustration and fury turned Walingame's face a poisonous shade of purple. His mouth opened and shut, and then, with a snarling growl, he brushed past Duff. Dougal was quick on his heels.

The outside door slammed a moment later, the crack of a whip was heard, and soon after, the rattle of a chaise as it picked up speed.

Peace descended on the parlor.

With a faint smile, Duff walked over to the settee, sat down, and calmly waited for Annabelle to return.

The marquis was sprawled in a comfortable pose, his eyes half shut, when Annabelle entered the room.

His lashes lifted, and pushing up into a seated position, he pleasantly inquired, "How is your mother feeling?"

"Very well now, thank you." Standing in the doorway, Annabelle surveyed the room and smiled. "They're gone."

His gaze was innocent as a saint's. "I told you I could accomplish the task diplomatically."

"And quietly," she breathed in astonishment. "I didn't hear a voice raised in protest."

"There was very little to hear. I told Walingame he wasn't welcome and he apparently understood."

Her brows rose. "That sounds very much out of character for Walingame."

Duff shrugged in a small, dismissive gesture. "I suspect Innes's voice of reason helped sway Walingame," he lied. "Innes pointed out there was no further reason for Walingame to stay, since you'd broken with him anyway," Duff added, both statement and query in his softly murmured addendum.

"I *did* break with him!" Annabelle replied emphatically, wanting no ambiguity on that score. "There was absolutely *no* question that I broke with him!"

"Well, then—everyone understands everyone else, I'd say," Duff quietly acceded. "They're gone, and for my part, I say good riddance."

"Oh, yes . . . absolutely!" Annabelle exclaimed, finally allowing herself to exhale a great sigh of relief. "It's really over, isn't it? I can't thank you enough," she quickly went on, answering her own question. "We *all* thank you!" She opened her arms in a sweeping, all-encompassing gesture. "My mother, Molly, and the babies thank you, too!"

"Then all's right with the world once again. Come, sit by me." Duff patted the settee seat, feeling a deep contentment, feeling like he did long before Waterloo. As though life held promise and pleasure was his by right. "If you don't think your mother will mind," he added, with inherent good manners.

"She's with Molly in the breakfast room having a cup of tea," Annabelle noted, moving across the room. "Walingame will be the topic of conversation for quite some time, I suspect. Neither Mother nor Molly found anything pleasing in him."

"There aren't many who do."

"Don't look at me like that." She stopped in her tracks and frowned slightly. "I was coerced—not that you have to believe me, but it's true."

"In what way were you coerced?"

Standing a little straighter, she met his gaze with unswerving directness. "I don't have to tell you."

"Of course you don't." Although restraint echoed in every syllable.

"Oh, very well," she said with a sigh, not knowing if she was giving in to that small hint of temper in his voice or her own better judgement. Duff had, after all, summarily dealt with Walingame. "I owe you a considerable favor, so if you wish an explanation, I shall give you one," she added, moving forward once again. "Also, I very much don't want you looking at me like that."

He smiled. "Like what?"

"Like you might be thinking of shaking the information out of me."

"Don't mistake me for Walingame," he murmured, a flash of umbrage in his gaze. "You needn't tell me if you'd rather not."

"What I'd rather do is forget any of this happened. I'd like to pretend you simply drove me home after a lovely, glorious afternoon at your lodge and my life will continue to be filled with more such joy."

Her voice suddenly held a note of desperate unhappiness, and without a care for whether the other occupants of the cottage saw him—a startling circumstance, had he noticed—he reached out, pulled her onto his lap, and wrapped her in a warm embrace. "I'm jealous of any man you've ever known." He didn't even blanch at the admission, nor did he question its veracity. "You may tell me as much or as little as you like about whatever you like. It makes no mind to me. As far as I'm concerned, the subject is closed. And on a more pleasant topic, if you don't think your mother will miss you too much, let's make plans for tomorrow."

"You offer me paradise, Duff. Truly—in every fathomable shape and form." And she allowed herself to dream for a moment that life could remain in this blissful state forever.

"You've given me back my life. Why shouldn't I offer you anything and everything?"

If only she could let herself believe that men like Duff were more than a fleeting pleasure. That paradise truly existed somewhere close enough for her to reach, that she would be allowed to dwell there and bask in its beauty. "Why don't I see what Mother says," she murmured in lieu of dreaming impossible dreams.

"And if I can help you in any way with Walingame, you need but ask." He was tactful enough not to say he wanted exclusive claim to her time and person. Nor did he fully acknowledge that such feelings would have been incomprehensible to him short days ago.

"Perhaps he won't be back."

"Perhaps." At her terror-stricken look, he quickly added, "I'm sure he won't be."

But Annabelle had been on the stage too long not to recognize unspoken nuances in others. Walingame would be back; she could read it in Duff's eyes. "In any event," she offered, not wishing to dwell on painful thoughts and also wanting Duff to understand why she'd tolerated Walingame so long, "I'd like to explain my relationship with him."

He should have said it wasn't necessary. He should have brushed off her attempt at disclosure. But he was no longer indifferent as he had once been to his ladyloves and because of that, he remained silent.

"Soon after I first came to London," she began, "I signed a note with a moneylender. I'd just begun my career at Drury Lane and was short of funds." She chose not to say she was desperate to send money home for her mother and Chloe. How could a man like Duff understand that degree of privation? "I went into debt, and not long ago, Walingame discovered my business dealings with Crasswell and purchased my note from him. There was scarce any balance remaining, but knowing Walingame was anxious to buy it, Crasswell charged him an exorbitant price that I was forced to assume. I sought legal help, but Walingame threatened to find my family and tell them all, so legalities became immaterial."

"When did all this transpire?" Duff asked as though he could tally the number of days she'd been obligated to Walingame and by so doing, allay his jealousy by commensurate degrees.

"Early this year. Before that, I'd always been independent. You know that. I've never lived under anyone's protection. Walingame was impossible, of course, threatening to embarrass me in a number of ways. I paid him off as soon as I could and left him."

He took comfort in her explanation. He felt better knowing Walingame had no further claim to her.

He was comforted as well, knowing if Walingame pressed his suit with Annabelle, he would kill him.

If necessary.

If the man didn't have sense enough to cease harassing Annabelle.

Duff was no better or worse than others when it came to the accepted codes of conduct in society.

It was a violent time. Life was cheap.

Men, women, and children could be transported for stealing a loaf of bread, sometimes hung for less. And while the aristocratic world was immune to the more brutal laws of England, beneath the elegant dress and fine manners, they had their will of each other in any number of barbarous ways. Wives were beaten by husbands. Husbands were cuckolded by wives. Men fought duels over the turn of a card or some senseless outrage.

Or over a woman.

Chapter

19

"Darley was ready to dispatch you on the spot," Dougal murmured, lounging in the corner of the chaise, his legs propped up on the opposite seat.

"I doubt it," Walingame muttered, uncorking a brandy bottle and taking a long draught.

"Deny it all you wish, it's true. You could see it in his eyes. And Darley has never had any scruples about putting a bullet in an adversary. Not to mention, most of his duels have been over some ladylove's so-called honor. You were lucky you came out of there unscathed."

"You run off at the mouth, Dougal. As for Darley, I'll see that he pays for his bloody insolence."

Dougal grinned. "Thinking about hiring some thugs again?"

"If need be," the earl growled, immune to issues of honor. Right and wrong were mere words to him.

"Keep in mind, Darley might be on the lookout for a crowd of roughs. He said as much."

"I don't care," Walingame spat. "All I know is that he's going to pay one way or another for fucking my mistress."

"He may not be fucking her." Dougal didn't add, *And it didn't look like she was yours.*

"Acquit me of stupidity," Walingame muttered. "They smelled of sex when they walked in."

"Not from where I was sitting."

Walingame snorted. "They'd spent the day in bed. I'd bet my stable on that."

Dougal grinned. "Since I'd like your stable, could we find out whether they had sex or not?"

"Very humorous, I'm sure. Remind me to mock your female attachments. Not only is Janet Ferguson so shapeless one can't tell if she's coming or going—she doesn't discriminate whom she takes into her bed. I hope you understand you're not alone in fucking her."

"Nor do I wish to be," Dougal drawled, his inamorata one of the hotter women he'd ever bedded despite her boyish form and indiscretions. "And I hardly think Annabelle Foster could be considered your exclusive property," he bluntly pointed out.

"Regardless, I intend to have her back in my bed in short order," Walingame declared firmly.

"And how do you propose to do that?"

Walingame smiled wickedly. "The usual way. Through guile."

Chapter

20

Duff had tea with Annabelle, her mother, and Molly before he left. He also asked Mrs. Foster for permission to fetch Annabelle the following morning and was speedily answered in the affirmative.

He stayed for some time, enjoying the company, making plans with them for the summer as though he was a member of the family. It was near sunset when he and Annabelle said their good-byes. They stood together at the garden gate, the sun pinking the horizon, the scent of flowers perfuming the air, a palpable serenity enveloping the scene.

"I can't remember when I've had a more pleasurable day," he whispered, taking her hand in his behind the shield of her skirts.

"Nor can I. I thank you again for my happiness and your gallantry in all things. It's delightful to have Walingame gone as well."

"Tomorrow, I'll send some servants over to help your mother and Molly with the children and a few men to stand guard as a precaution."

She shook her head. "I wish you wouldn't. Such actions might unduly alarm Mother."

"Your mother won't mind one or two maids, will she? Come,

say yes to that, at least." As for the guards, he would see that they stayed out of sight. But they would be there for his peace of mind, if not hers.

"Very well," she replied politely, not wishing to continue the argument.

"Good." He gently squeezed her fingers. "Tell me you'll think of me tonight," he murmured.

She smiled. "How could I not?" A man like Duff was not easily forgotten.

"I'll be here at ten to fetch you. I wish I could kiss you good-bye."

"No more than I. But Mother and Molly are probably peering out the windows."

He sighed softly. "So I must be well behaved."

"I'm afraid so," she whispered, her eyes suddenly filling with tears.

"Darling, don't cry—don't—especially when I can't take you in my arms and comfort you."

She sniffled and snuffled and a moment later offered him a quivering smile. "There. I'm fine. I'm probably still rattled by all that has happened."

"Walingame won't bother you again. Don't worry about him another second."

She nodded, forcing back her tears. "I shan't. 'Til tomorrow, then." If Duff didn't leave soon she was likely to burst into a veritable fit of weeping.

He released her hand, bowed faintly, and with a smile took his leave.

As his phaeton drew away from her gate, he waved.

She managed to maintain her smile until he was out of sight. Wiping away her tears, she turned and with a determined tread, briskly walked back to the cottage.

They would have to be gone by morning.

There was no question of staying now that Walingame knew where she lived.

He would be back. She had no doubt.

And even if Duff could protect her—not necessarily a certainty with a man of Walingame's treachery—she didn't want to put herself under the marquis's protection simply because of Walingame.

She'd always avoided the position of "kept woman."

She'd decided long ago that as compensation for her way of life, she would at least retain her independence. And much as she'd enjoy Duff's company—a tame word for the glory he offered—he would be the same as any other man if she allowed him to put his mark on her.

She'd long adhered to a set of rules, first among them that she bestowed her favors where she pleased. Second, that no man made demands of her. And third, that she alone determined when a liaison was over.

In many ways, she was no different from aristocratic ladies who played at amour. She'd just had the misfortune to be born into a craftsman's family rather than into wealth. Noble ladies amused themselves with a variety of bed partners, their leisure activities often largely devoted to amorous play. Once a peeress had borne an heir, society was inclined to overlook extramarital affairs so long as scandal was kept to a minimum.

Not that comparisons of her life to that of noble ladies mattered at the moment. All that mattered was deciding on an explanation for a swift departure that wouldn't alarm her mother.

She wished to be gone by midnight at the latest. She wanted to be well on her way before Duff arrived in the morning.

She most regretted leaving him. If there had been a way to say a proper good-bye without complicating her plans, she would have. But sweet as Duff was, wonderful and enchanting as he was, a fleeting love affair was all he offered. She chose to live her life another way.

Perhaps the Isle of Wight would do nicely, she thought, determined not to dwell on what could never be with Duff. It was a wholly useless endeavor, in any event, to pine over lost pleasures. She had many more relevant issues facing her.

The sea air would be bracing, she decided, the distance from London sufficient, the secluded location perfect for anyone wishing to disappear.

And her mother knew the island. As a child, she'd spent time there with her grandparents.

All in all, summer should be an ideal time to enjoy the seashore.

Chapter

21

The duke and duchess were sharing a moment of quiet after luncheon. Their children and grandchildren had all gone off in a variety of directions, and before leaving the table themselves, they were having a last cup of tea when a footman carried in a note and handed it to the duke.

Quickly unfolding the rumpled scrap of paper, the duke scanned it. "It's from Duff." Turning it over to his wife, he glanced up at the servant who had delivered the note. "Who brought this to the house?"

"I don't rightly know, Your Grace."

"Is the person still here?"

"He may have left, my lord."

"Find him. Bring him back. Quickly." Crisp words, crisply uttered.

As the servant left at a run, Julius turned to his wife. "Duff doesn't explain why he's going to London."

"You and I both know why," the duchess replied, although mouth pursed, she was clearly beginning to think of other things.

"Perhaps the messenger may be able to shed light on our son's precipitous departure."

"I'm sure he can," she murmured. Then her expression

brightened, and quickly pushing back her chair, she came to her feet before a footman could jump to help her. "While you're waiting for the messenger, dear," she said pleasantly, "why don't I go upstairs and tell the girls we're off for the City. I'll send word to the stables that we need Giles back at the house."

"Duff might consider you're meddling," her husband cautioned.

Elspeth smiled. "Now, darling, meddling is every mother's right. We like to think of it as being helpful."

"Your help may all be for naught if Duff returns before we reach London," he said kindly. "Have you thought of that?"

"Really, darling, didn't you read the note? There's some trouble brewing."

"How in the world did you fathom there was trouble from those few brief lines?"

His wife offered the duke a beatific smile. "Mother's intuition, my sweet. Trust me. But do let me know what the messenger says. In the meantime, I'll see that the girls get their families ready for travel. You might want to order the carriages brought round."

The duke had learned long ago not to ignore his wife's motherly intuition. She generally knew of what she spoke. But after talking to the local farmer who had delivered the note, he did have added information to offer Elspeth apropos the time of their son's departure.

"The man lives on a small holding near the hunting lodge," the duke related. "He was out tilling his garden shortly before noon when two men on horseback rode up and asked him to relay the note to us. Apparently Duff was already in transit when he remembered to apprise us of his plans."

"That explains the pencil and rough hand. He was writing from horseback. How sweet of him to think of us," his mother said, in that doting way of mothers that overlook all their children's infractions.

"No doubt we should count our blessings that he thought of us at all," the duke said ironically.

"Exactly, my dear," Elspeth replied without an iota of irony. "He's a most charming boy. Now, did you learn anything more—about Miss Foster, who we all know is the reason Duff has quit his life of seclusion for the bright lights of London."

"The yeoman knew nothing of her. I asked in a roundabout fashion."

"Then, perhaps it wouldn't be amiss to drive through Shoreham on our way south. In the way of a small reconnoitering mission."

"Perhaps you and I should do that alone."

"You're absolutely right. Much as I adore our girls, they are prone to gossip, and darling Duff doesn't need that sort of mischief right now. When he's still . . . well . . . recuperating." The duchess had never allowed herself to use more than the most benign language to describe her son's emotional state.

The duke had been more realistic about Duff's debility. He knew there were men who came back from war broken for life. And while he wished a full recovery for his son, whatever the outcome, he would have protected and supported him. That seemingly, Miss Foster had performed a miraculous transformation in a matter of days would forever garner his gratitude, not to mention his indebtedness. "We'll have Giles escort the girls. I've had the traveling coach readied. There's room for them all, although I suspect Giles will prefer riding instead of joining a swarm of children inside the confined space of a carriage."

"I'm sure he will," the duchess noted with a faint smile. "And since everyone knows how I can dither about closing up the house before traveling, they won't mind going on ahead."

"What do we say to Miss Foster if we chance to see her in Shoreham?"

"We won't see her. Really, darling, you don't actually think our son would run off to London if Miss Foster was still in the country, do you?"

His brows lifted slightly. "And yet, you're stopping by."

"Insurance, darling. That's all. Now be a dear and tell Giles he's to play escort when he comes in and I'll see that the girls and children are informed of our plans."

In less than three hours the entire D'Abernon family was on the road to London. A half hour later, having detoured to Shoreham, the duke and duchess were standing at the door of Annabelle's mother's cottage.

"There's obviously no one here, darling," Julius noted. "You needn't knock."

"I'd feel better doing so." And she did.

"Why don't I check the back door," the duke offered.

"See if they left any servants behind, although it doesn't appear to be the case. Strange, that," the duchess murmured, her mind racing with possibilities.

She said as much a short time later as she and her husband were bowling south in their comfortable chaise. "Didn't you think the cottage had an air of abandonment? There wasn't a servant in sight. It almost gives one the impression the family wished to disappear," she said, a musing note in her voice.

"Perhaps they don't have servants."

"Miss Foster is not destitute. Everyone knows she paid a tidy sum for her London house. I'm sure she could afford a cook or maid for her family—such as it is. Duff never did mention the exact makeup of the family."

"We shall find out once we reach London, I expect."

"Thank you for your calm counsel and support, darling. I appreciate your understanding."

"I worry about our son as much as you do, sweetheart. We shall see that all remains well with him"—Julius smiled—"and possibly with Miss Foster, too."

While his family was still on the road to London, Duff was tossing his reins to a young flunky on King's Place. He'd already been to Annabelle's town house. It was closed, so he'd checked for Walingame at his clubs and was now at the earl's favorite gambling hell.

That Walingame had abducted Annabelle he didn't doubt for a moment. That he'd make the cur pay for that transgression was also not in doubt.

"Wait here," the marquis said to Eddie, who had dismounted behind him. "I'll let you know whether we stay or go." Then he strode to the stairs fronting an elegant colonnaded facade, took the steps in a leap, lifted the brass knocker on the door, and let it drop.

When the door opened, an imposing butler surveyed Duff's dust-covered garments and boots with disdain. But as his gaze eventually came to rest on the marquis's face, the man's expression abruptly changed. "My Lord Darley!" he said with considerable warmth. "What a pleasure to see you again! Miss Abby will be gratified to hear you're back in town. Please"—he waved Duff in with a wide smile. "She's upstairs. You know the way."

"Thank you, Willis. The usual crowd, I see," Duff said with a nod at the adjoining rooms.

"Miss Abby's games are honest, my lord. It makes for good trade."

"A wise businesswoman," Darley murmured, already striding toward the curved staircase, alight with a splendid crystal chandelier. Familiar with the house, Duff raced up the carpeted stairs, turned right as he reached the first floor, and strode down the corridor until he reached the last door on the left. Rapping twice, he pushed the door open without waiting for an answer, and walked in.

"If you don't mind," a waspish voice intoned, the lady in question's back to the door as she plucked a book from her library shelf. "Kindly wait to be granted entree."

Duff shut the door behind him. "And if I don't?" he murmured with a smile.

"Duff! Darling Duff!" Abigail Fleming, the flame-haired proprietress of the preeminent gambling hell in London, swung around, opened her arms wide, and laughed in glee.

"You've finally come back, you darling man! Come give me a kiss, you rascal! Life has been interminably dull without you!"

"You're looking excessively fine, Abby," Duff said with an appreciative glance at her splendid form in a jonquil yellow gown with a fashionable low decolletage. Reaching her in three long strides, he took her in his arms and kissed her lightly on the cheek.

She leaned back slightly and gazed up at him, a teasing glimmer in her violet eyes. "You certainly don't call that a kiss after how many years—four? Surely," she purred, "you can do better than that."

He let his hands drop away, stepped back, and smiled faintly. "You must acquit me of my prodigal past, Abby dear. The thing is"—he hesitated, then with a deprecating shrug, said, "there's a possibility I may be at least thinking of falling in love. Indeed you may look at me like that. I find it equally shocking."

Concealing her chagrin at perhaps losing one of her favorite lovers, Abby took his hand and offered him a charming smile. "So England's premier Corinthian might have been felled by Cupid's dart. I'm astonished to hear it, but come, my pet, sit with me and tell me of this divine who has stolen your heart." Leading him to a chair, she took one opposite him, leaned back, and with a graceful little wave of her hand, prompted him to speak. "Start from the beginning, my dear Duff. I want to know everything about this incredulous matter."

"Actually, I only just met her four days ago—well, met her again, I suppose one would say—or more precisely, spoke to her for the first time in—" He shifted uncomfortably in his chair. "You wouldn't happen to have a brandy?"

"Of course, darling." She'd heard of his troubles since Waterloo, and now this—Darley contemplating love after only *four days*? She didn't wonder at his restiveness. In an effort to ease his discomfort, she chatted superficially about the current gossip going about town as she poured them both a drink.

Handing Duff his brandy a moment later, she sat down again and lifted her glass in salute. "To your return, Duff." She smiled. "And to the possibilities of love."

"Thank you. It's good to be back." With a flashing smile, he raised his glass, then drank it down in one gulp and set it aside. "You needn't worry," he said, dipping his head as though in acknowledgment of her assessing gaze. "I scarcely drink these days."

"So much the better. Drink is the devil. And I know that better than most. Everyone downstairs would do better to drink less; they'd win more."

"But then you wouldn't profit as much."

"True—although I'm long past concerns about money. You only just arrived in town, I take it," she went on, indicating his travel clothes with a lift of her hand.

"Eddie and I rode in an hour ago."

"You haven't been home yet?"

He shook his head. "I've been looking for her."

"I gathered as much. Your inamorata wouldn't be here, though. Or at least I doubt she would. Who is this creature who can turn your head in four days when no one so much as held your interest for four hours all these years?"

"Annabelle Foster."

It was a considerable achievement not to look stunned. On the other hand, Abigail Fleming hadn't made her way to these lofty heights of business and financial success without a good deal of sangfroid. "No one can fault Miss Foster for her grace and beauty," she noted pleasantly, leaving everything else about Miss Foster unsaid.

"Unfortunately, she's disappeared."

His blunt admission was as shocking as his confession of love. Abby couldn't possibly say what she was thinking—that Annabelle Foster often made herself inaccessible to men she didn't wish to see. On the other hand, Duff was not like other men—definitely not, she reminded herself, knowing well his versatile talents. To that point and another having to do with

Miss Foster's well-known aversion to a certain earl, she delicately inquired, "Might there be some other reason she chooses to secret herself from the world?"

"Fucking Walingame. He found her yesterday at her mother's."

"Ah—and you were there."

He nodded. "Naturally, I sent him on his way. But she was gone this morning." His jaw went taut. "I think he's taken her."

The curtain had rung up, the play fully revealed. Abby set her glass aside as though suddenly she must needs keep her wits about her. "He comes in here regularly," she said, watching for Duff's reaction.

"I know. Is he here yet?"

"It's too early for him." She held Duff's gaze. "I hope you don't mean to spill blood in my house."

He suddenly looked like his old self, all cheeky insolence and swagger, his dark gaze audacious. "I wouldn't think of it, darling. I'll drag the bastard outside."

She couldn't help but smile. "He won't fight you fairly, you know. Just a warning."

"I'm well aware of his lack of principles. Don't worry, I am vigilant."

"Tell me what makes you so sure Walingame has something to do with Miss Foster's disappearance?"

"I just do."

"She's left any number of men in the lurch. You know that."

"Yes."

"But she wouldn't leave you?"

"No."

"You've always been shamelessly arrogant." Her smile was familiar and warm. "But with good reason, as you well know."

He was polite enough not to agree. He only said, "Do you mind if I wait up here for him to arrive?"

"Not in the least." She would have liked to say *I'll have him disposed of for you*, but knew better than to interfere in a gentleman's debt settling. "Have you eaten?" she said instead. "You look as though you could use a good meal."

"I haven't—nor has Eddie. He should be brought in and fed. Tell him I'm staying here for a time."

He spoke in short, succinct phrases, as though he were conserving his words or his energy, she wasn't sure which. "I'll see to some dinner for you and Eddie," she said, rising from her chair. "Would you like another drink while I'm gone?"

He shook his head. "My aim is better if I'm sober."

"I'm not sure it's ever mattered, has it?" Duff was more drunk than sober for many years and yet always managed to hit his mark with deadly accuracy.

"Let's just say, with Walingame, it's best not to take chances. He won't play by the rules."

"The man doesn't know the word."

"I agree. In fact, I might just shut my eyes for a minute while you're gone. I haven't slept much lately."

"Get up on the bed. It's more comfortable and you needn't frown. I don't care about a little road dust. That's what I have servants for."

"You're sure?"

Duff had always been exceedingly polite, even in his cups. "I'm sure. Now, go lie down. I'll see that Eddie's taken care of and I'll be back with some dinner for you."

"Let me know if Walingame comes in."

"I shall. Sleep, now." He looked exhausted, but then she hadn't seen him since he'd left for the Peninsula four years ago. Maybe it was more than his travel to London that made him look weary; maybe the war had taken its toll.

Chapter
22

Two hours later a burly footman came to Abby's room with the message Duff had been waiting for.

Walingame had arrived.

"He's not been here more than five minutes," the footman said with a frown, "and he's already in a row with the dealer at table ten. Do you want me to have him thrown out, Miss Abby?"

Duff came up out of his chair like a shot. "I'll take care of it," he said briskly. "Have Eddie bring my pistol case round back to the garden."

Abby stopped Duff with a hand on his arm. "You could let this go for a day or so." The marquis had rested and eaten, but no one would have mistaken him for the same man who had left for the Peninsula three years ago. "There's no need to beard Walingame tonight."

"I'm fine, Abby," Duff said, leaning over and kissing her rosy cheek. He smiled. "And you know as well as I do that this should have been done a long time ago."

"I won't argue with you there. But I'd like to see you less fatigued when you face him."

"It doesn't take much to aim a pistol. Not to mention, mine have hair triggers." He grinned. "It will be a simple matter."

"I'm pleased to hear it," she said with grace, when she knew it could end disastrously for both men. Walingame, while he chose not to duel when other means were available, had on occasion—when his adversaries were sufficiently weak—stepped onto the dueling field. He'd killed young Addington with a clean shot to the heart from twenty paces without so much as a scratch for himself.

"When it's over, I'll drink a glass of champagne with you," Duff said, unruffled and cool.

"Is that a promise?" Abby murmured, unable to keep the tremor from her voice.

He grinned, pulled her in his arms, and kissed her like he had in the past. "Is that better?" he teased, hoping to allay her fears. "Now, don't worry." Releasing her, he bowed gracefully. "I shall be back for champagne before you know it."

But as Darley walked from her apartments, Abby called her footman to her side and issued a few rapid instructions. "I want everything to go smoothly. You understand," she said at the last.

"Yes, Miss Abby. Don't worry none. We know what to do."

Duff strolled into the room where Walingame was gambling and stood just inside the doorway for a moment, surveying the throng. He knew most everyone. A few wealthy merchants who could afford the play were in the mix, and a few out-of-town gentry were trying their luck at Abby's, but other than that, the players were men of his acquaintance.

Having brought gloves in from his saddlebags, he'd tucked them into the pocket of his riding pants. He touched them briefly, as though reassuring himself they were in place, and moving from the entrance, slowly threaded his way between the tables to where Walingame sat at cards.

Walingame caught sight of Duff before he reached him and had time to school his features. The earl set down his cards with a studied nonchalance.

Everyone at his table wondered at Walingame stopping in

the middle of play until they looked up and saw a grim-faced Duff coming near. An uneasy hush rippled out from table ten, a muzzled silence slowly pervading the room. By the time Duff finally came to rest beside Walingame, one could have heard a pin drop.

"Where is she?" Duff's voice was measured and mild, his gaze in contrast hard as flint.

"I don't know."

"Liar." A knife blade of a word.

Walingame didn't knowingly put his life at risk. "Perhaps," he said with a dip of his head. "But not about that. I have no idea where the jade is."

"I could beat it out of you."

Walingame's mouth turned up in a sneer. "I doubt it. You're not carrying enough weight anymore. If you want me to say I'm sorry the bitch ran, I will, but otherwise I can't help you. She sure as hell didn't run to me." He wasn't interested in shedding any blood tonight or any night over a woman, and to that end he was willing to mollify Duff.

Duff wasn't inclined to be mollified. If Annabelle was gone, Walingame had to be party to it, his denial notwithstanding. "I'm calling you a damned, bloody liar," Duff said so softly, the men at the table strained forward to hear the words. And drawing out his gloves, he slapped Walingame's face.

A red welt rose on Walingame's cheek, but he didn't move from his chair. "I'm not fighting you over that doxy."

"Then you're a liar *and* a coward." Duff shifted his stance as though provoking him to rise. "Get up, you spineless cur." He slapped Walingame a second time—harder.

Walingame came to his feet in a surge of fury, goaded beyond even *his* sense of self-preservation. "You're dead, Darley," he snarled. "And I'll fuck the bitch on your grave for good measure."

Duff gave no indication he'd heard him. He only nodded toward the terrace doors. "I'll see you outside."

Everyone within earshot was rapidly coming to the same

conclusion concerning the identity of the female at the center of this dispute. Had Darley been the reason Annabelle Foster had left London? Was Walingame the cuckold? If so, why was Darley at his throat? That Annabelle was worth fighting over was not in question. She'd even brought Walingame up to the mark.

While Walingame had been driven to accept Duff's challenge, he wasn't without options. Aware of Darley's history on the dueling field, as well as the fact that he might be a target of the marquis's displeasure since Shoreham, he'd taken appropriate measures to protect himself. "Are we using seconds?" he inquired, in control of his emotions once again, playing the gentleman for practical reasons.

Duff looked right through him. "What for?"

"After you, then," Walingame said in silken accents. As he spoke, he casually moved his arm at his side, reassuring himself the pistol in his coat pocket was conveniently near. *Fortune sides with him who dares*, he mused, finding Virgil highly appropriate at the moment.

"We'll go out together." Duff had no intention of walking in front of Walingame.

"Very well." Walingame's plans would require a slight adjustment, but nothing untoward, he decided, taking his place beside Duff with an air of equanimity.

It would soon be over in any event, he reflected.

Darley's insults would be avenged.

As the men walked through the terrace doors, a fully illuminated garden lit with numerous flambeaux met their gazes. Footmen were stationed in neat rows on either side of the open green in the center of the garden. And Eddie waited on the manicured grass with Duff's pistol case in his hands.

"My, my," Walingame murmured. "Do I detect a calculated plan?"

"My servants are simply here to assure compliance with the rules," Abby noted, as she stood near the terrace balustrade. What was left unsaid was the fact that governance was needed to be sure those rules were observed.

Walingame suddenly found the odds unacceptable. Any hope of utilizing his concealed pistol on the field was seriously curtailed by the blazing lights, not to mention all the footmen witness to the scene. Which left him diminishing options. And less time than he'd thought to play out his game. The pistol in his pocket was meant to be a deadly surprise.

With footmen posted like guardsmen on the green, even if he managed to shoot Darley with his hidden weapon, escape would be impossible.

His life was clearly at stake.

There was no time to let events unfold.

Jerking the small pistol from his coat pocket, Walingame leaped in front of Duff, and as Duff's arms flew up to protect himself, Walingame fired twice from point-blank range.

Duff was flung back by the powerful impact of two fifty-caliber shots.

Walingame spun away and sprinted toward the darkness at the end of the terrace.

Pandemonium exploded around Darley.

Fuck. He'd been gulled like a simpleton, Duff thought bitterly, as his knees began to give way.

"Get a doctor!" Abby screamed, running toward Darley.

Abby's scream seemed to be coming from far away, the high-pitched cry competing with the corrosive pain ripping through his body, the agony so raw he couldn't breathe. Although, maybe it was better if he didn't breathe, Duff thought, if he didn't move—the hellish torment might be more manageable. But as he collapsed, the downward motion jolted his body with nightmarish intensity, and he gritted his teeth against the scream rising in his throat.

Two men caught him just before he hit the ground, and Eddie was at his side a second later.

"Get Stewart," Duff breathed, the effort it took to speak almost insupportable.

Then his eyes went shut.

Duff was still conscious as they carried him back into the

gaming room, but his eyes hadn't opened and his wounds were bleeding profusely. His shirt and waistcoat were soaked through, the coat sleeve of the arm through which one of the balls had passed before entering his chest drenched with blood.

He was carried up to Abby's rooms while Eddie instructed a messenger to fetch Dr. Stewart. Then Abby and Eddie set about trying to stanch Duff's bleeding.

Scottish doctors weren't allowed to practice in England. Their less competent English colleagues didn't like the competition. But at this juncture, no one was concerned with legalities.

Very soon after being placed in Abby's bed, Duff lost consciousness.

Abby was quietly crying as she kept handing clean towels to Eddie.

Eddie's mouth was set in a grim line as he kept pressure on the wounds in an effort to stop the bleeding.

The arm wound was clean—no major arteries had been hit. Eddie had wrapped it tightly and left it. The chest wounds were more daunting, the clear shot deep and very close to the heart. The second ball had lost momentum as it passed through Duff's arm, although a fifty-caliber projectile was powerful enough to do serious damage, deflected or not. "No arteries have been hit, thank God," Eddie muttered, easing another blood-soaked towel from Duff's chest, the hole left by the bullet seeping blood but not pumping it out. Quickly putting a clean towel in place, he leaned on the wadded towel with both hands. "He's led a charmed life, he has," he murmured. "Lady Luck might still be on his side."

"Pray God she is. How far did you say it was to the doctor's house?" Abby asked as though she might hurry the doctor along with her repeated queries.

"Ten blocks, maybe a few more," Eddie answered patiently. "I told your man to ride anyone over who gets in his way. They should be here soon." Fortunately, Dr. Stewart was a stay-at-home family man. He wouldn't have to be chased down at some club or social engagement.

"How long has it been?" Abby asked again, like a child might, repeating the question until she received the answer she wished.

"He should be here soon," Eddie replied kindly, having no more idea of the time than she did. It seemed like a hundred years since Duff had been shot—or maybe just months, memories of the horror of Waterloo suddenly flooding into his brain. But even then, Duff hadn't been shot in the chest.

Eddie wasn't a praying man, but these were the kind of wounds that required prayer. Before he'd run out of words— his religious vocabulary spare from disuse—a soft knock was heard, and a second after that, one of Abby's footmen entered. Walking over to his employer, he whispered in her ear.

Since it wasn't the doctor who'd arrived, Eddie paid no further notice. He went back to his harrowing business.

When the man finished talking, Abby nodded in understanding. "Thank everyone," she said, keeping her voice low in the sickroom. "Have Dudley make the appropriate payments, then I want everyone concerned to leave London immediately. No one is to return until they hear from me."

The door softly shut a moment later, and as Abby returned her attention to Duff, she said without expression, "Walingame was shot and thrown into the Thames. I wish he would have suffered more but there wasn't time."

Eddie grunted in acknowledgment.

"If only revenge were sweeter," she murmured, her voice heavy with grief.

"If Duff lives, it will be sweet." Eddie turned his head for the barest second and met Abby's gaze. "Good work," he said. Then he softly exhaled. "Now, you might want to pray."

"Don't say that," Abby cried softly.

Eddie shook his head in the slightest of movements. "I don't know what else to do. I don't dare dig out the shots when they're so close to his heart."

"Then I'll pray that the doctor comes," Abby replied firmly. She refused to give up hope. She wouldn't allow herself to even consider it. Duff was too full of life to die, too good and bonny and kind. Someone as cursed as Walingame shouldn't be allowed to take his life.

She began to pray, pleading, promising anything, offering supplications of every kind if only God would hear her prayers.

Duff was more than a friend; she owed him her life. Years ago, he'd saved her from cruel treatment at the hands of Lord Sheldon. He'd given her the funds for her first gambling house and refused to accept payment in return. Not that offering him her favors hadn't been a gratifying way of repaying him in some small measure.

But, in addition to praying for the doctor, she decided to pray that Duff lived so she might settle her debt to him in a more substantial way. Once Duff recovered, she decided, refusing to give in to despair, she would ask him what charity he preferred.

She immediately took comfort in the thought of Duff's charity, or maybe God had answered her in his own way. Whatever the case, the door suddenly opened—young James Stewart walked in and calmly said, "Let's see what we have here."

The doctor immediately took over, issuing orders in a brisk staccato, his manner both efficient and confident. He appeared neither worried nor harried, a distinct balm to the fear of those in the room.

He'd brought ether—first synthesized in 1540 and used in various compounds since then—and Duff was given a small amount to dull the pain. Due to his extensive bleeding, the doctor took care not to put the marquis into too deep a sleep. But once the narcotic was administered to his satisfaction, he swiftly and deftly plucked the shot from Duff's chest with delicate forceps of his own design. The lead balls landed in the basin Abby held with a heavy thud in what seemed a miraculously brief procedure, and then the doctor cleaned and dressed the wounds.

Stepping back from his handiwork, James Stewart smiled. "I believe we're done now."

"Will he live?" Abby asked, apprehensive in every word.

"Do you think me incompetent?" But he was clearly teasing, his clear blue eyes gleaming with amusement.

"What if the wounds fester?" Abby needed guarantees.

"You must see that they don't. No, no, my dear, don't take alarm. I can see you don't like my humor when you're so distressed. I will leave instructions for the wound cleaning," he added as he washed his hands. "I have studied in the Levant and their medicine is much superior to ours. The wounds will not fester. My word on it."

"What about all the blood he's lost?" Eddie asked, still concerned despite the doctor's high spirits.

"Come now, Eddie, Duff has the constitution of a horse. Don't worry. As for his blood loss, we will see that he is fed some bracing broth." The doctor set down the towel, ran his hands through his sandy hair, and smiled at Abby. "I will leave recipes for your staff."

"Your confidence is reassuring, Doctor." Abby allowed herself the smallest sigh of relief. "And it seems as though you know Duff."

"We met several years ago—on a caravan to Timbuktu. Eddie found us both when we became lost in a sandstorm. We stayed in touch, and when the marquis came back from Waterloo, Eddie consulted me."

"With excellent results," Eddie acknowledged.

The doctor dipped his head and smiled.

"Might I ask you to stay the night with us?" Abby asked. "In the event of complications," she added. "You could have your own room, of course. I would just like you nearby should we need you. And if you'd be interested in one of my girls, you may have your pick."

"Certainly, I'll stay if you wish. And while I appreciate your offer of female company, I'm happily married, so I shall politely refuse."

"You're a rare novelty in my business, Doctor. I don't often see your kind. It's refreshing to know happy marriages exist."

"We who live outside the peerage can marry for love. With no grand acres or titles to consider, settlements and dowries are inconsequential."

Abby smiled. "I feel as though I've witnessed two miracles tonight. Duff's life is saved and I've met a happily married man."

"And don't forget, Walingame is gone," Eddie added. "Good things come in threes, ain't that true?"

"True indeed," she replied cheerfully, suddenly feeling as though Duff was assured a future. "Now, gentlemen, allow me to have a bottle of champagne sent up. We should offer a toast for Duff's speedy recovery."

Everyone agreed, but before they enjoyed their toast, Eddie had a message sent to Duff's parents.

Chapter
23

Duff's parents didn't receive Eddie's message until the following day, the missive having traveled north and then south again before reaching Westerlands House in Portman Square.

The duke and duchess had already become mildly concerned about Duff's whereabouts by the time the message was delivered. While he'd ostensibly come to London, Duff wasn't at his home in St. James Square, nor was he at theirs, or anywhere else he might have normally been found.

When the messenger arrived, by good fortune, the duke was alone in his study. After absorbing the shocking news, he immediately asked where he might find his son. Reassured that Duff was in good hands with Dr. Stewart, he quizzed the man about the details surrounding the shooting. After being apprised of the events, he graciously thanked the man, told him to relay the message to Miss Fleming that they would come to fetch Duff forthwith, and, in a great show of courtesy, walked the man out himself.

But once he returned to his study, he shut the door, and, leaning back against it, felt the blood literally drain from his face. He stood very still for a brief time, silently rendering thanks to all the divinities on high, grateful to the depths of his soul that his son still lived. Then, drawing in a sustaining breath, he absently ran his hands down the front of his waist-coat, pushed away from the door, and left his study. Elspeth must be told. The question was how best to tell her. As he de-bated his options, he took the stairs to the first floor, walked to the back of the house where his wife's sitting room overlooked the garden, and opened the door.

The duchess looked up from her letter writing as Julius walked in. "Have you seen a ghost?" she asked, immediately coming to her feet. "It's Duff, isn't it? Tell me, tell me this in-stant—is he alive?"

"He's alive." He didn't question how she knew. She had a sixth sense about their children.

"Thank God," she whispered, sitting down suddenly as though her legs had given way, the frothy blue muslin of her gown following her down in a pouf.

"But he's been shot," Julius said, moving toward her.

Her gaze came up. "Shot?" While she'd always feared her son's involvement in dueling, Duff was never hurt. "It could only have been treachery. It was, wasn't it?"

"Walingame shot Duff, and yes, treachery was involved. The earl is dead by other hands, I was told."

"Good. He deserves to die," the duchess said with steely resolve. "Not just for harming our son, but for a lifetime of in-famy." The duchess was a lioness when it came to her chil-dren. "Where is Duff? How is he?" She seemed to rally herself in order to ask, in a very small voice, "Tell me honestly—how grievous are his wounds?"

Having reached his wife, the duke bent down and scooped her into his arms. "He's alive—that's all that matters." Sitting down on her chair, he settled her on his lap and held her close. "He's at Abby Fleming's gambling house, where this disgrace took place. I'm having the carriage brought around and we'll go and fetch him."

"Isn't Miss Fleming Duff's friend from years ago?" Elspeth said as though she needed to make mindless conversation in order to keep her fears at bay. "I remember him speaking of her just recently. Or was it—"

"She *is* an old friend," the duke interposed soothingly. "But not a woman of conventional form," he added guardedly.

"You needn't be so cautious, Julius. I know who my son's friends are. Oh, dear," Elspeth softly exclaimed, feeling as though the angel of death had suddenly entered the room. "Tell me our boy is going to be fine."

"He will be, darling. Don't worry."

"Promise me?" Her eyes were huge with worry. "You must promise. I just felt the most terrible sensation."

"I promise," he murmured, dropping a light kiss on her forehead.

"Thank you, darling," Elspeth whispered, resting her head on his shoulder. Julius always dealt with the world with such certainty. He was her unassailable refuge, and always had been. "And forgive my nerves. But Duff has skirted death so many times, one wonders when fate might turn on him. However, today is not the day, is it?" she said more briskly, sitting up again. "There now—I'm better," she added, patting her cheeks to bring back the color.

For a moment Julius was reminded of the first time he called on her at her first husband's home. Ultimately, she'd dismissed her apprehensions in the same determined way. "We have had our share of crises, darling," he said with a faint smile. "And we've survived them all."

"This too will pass, won't it?" And before he could answer, she jumped to her feet. "Do let's go and bring our boy home."

Rising from the chair, he took her hand in his and moved toward the door. "I also called for a dray wagon," he said. "I doubt Duff's in any condition to sit in a carriage."

The duchess smiled. "And think—we'll have our darling

boy back home by the time the rest of the family returns from their shopping and clubs. Although, I'm not taking this lightly," she attested. "I'm just vastly pleased our Duff is alive."

"As am I, darling," the duke agreed. "He took two shots very near to his heart, though, so there's still a certain element of danger."

"Eddie's with him now?"

"Yes, of course," he replied as they moved out into the hallway. "And Dr. Stewart tended his wounds."

Elspeth gave her husband a fleeting look of reproach. "Why didn't you say Dr. Stewart was with him? Really, my dear, you could have saved me considerable apprehension." Then her tone brightened. "Young James is quite extraordinary, though, so all is well. He will have Duff back in good health in no time."

Not inclined to argue with his wife, the duke only smiled. "I'm sure you're right, my dear." Although the messenger had conveyed a more sobering report. But sober or not, Julius was sanguine about his son's recovery. After what Duff had survived at Waterloo, clearly, he wasn't a man who would ease into his grave with any complacency.

And on another positive note, the duke mused, with Walingame dead, he was saved the trouble of killing him.

At the same time the Duke and Duchess of Westerlands were en route to King's Place, Annabelle Foster and her family were aboard a ferry taking them from the mainland to the Isle of Wight. They'd pressed straight through on their journey south, sleeping and eating as best they could in the coach. Concerned with possible pursuit by Walingame, Annabelle refused to tarry any longer than it took to change horses at the post stops.

It was a glorious, sunny day, with a light breeze off the sea, the docks at Ryde in sight across the sparkling water. With luck, they would find a cottage to rent on the far side of the island where they could settle in and enjoy the summer. Molly's beau Tom had come with them, both for Molly's comfort and as a male escort to the small group of females. He was young, strong, and devoted to Molly and his daughter. As for Annabelle, she welcomed the protection he offered.

She was hoping, of course, that Walingame would relinquish his pursuit. But knowing him as she did, she didn't allow herself to let down her guard. Constant vigilance was called for when dealing with a man like the earl.

Duff was lightly sedated when the duke and duchess arrived. While Dr. Stewart had returned home that morning, he'd left instructions for the care of his patient. The doctor was of the opinion that the body healed best when not constantly battling pain, and with the severity of Duff's wounds, he'd prescribed a mild narcotic regimen.

At the sound of his mother's voice, Duff's eyelids fluttered open and he came awake enough to recognize his parents.

"We're going to take you home, darling," Elspeth said, leaning in to kiss him gently on the cheek.

He smiled faintly before returning to his morphine-induced doze.

Turning from the bed, the duchess offered her hand to Abby. "I wish to thank you for helping save our son's life. We are most grateful. Duff always speaks highly of you, Miss Fleming."

"Thank you, ma'am," Abby replied, blushing when she hadn't known herself to blush in years. In fact, if Eddie hadn't insisted she stay, she would have been elsewhere. "Lord Darley is a very special man."

"We think so as well, don't we, Julius?" The duchess addressed her husband informally when most in the fashionable world didn't.

"Yes, my dear. He's very special. And allow me to express

my gratitude as well, Miss Fleming," the duke said, bowing faintly to Abby. "We are in your debt."

"Feel free to come and visit Duff whenever you wish," Elspeth offered, smiling brightly. "I'm sure he would enjoy seeing you."

"I would like that very much." Abby understood from whom Duff had inherited his great charm. His parents were uncommonly genuine for persons of wealth and rank.

In due course, Duff was conveyed downstairs on a stretcher, and placed in the wagon that had been cushioned with feather beds. After taking leave of Miss Fleming with further promises to see each other again, the Westerlands made their way home.

Duff, still dozing, was installed in his former rooms. Eddie went off to sleep for the first time in two days. And the duke and duchess retired to an adjacent sitting room so they would be near their son should he wake.

"Dr. Stewart will come to check on Duff tonight," Julius noted. "He sent a message."

"Eddie says there was no question that Dr. Stewart saved Duff's life." Elspeth exhaled softly. "How fortunate for Duff that he was in the city when this terrible event transpired."

"Yes, it was fortunate indeed. But, as you suspected, he was in London looking for Miss Foster. He wants us to find her. You heard him as he was being placed in the wagon."

"The sweet boy could barely speak or think and yet he insisted she be found," the duchess said with a benevolent smile. "How like Duff to be so single-minded," she added like a doting mother, questioning neither her son's motives nor reasons. "Naturally, we must find her."

"I assume she ran from Walingame. Or so I gathered from Miss Fleming."

"Is that what you two were talking about so earnestly while Duff was being carried downstairs?"

"Duff confided in her about his feelings for Annabelle Foster. He talked of being in love. Miss Fleming was surprised, naturally."

"I should think so. You must admit, the word *love* and Duff have not had even a nodding acquaintance all these many years."

"You know Annabelle Foster has a certain reputation," the duke cautiously pointed out.

"Of course she has a reputation. She's an actress. As was Lady Derby before she married the earl, and Mrs. Jordan even as she presented the Duke of Clarence with his tenth child. I must say, I've never liked the disparity between the scandals of the aristocracy and those of people of lesser means. It's quite unfair."

The duke's heavy-lidded gaze was measured. "Nevertheless, it exists."

"Pshaw. I care nothing for scandal." Elspeth cast an amused look her husband's way. "If I did, would I have fallen in love with you? Really, darling, your scandalous reputation was quite enticing, if you must know. Or perhaps you did know."

The duke met her gaze with a look of improbable innocence. "All I knew, my dear, was that my pursuit of you was in the way of a *force majeure*. You enchanted me completely."

"How very pretty of you," Elspeth said with a grin. "And do I still enchant you?"

"Need you ask? It's quite unfashionable to be in love with one's wife and yet I am, still and always."

"We are very lucky, are we not?" Elspeth softly murmured. "Do you think," she went on in a musing tone, "that Duff might truly be in love with Miss Foster?"

The duke had his doubts, but he said instead, "He seems to think so."

"Well, then, we must bring her to him. How do you propose to find her?"

The duke shrugged faintly. "England is large and it appears she doesn't wish to be found."

"Surely you're not going to let a little difficulty like that deter you," his wife said with a challenging look.

The duke laughed. "I gather I'm not."

"No, of course you're not. If our darling boy thinks he's in love with Miss Foster, surely you understand what a boon her presence would be to his recovery. I daresay, just seeing her will immediately revive his spirits."

"No doubt," the duke replied drily. "In any event, I propose to hire some Bow Street Runners. They have contacts throughout the country. And with Miss Foster's celebrity, she will find it more difficult to hide. In fact, the next time Duff wakens, I shall ask him how many people might be in Miss Foster's party. Although, in the way of a small warning, my dear—the lady may not wish to see Duff."

"Surely, you jest. Our son? You are quite mistaken, my dear. And didn't you say that she was running from Walingame, not Duff?"

"It was information I received third-hand from Miss Fleming. I can't be certain of its accuracy."

"Well, I am most certain. Mark my words, she will be overjoyed to see Duff again."

"And you are prescient in all things?" he said with amusement.

"When it comes to our children, I am, my dear, as you well know. Speaking of children, we must decide how much or how little to tell the girls and Giles. Until Miss Foster is found, I suggest we say nothing about her. Gossip will be rampant enough about this terrible shooting without adding more salacious details to the mix. And it does no good to ask people to keep such things confidential. Even if the children scrupulously adhere to our wishes, the servants hear everything. If we tell anyone that we are looking for Miss Foster, the news will be bruited about at every breakfast table in London tomorrow." She lifted one brow. "If not sooner."

"I agree."

"You always agree," she said with a teasing smile. "That must be why we get along so well."

He winked. "It's exactly why we get along so well."

Chapter
24

A week later, Annabelle answered a knock on the door of their rented cottage and blanched. From the parlor window, she'd watched a single man walk up the path to the door. But now, standing in the open doorway, she found not one but *six* men in her small yard, five of them sporting the red vests of Bow Street Runners.

That five large men could have so effectively concealed themselves from sight was both awe-inspiring and frightening.

And even more frightening, they looked grave.

"Miss Foster?"

While the spokesman's voice was polite, he wasn't asking a question. It was obvious he knew who she was. "I am Miss Foster," she said in her best Lady Macbeth manner.

"The Duke of Westerlands has commissioned us to deliver this note to you." He offered a sealed letter that had clearly suffered in transit, the superior paper much creased and wrinkled. "If you please, we'll wait for your reply."

Not wishing to give anything away, Annabelle allowed herself only the smallest sigh of relief. At least she was not to be carried off by Walingame's men. Nor by Westerlands'. Perhaps she yet had choices, despite the six Bow Street Runners in her garden. "Allow me a moment to read this," she directed, and with a nod, she turned and walked back inside, shutting the door behind her.

"Who is it, Belle?" her mother called out from the kitchen.

"Nothing, Mother. I'll be right there." Tearing the seal open, she unfolded the letter and read:

> *My dear Miss Foster,*
> *Our son, Duff, was shot by Walingame. He is asking for you. The state of his health is serious, but not, at this moment, critical. However, if you would be kind enough to return with the runners, we would be very grateful. Also, Walingame is dead, should you be concerned for your safety. He is no longer a danger to anyone.*

It was signed *Westerlands*, and a postscript had been added by the duchess imploring Annabelle to come to London with all possible speed.

Stunned and confounded, her thoughts in a tumult, Annabelle stood frozen in place. Not only shocked by the events disclosed in the letter, she was disquieted at the seriousness of Duff's condition, not to mention having to make a decision concerning this information and her family. Did she tell them or not?

As if the choice had been taken from her by the hand of fate, another rap on the door echoed in the hall just as her mother appeared carrying a plate of piping-hot scones.

Her mother dipped her head toward the door. "Open the door, dear. And invite whoever it is in. Hetty just made the most delicious scones we can share with company. Is that a letter?" she inquired, indicating the sheet in Annabelle's hand with another nod.

"A bit of a crisis has arisen, Mother." It was impossible to dissemble at this point.

"You do look a bit harried, my dear. Is it something I can help you with?"

Her mother's senses were completely normal once again,

Duff's initial visit having been the opening breach, as it were, toward a full recovery. Since then, her mother had steadily improved—a veritable blessing for which she owed Duff her thanks. "I just received a letter from the Duke of Westerlands—Duff's father," Annabelle announced. "It was brought here by men he'd hired to locate us."

"And they're knocking at the door? Why don't you invite them in?"

For any number of reasons, none of which she chose to mention to her mother. Could she return to London without her family? Or would her mother insist on going with her once she heard of Duff's condition? Would her entire life come tumbling down around her ears if her mother accompanied her to London? Did she have to go at all?

"Really, dear," her mother admonished. "Open the door. Never mind, I shall." And to the very large man who was standing on her stoop, she cheerfully inquired, "Would you like a scone? And do bring in your friends," she added. "You're Bow Street Runners, aren't you? How very exciting."

If her options weren't so fearsome, Annabelle might have been tempted to laugh at her mother's delight in meeting the men who might turn out to be her warders. But at the moment there was nothing to do but play her role calmly. While her mother served the six men tea and scones and asked them myriad questions about London, Annabelle sat quietly in a corner of the parlor, debating how to deal with the duke's letter. Until her mother suddenly came to her feet, said, "I shall get us another pot of hot tea," sent a piercing gaze her daughter's way, and added, "Do help me, dear." Then, her mother nodded toward the kitchen and winked as though she was participating in a broad farce.

There was nothing to do but try not to blush too noticeably and follow her mother into the kitchen.

"Now, tell me this instant what is going on," Mrs. Foster insisted, pointing her finger at Annabelle as she had when her daughter had been caught in some mischief as a child. "You have a letter from the Duke of Westerlands. That, however, does not require six men to deliver it, when England has a very reliable post."

"The duke would like me to return to London with these men."

"Whatever for? You're not in some trouble, are you?"

"No, no, Mama." She exhaled and then, realizing there was no way out, said, "Duff has been shot—don't worry . . . they say he is not critical. But apparently, he would like me to come and visit him."

"My goodness gracious!" her mother exclaimed softly. "My goodness gracious," she repeated, this time in breathless wonder.

"Now, Mama, don't begin to imagine things. We're just friends. He must be in need of company during his recuperation."

"Company indeed. As if London isn't filled with a million souls. We're going, of course. I don't know how you could even hesitate. The poor boy has been shot, and his family is asking you to come to his bedside as a ministering angel."

"This is not a play, Mama," Annabelle said firmly. The last thing she wanted was for her mother to put this summons into some fairy tale context. "We are in the real world, and as you know very well, people like us are well apart from the *beau monde* and its privileges."

"For heaven's sake, I'm not a dunce, my dear. But you know as well as I do that Lord Darley is a most well-mannered, amiable man. There's no reason in the world why we can't go up to London to visit him when his father has requested your presence so nicely."

"The request may not be so nicely couched, Mama. If I were to refuse, I'm not so sure I might not be coerced into going."

"Nonsense. A cultivated man like Darley surely can't have parents that are barbarians."

"Why don't we find out," Annabelle declared, rankled by

her mother's benign view of the fashionable world that was, in her experience, far from benign. "Then we needn't argue uselessly."

But when she asked, she was told that the men had no orders other than to relay the message to her. "Not that the duke wouldn't be right happy if'n you were to come back with us," their spokesman said. "An' the duchess, too."

Nonplused, Annabelle was left speechless.

"I do believe I said as much," her mother murmured with a triumphant glance at her Annabelle. Then she added, with such conviction that Annabelle suppressed a gasp, "My daughter would be pleased to return to London with you."

"I'm not sure, Mama," Belle quickly interposed, her gaze heated.

"I will be sure for you, my dear," her mother airily replied, giving as good a rendition of divine right as the Regent.

Annabelle's voice took a note of impatience. "But what about you and the children? I couldn't possibly leave you."

"We shall be perfectly fine here with Tom and Molly." The Regent could have taken lessons from Mrs. Foster in noblesse oblige as well.

The Bow Street Runners' spokesman glanced from woman to woman before clearing his throat loudly. "The thing is, Miss Foster, I was authorized to invite your entire family," he said respectfully. "The duke was quite particular in the invitation. He sent along his well-sprung and commodious traveling coach in order to accommodate your family."

"Well, well," Mrs. Foster proclaimed, her point of view having prospered. "It looks as though we'll be going to London. And such a lovely time of year for travel. Molly!" she cried out. "Do come in and hear the good news!"

At which point, Annabelle realized, any further plans were out of her hands.

Even the Bow Street Runner was smiling. "The duke and duchess will be most grateful to see you, miss," he said quietly, as her mother began gaily telling Molly of their plans.

"And I was expressly directed to give you this." Slipping a small box from his coat pocket, he handed it to Annabelle.

She recognized the red leather box and couldn't help but smile, no matter that she was exasperated that any further resistance had been rendered useless by a great many people, she suspected. "Thank you," she said, slipping it into her skirt pocket without opening it.

But when she did a short time later in the quiet of her room as the house was all abustle with packing, she found a small rose brooch in yellow diamonds and couldn't help but smile.

He'd remembered.

Chapter
25

The message that Duff and his family were to expect company was received fully two days before the Westerlands' traveling coach reached London. A rider had galloped ahead with the news.

But on one point in this unscheduled journey to London, Annabelle had exerted her authority and would not compromise. She and her family were to be conveyed to her London house, *not* Westerlands House.

As the coach passengers alighted in Mayfair shortly before teatime three days later, Mrs. Wells, Annabelle's longtime housekeeper, greeted them, her face wreathed in smiles. "We received your message and now here you are!" she exclaimed. "How nice to have you back, Miss Foster!"

Annabelle smiled. "It's good to be back." And despite the serious matter that had brought her to London, Annabelle found she really was pleased to return to her home. Her entire staff—some having been with her from her first days on the stage—were like family, and her elegant little town house had a cozy charm all its own.

Annabelle introduced her mother and the others to Mrs. Wells and the servants, who were all lined up in the entrance hall to greet them. The coach was unloaded next and sent away; Molly, Tom, and the babies were shown to their rooms and her mother and Mrs. Wells had gone off arm in arm, chatting like old friends. Annabelle suddenly found herself alone in the entrance hall.

She was relieved that the women were getting along. Mrs. Wells had always reigned supreme in her household, and Annabelle had worried how the two women would receive each other. But apparently, exceptionally well. Since she had myriad personal issues to deal with, she was gratified.

Of course, the dilemma of Duff's impact on her life was first and foremost. How much or how little did she care—or, more to the point, how much would she allow herself to care? Or did her feelings even matter when the Westerlands were in command?

Then there was the matter of concealing from her mother the more indecorous incidents in her past. Although, having renounced that necessitous period of her life quite some time ago—Walingame's recent blackmail notwithstanding—it was annoying even to have to consider it. But since gossip was what it was, she dared not be cavalier.

Lastly, a flood of invitations was bound to appear, now that she was home. Did she answer some or none? Did she turn away all visitors or only select ones? Did she enter the social whirl or ignore society completely?

Brought from her musings by a knock on the door, she glanced up. Her footman was already opening the door, and a moment later a flunky in Westerlands livery was visible on her stoop. The flunky informed her servant, who, in turn, informed her—although she could hear the exchange well enough from where she stood—that a carriage was outside waiting to convey her to Westerlands House.

Their traveling coach could have scarcely reached Portman Square yet, she thought peevishly, and she was already being summoned.

For the briefest of moments she debated playing the prima donna. She'd barely had time to catch her breath. Nor had she ever been at the beck and call of aristocratic personages. In fact, she'd had the luxury of refusing more noble invitations than any one woman in London.

As quickly as she'd taken a pet, however, she overcame it, understanding the circumstances this time were very different. She wouldn't be turning down an invitation to some frivolous entertainment—Duff was seriously wounded. It was only natural that his parents would be interested in having her appear with all speed.

Regardless of the need for haste, however, she couldn't present herself at Westerlands House in her disheveled state, two days on the road having left her unpresentable. "I shall be ready in forty minutes," she informed both servants together. Even then, she knew she would be leaving her house with wet hair.

And so it transpired, after she'd bathed quickly and dressed and assured her mother countless times that she would not put a foot wrong in the presence of such exalted nobles. Exiting her house with damp curls, she descended her front steps, walked across the pavement, and stepped into the elegant carriage parked at her curb.

Fortunately, with short hair, by the time the carriage came to a stop at Westerlands House, her tousled ringlets were nearly dry. Her simple, white dimity gown was fashionably trimmed with several rows of lilac ribbon at the hem, her hair held back from her temples with lilac ribbon as well. She was as presentable as one could be on such short notice.

Except, perhaps, for the high flush on her cheeks that was definitely not viewed as *à la mode*.

And whether her pinked cheeks were from having rushed headlong to arrive posthaste or because she would be seeing Duff again, she chose not to question. Such debate was pointless, in any event. Unlike her mother, who still clung to fanciful dreams, she had long ago given up such whimsies.

That a nobleman would want her company, she understood.

That he wanted more than transient pleasure, she'd learned long ago was not the case.

But for all her cool pragmatism and reasoned argument, she was shaken to the core when she first saw Duff lying in his bed. He was white as death, his eyes were closed, his breathing barely noticeable.

His parents, who had been seated by his bed, quickly rose to greet her.

"Thank you so much for coming, Miss Foster," the duchess murmured, rushing forward to take her hand, the relief in her eyes profound. "Duff has been impatiently waiting for you. We all have."

The duke came up and thanked Annabelle in turn for coming to London with such dispatch. "As you see," he said, his deep voice filled with emotion, "our son is in delicate health. I expect," he said with a pleasant smile, "your arrival will hearten him."

"We do all hope so—most earnestly," the duchess agreed. "Please, sit," she offered, indicating an arrangement of chairs by the windows. "I'll send for tea—or would you like sherry? The doctor is keeping Duff mildly sedated," she added, fluttering her hand in the direction of the bed. "But he's scheduled for some broth shortly and you'll see him awake."

"A sherry would be agreeable. I've been on the road for quite some time."

"Of course. We are exceedingly grateful you came. Most grateful. Sit, please. I'll ring for sherry and some brandy for you, dear," she added with a smile for her husband. "Julius detests sherry, but then so many men do, don't you think?"

The duchess kept up a running commentary on Duff's health and nursing regimen as they waited for their drinks; then they drank their sherries and waited for Duff to be wakened. The duke added his voice to the conversation from time to time, his quiet delivery reminding Annabelle powerfully of Duff.

In the course of what was essentially the duchess's mono-
logue, Annabelle learned of the duel, its aftermath, and what
little information they had concerning Walingame's death.
That Duff was looking for Walingame at Abigail Fleming's,
she briefly pondered, knowing the gambling hell offering
other services as well. But those were not questions she could
ask.

"I believe Miss Fleming's people were the instrument of
Walingame's demise," the duchess was explaining. "And I
must say, I heartily approve of her actions. He was a complete
blackguard to shoot an unarmed man."

"I confess, it is comforting to know he is gone," Annabelle
acknowledged, feeling relief again even as she spoke. "He
was quite without virtue or humanity."

"Most in London would agree," the duke noted. "Although,
scoundrels must run in the family. Some cousin has appeared
to claim the title, and rumor has it, he has even fewer qualities
to recommend him."

"Enough of such miserable rogues," the duchess implored.
"Tell us instead, Miss Foster, how your family does."

"They are settling in nicely. As you may know," Belle went
on, since the makeup of passengers traveling to London
would have been reported by the Bow Street Runners, "we
are quite a little miscellany. My sister died in childbirth recently, so my mother and I have been caring for little Celia.
And then we have our wet nurse, her child, and her beau with
us as well."

"I expect you're kept exceedingly busy with your family.
Babies, for one, like constant attention."

"Indeed, I quickly came to understand that. But little
Cricket, as we call her, is a sheer delight."

"How nice for you. Once everyone has acclimatized themselves to the city, you must invite your mother to take tea with
us and bring Cricket along. I adore babies."

Having been made comfortable enough by the duke and

duchess to make a personal observation, Annabelle remarked, "Duff is surprisingly adept with babies. He immediately charmed both Cricket and Molly's baby when he came to tea."

"Duff is vastly familiar with children, since his nieces and nephews have always been underfoot. And he takes after his father," Elspeth said, reaching over and patting her husband's hand. "Julius was very good with all our babies. He'd take on any task required, wouldn't you, my dear?"

"I don't see any point in having servants raise one's children," the duke declared.

"Exactly. You see how modern he is," the duchess said with a smile. "We are quite averse to all the old-fashioned rules of child rearing."

"Or in the case of my wife," the duke murmured with a gleam in his eyes, "averse to any rules at all."

"You may tease all you wish, darling, but look how wonderful all our children are. Every one is quite lovely and intelligent and kind."

"Indeed," the duke said with a wink for Annabelle.

Annabelle smiled, feeling as though she been taken into a charmed circle, understanding more than ever why Duff was as sweet and amiable as he was, as self-confident and assured. The duke and duchess adored their children and each other. The Westerlands household must have been a perfect environment in which children could thrive.

"All this talk of babies is making me vastly sentimental," the duchess noted. "You must bring Cricket over soon so we may enjoy her company."

"Did I hear the name Cricket?"

The voice coming from the bed was hoarse with sleep, but a familiar teasing note underlay the query. "Come here and let me see you." This time there was no question of the warmth and affection in his tone.

The duchess immediately came to her feet, glanced at her husband, and said with polished grace, "We'll let you two chat."

Moments later, the bedroom door shut.

"What took so long?" Duff whispered. "I've been dying to see you."

"Very amusing, I'm sure," Annabelle replied drolly. But as she walked toward the bed, she had to forcibly suppress the heady rush of emotion warming her senses. "You might have found a less lethal way to coax me back to London," she admonished.

"I thought you'd appreciate the drama."

He was smiling as he lay, pale and white, in his bed, his dark, ruffled curls in wild disarray on his pillow. "A man like you doesn't require added drama," she said, smiling back. "You're quite dynamic on your own."

"And yet you left." His dark gaze held a question.

"I had to because of Walingame."

"You should have told me," he said, his voice stronger now, a little more like his old self.

"I didn't want an argument."

"Ah."

"Don't look at me like that. You know I'm right."

He tried to shrug and grimaced instead. "Nothing moves very well, yet," he explained with a flicker of his brows. "And you were right—I would have tried to stop you."

"No argument?" She smiled. "You surprise me."

"You don't actually think I've waited days for you to arrive only to have an argument," he said with a grin. "I'm not so foolish." His voice drifted lower, took on a softer note. "Come closer, so I can touch you."

It shouldn't have mattered—his wanting her, nor the beauty of his sweet smile and dark gaze. She should have been able to shrug off his breathtaking, swarthy good looks, see him simply as another suitor and nothing more. But she wasn't so adept as she always had been in the past, and as she moved forward, she ached to touch him as well.

He moved his hand gingerly as it lay atop the coverlet, easing it toward the side of the bed, his struggle to move his hand even that small distance starkly evident on his face.

She could feel tears welling in her eyes, but she forced them back and smiled instead. "I'm pleased you had such an excellent doctor," she said, speaking casually to hide her emotions, drawing on all her experience as an actress to project the proper sensibility. "Your parents told me of James Stewart and all he did for you."

"At the range Walingame chose to fire at me, I wasn't about to put myself in the hands of an English doctor. Especially since I was planning on seeing you again and continuing our delightful friendship."

"You haven't lost your ability to charm, I see," she said lightly.

"I haven't lost my ability for anything," he said with a grin.

"Perhaps I should keep my distance."

"You're safe, darling. If I moved that much—not that I'm not sorely tempted—I'd bleed like a stuck pig and my mother would ring such a peal over my head it would be heard clear to Brighton.

"So I am currently in no danger."

"*Currently* is the operative word. Now that you've arrived, I have considerable incentive to recover."

His parents had said as much, although in more polite terms. Not that she took issue with wanting to help Duff regain his health. She was more than willing. Just how willing and to what extent she was willing, she wouldn't allow herself to contemplate. In any event, it didn't pay to make long-range plans; life was uncertain, a lesson she'd learned at thirteen when her father first became ill.

But a moment later, when she touched Duff's hand and gently twined her fingers in his, the sense of having come home struck her viscerally. She'd never felt such trenchant emotion. It was part compassion and tenderness, and more—a potent, pure, hedonistic pleasure so shocking it sang through her senses at fortissimo pitch.

"Stay with me," he said, his gaze as bold and presumptuous as ever.

She didn't answer. She couldn't when every particle of her being was thinking how *impossible* it would be to stay.

"Just say yes."

No, no, no! "Yes," she whispered, her heart triumphing over reason.

His smile warmed the room, her soul. And perhaps in a way too illusive to recognize, it erased her past as well.

"Now, I'm going to get well very, very quickly," Duff proclaimed, a new vigor in his voice.

Her smile reflected the depth of her feelings. "I'd like that," she said simply.

"Your family is with you, I hear." He spoke briskly, like a man on a mission. "Have them move in."

"Are you mad?" Shocked back to reality, her gaze took on a willful stubbornness. "Every tongue in town would take up the scandal."

The marquis rarely had his wishes thwarted. "I'll have my mother invite them," he calmly proposed, equally stubborn. "Surely that would comply with all that is proper."

"Absolutely not! Duff, don't be impossible! My mother knows little of my past life and I prefer it that way. If we live at my house, where I've given orders to admit no visitors, the possibility of gossip will be considerably lessened."

He scowled. "Male visitors, you mean."

"No. As I already told you, those days are past. I have no male friends."

Except for me, he wished to say. But he wasn't about to make comparisons when what he felt for her was so far outside her former way of life—and his . . . that it was virtually inexpressible.

"I also have turned over a new leaf. You have no male friends and I have no female friends. So stay."

"You needn't change anything for me, Duff." She waved

her hand in a little dismissive gesture. "Truly, I have no expectations."

"Nonetheless, I have changed."

"When you've recovered, you'll think otherwise." She smiled. "You are still weak from loss of blood, my lord."

He wasn't amused. "You think my brain is not functioning?"

"I simply wish to point out that I don't require flattery. I'm pleased to be with you and no more need be said."

"It's not flattery," he grumbled. "I'm quite serious. As I am about you staying here with me."

"Duff, really, you and I both know better. Such news would be all around town within hours."

"So you were just leading me on when you agreed to stay," he said sharply.

"If it were possible, I would," she replied gently. "It just isn't. Nor would your parents appreciate such an irregular arrangement."

"You don't know my parents. Their courtship was so far outside the ordinary, people occasionally still talk about the scandal."

"Nevertheless, I have my mother to consider. If it's any consolation, I'm quite willing to visit you as long as you wish each day. I'll only sleep at home."

His mouth set in a pout.

Annabelle smiled. "You don't think that's going to alter my thinking, do you?"

He broke into a grin. "It used to work on my mother."

"From what I've heard from your mother, you can do no wrong."

"Nor have I ever," he noted with an angelic gaze.

She laughed and inadvertently squeezed his fingers.

He gasped.

"I'm sorry, I'm sorry," she whispered, easing her fingers away. "I'm so very sorry. Where does it hurt?"

He tried to laugh and grimaced instead. "Where doesn't it hurt?" he breathed. "I need a kiss to make it all better."

"You're incorrigible," she chided, her mouth twitching into a smile against her better judgement.

"But you like me anyway," he said, smiling back.

More than that, she thought, already half in love when she should have known better. "Very well—just one kiss until you're stronger."

"Whatever you say."

She laughed. "It appears you may be very agreeable in your invalid state."

"Just don't plan on my weakness lasting long. I have enormous incentive now to heal with all speed."

"Because of sex, you mean."

"So I can hold you again," he said softly. "The rest is up to you."

It always was with him, she thought. Duff had no need to implore. He had but to smile and crook his finger and every woman was lost.

"Kiss me, please," he said, soft and low. "I've missed you."

If she didn't know his reputation, if she hadn't heard all the stories, it would have been tempting to take his words to heart. And maybe she would—now, this moment, at least. "I've missed you, too," she murmured, bending low, brushing his lips in the lightest of caresses, and even then—with that minute, skimming contact—she felt herself being drawn inexorably toward temptation.

"More," he whispered, feeling his own provocative siren song.

And one kiss led to another and yet a third, the flame of desire blind to debilities or reason until, breathing fast, Annabelle wrenched herself away.

"This is mad," she whispered.

"But a glorious madness," he noted, hot-blooded desire coursing through his veins, every sensibility renewed, revived, Belle's kiss the curative of all curatives. "You are, my sweet, the perfect medicine," he murmured with a wink. "Ring for a maid," he ordered. "I want to eat—and no broths and gruels. I want real food."

She laughed, his sudden volte-face both gratifying and amusing. "Soon, I shall have to fight you off," she said over her shoulder as she turned to reach the bellpull.

"I doubt that," he drawled.

"Arrogant man." Jerking the embroidered strap, she turned back around. "I may surprise you."

The only thing that would surprise him after their heated kisses was if she gave him time to fully recuperate. But he was inclined to be tactful. "If you do choose to fight me off, then might I suggest you get fit? Because I intend to take you on in a matter of days. Or seduce you." He grinned. "Whichever you prefer."

It was astonishing how his words alone could arouse her, how she could feel the heated implications of his threat melt through her senses in a fevered rush of pleasure. "I'll let you know later which I prefer," she replied, skittish and flushed.

It was impossible not to hear the longing in her voice, a familiar enough inflection to a man of his repute. "Take your time," he murmured, smiling faintly. "It may take me a day or two to get out of bed. Although, I don't suppose I'd have to get out of bed," he drawled. "In fact, if I asked you nicely, perhaps you'd oblige me in my infirmities—say, perform more of the—er—vigorous activity, for instance. I'd be more than happy to make it up to you at some later date. You might even be able to talk me into taking orders from you . . ."

"Enticing as your offer is, my lord, allow me to refuse," Annabelle said with equal drollery, having marginally restrained her desires. "And for your information, I have no dominatrix tendencies. I hope that does not deter your interest in me."

"Vixen. You toy with me when I am deep in love."

"You are merely in rut. Pray don't confuse the two."

"I don't in the least."

She flushed before his steady gaze and opted for mockery rather than admit the extent of her own involvement. "I daresay your feelings will change once you climax."

"If I could move, I'd throw something at your head for your rudeness," he said with a roguish grin, taking his cue from her. Who better than he understood a reluctance to speak of love?

She stepped back. "Then I am fortunate to be out of range."

"But not for long, darling," he murmured. "Not for long . . ."

Chapter

26

True to his promise, Duff forced himself to sit up the next day, and the day after that, he was on his feet. Shakily, but unaided. Although his teeth were gritted against the pain, his forehead beaded with sweat, and the moments he was upright were brief.

But he refused to be deterred and as the week progressed, he became increasingly stronger. His appetite had returned as well, and the cook was kept busy supplying him with nourishing food. In short, his recovery was moving by leaps and bounds. Even Dr. Stewart described it as phenomenal.

His parents thanked Annabelle on so many occasions, she indeed felt like some ministering angel, a role she accepted with the full knowledge that her input was minuscule compared to Duff's Herculean efforts.

She was in constant attendance because Duff wished it, and she could no more have refused than she could have stopped the sun in its tracks. Nor did she wish to. Nor did her mother or Molly, from their unsubtle comments about Cinderella and the Prince and all such fantasies.

But Annabelle took her role as companion in the sickroom as she would a role in a play that had perhaps a long, but ultimately a limited, run. In real life she understood Cinderella stories didn't exist, and even in those cases where women of lesser rank married into the nobility, the resulting marriages were rarely, if ever, ideal.

Her duties were pleasant, though, more than pleasant, and she looked forward each day to her time at Westerlands House.

In the early days, she'd asked if Duff wished her to read to him during those times he was abed.

"No, thank you," he'd said. "Talk to me instead."

She hadn't thought they would have had so much conversation. She knew him so little. And truth be told, many of her relationships with men hadn't revolved around conversation.

Nor had Duff's with women.

They were both treading on virgin ground, but they found the experience both enjoyable and enlightening. They spoke at length of their childhoods. His was idyllic; there was no other word for it. Hers had been equally pleasant in her early years when her father's business had prospered and the family had lived in comfort. Her education was excellent, Cambridge offering more than its share of tutors in every discipline. And until Annabelle was fourteen, her life had been cosseted and free of suffering.

As her father's illness had progressed, however, everything had changed. She spoke of some, but not all, that had transpired. Nor had she ever to anyone.

"When my family situation required it," she said, editing her version of events to avoid words like *destitute* and *desperate*, "I came down to London to seek my fortune." She smiled, as though her tale followed the pattern of triumphant conquest and victory so often portrayed in the popular fiction of the time.

"That's when I saw you at Drury Lane," Duff noted.

"Yes," she said, neglecting to say that she'd already spent a year as a governess at a salary that had barely kept her family from starvation. Nor did she mention she'd had to constantly avoid the master of the house, who thought all female servants were fair game to his lust. But when a question came up regarding that lapse of time between Cambridge and Drury Lane, she conceded, "I did try the life of a governess first. It turned out to be too challenging."

"No doubt," Duff observed drily. "As if you'd last a fortnight with your looks."

"Actually, I lasted a year."

"Astonishing. Did your employer prefer young boys or did his wife shackle him to her leg?"

"The baroness *did* hold the purse strings. She was an heiress who married a penniless title, but when it came to authority—"

"Money won out, of course. That at least explains why you lasted so long."

"The situation finally became untenable."

"I don't doubt it. The man must have been near to raving mad by then. And I say it as a compliment, darling. You are exquisite. Not that you haven't heard as much before. So who was this brute?"

"I'd rather not say."

"I won't call him out."

But Duff's voice had taken on an edge, and in the interests of prudence, she said, "I believe the family went abroad."

He grinned. "Liar."

"You've only just begun to heal. Be sensible. And consider, if this man, who shall remain nameless, hadn't driven me to the life of an actress, we never would have met."

"At least, not until the horse fair."

She made a small moue. "Argue if you wish."

"Truly—I don't mean to argue." He gently patted the bed. "Come sit with me."

Since Duff could traverse the entire upstairs corridor unaided and without stopping, it wasn't likely she was going to accept his invitation. "Your parents might walk in," she equivocated.

"No, they won't."

"How can you be so sure?" Her voice held a note of suspicion.

"I told them not to bother me unless I called for them."

Why had she even asked? "Nevertheless, I shall not sit with you," she firmly declared.

His smile was teasing. "Afraid?"

"Yes, as a matter of fact. I'm afraid I'll be embarrassed should someone come in, regardless you assure me no one will. What about servants?"

"They have orders, too."

"Everyone has orders, I see."

"Now if only *you* would bend to my will," he said with a boyish grin, "I would be vastly content."

"Where would I be, however, if I let you bend me to your will?" she answered with a faint haughtiness that smacked of the actress.

"Under me, if I had my preference." He grinned. "Snobbish airs and all."

"Very amusing. But I'm afraid I don't have similar carnal urges." Although seated on his bed as he was, handsome as sin in his buckskin breeches and open-necked shirt, his feet bare and his smile enticing, perhaps she wasn't being completely candid.

"Allow me to disagree," he murmured, smiling faintly. "After our afternoon together at my hunting lodge, I would say our carnal urges are much in accord."

"Please, Duff—stop." Putting up her hand, she leaned back in her chair as though distancing herself from temptation. "Don't remind me of such things when I'm trying to maintain a modicum of control. I do not have your exhibitionist tendencies in this, your parents' house." She took a deep breath, as though in restraint, and added, "I am quite firm in that regard."

He groaned softly, then sent her a quizzical glance. "What are your feelings about the garden house outside?"

"I should slap you for your insolence," she muttered.

"Come slap me," he said, velvety soft.

"Duff—for heaven's sake . . . don't," she whispered. "We're supposed to go downstairs for tea in scarce an hour," she added, finding herself tremulous and fainthearted and altogether too ready to throw herself into his arms. "And my mother is coming to visit for the first time." Panic colored her words. "I'm quite nervous enough about that already. I don't need any further pressures."

"I'm sorry, darling," he said, instantly contrite. "Forgive my selfishness. It's just that I'm going out of my mind. Don't be alarmed." This time he was the one to put up his hand. "I shall survive well enough. And you're right, of course. We wouldn't want to be all rumpled and mussed with your mother coming."

"Don't even say such things!" Annabelle cried, horrified at the mental image of appearing thusly at teatime. "I already live in constant fear that my mother is going to hear some scandal about me."

He couldn't so easily empathize in regard to scandal. "Darling, you worry too much about such things," he noted casually. "As if everyone I know hasn't been implicated in some scandal at one time or another."

She made a wry face. "That may be acceptable behavior for the aristocracy. Unfortunately, persons of lesser rank are held to a different standard."

"That's stupid, of course. I can protect you from any scandal."

"But perhaps not from my mother's distress," she answered as resolutely.

On that point she might be right. Although from what little he knew of Mrs. Foster, she seemed very much a woman of the world rather than a martinet for propriety. But obviously, Annabelle was distrait about possibly disgracing her mother. "Don't worry, darling," he immediately said, his voice soft as silk. "I shall be circumspect in all things. You will find me prudent as a vicar at tea. Should I discuss passages from the prayer book?"

She couldn't help but smile. "Please, no. You hardly look the part. And truth be told, our vicar was of the 'buckish' type. He drank rather a lot and kept a race stable while his curate carried out his duties. We all went hunting or to the races together on Sundays." Holy Orders were often the last resort of younger sons who chose to avoid the army or navy and found the practice of law beneath them. No religious training was required.

Duff laughed. "I can see that we are destined for a long and happy friendship. My family, too, spent Sunday at the races or hunting. The afternoon will be a great success—just wait and see. Your mother and I shall talk horses."

Chapter

27

The conversation at tea did turn to horses, but only after Cricket had been admired, passed from lap to lap, and oohed and aahed over by everyone in the room. She finally came to rest in the duchess's arms, where she dozed off so angelically, she could have posed as a metaphorical image of heavenly peace.

The duchess glanced at her husband and smiled. "It seems ages since we've had a baby in the house."

The duke met his wife's gaze. "I remember the day Duff was born."

A look of such intimacy and love passed between the duke and duchess, a sudden, embarrassed silence filled the room.

"As well as the day each of the other children entered the world," the duke noted affably, turning a casual smile on his startled guests. Society, as a rule, took exception to such public displays of affection, but then the D'Abernon family had always lived as they pleased.

"I understand completely," Mrs. Foster returned smoothly, like her daughter quick on her cues. "It seems only yesterday my girls were babes."

Annabelle took pleasure in the fact that her mother could mention Chloe now without distress.

"Indeed," the duchess agreed. "You turn around and they're all grown up."

"Or marginally so, in Giles's case," the duke observed. Giles had just run up another large gambling debt his father had settled. "Our youngest son plays too high."

"Too intemperately, you mean," Duff murmured.

"One worries, of course, when children associate with the wrong people," the duchess said with a smile. "But it seems it's all in the way of growing up."

"I daresay," Mrs. Foster returned politely. "Girls don't as a rule gamble, so it wasn't a worry for me. And both my daughters were very dutiful," she added, smiling at Annabelle.

Annabelle flushed under her mother's praise, not sure her mother's notions of dutiful coincided with hers.

Taking note of Annabelle's discomfort, Duff stepped in. "Would you like to go to the races some day, Mrs. Foster? Annabelle and I were planning on going to the track next week. I believe my family has some horses on the schedule."

Mrs. Foster beamed. "I should enjoy that immensely."

Julius looked at Elspeth, and she at him, their surprise apparent.

Annabelle was equally surprised. The races were a very public venue.

"I shall be quite recovered by then," Duff explained casually, as though in answer to the various looks of amazement. "We can make a day of it." He glanced at his mother and father. "Would you care to join us?"

"Of course. We would be delighted. Wouldn't we, Julius?"

"Indeed." The duke lifted his brandy glass to the room at large. "To a day at the races."

At which point, the discussion turned serious and all the various horses of note were analyzed as to speed, stamina, training, and which jockeys would be up. Mrs. Foster had been keeping abreast of the racing news once again, and she held her own in the conversation that turned on details only those with a particular interest in the sport would know and appreciate.

It was an agreeable afternoon tea with agreeable conversation, and only when Cricket woke, crying for her next feeding, did Mrs. Foster depart. Molly was called up from the servants' quarters and as she, Cricket, and Mrs. Foster took their leave, plans were confirmed for the day at the races.

Those below stairs loved to gossip about their betters, and in this case, the fact that *an actress's mother* had come to tea was startling. Not that Molly had contributed much, even with the grilling she'd encountered, but speculation went apace regardless, the buzz of tittle-tattle filling the Westerlands' kitchen.

How the gossip passed from the ducal household to *The Morning Post* was never clear. One servant talked to a friend in another aristocratic home, a tradesman happened to stop by and heard the news, even the newspapers had their paid sources. That it was impossible to keep anything secret in London was well known. And so an item appeared the following day in *The Morning Post*.

Yesterday, the Duke and Duchess of Westerlands and the Marquis of Darley had, as guests for tea, the celebrated actress Miss Foster and her mother, Mrs. Foster, along with the latter's charming infant granddaughter. The marquis and Miss Foster have recently returned to town after lengthy sojourns in the country.

Annabelle saw the paper before her mother and burned it, knowing full well what mention of a child implied. The suggestion was unmistakable: she had been absent from London for her confinement and Darley was the father.

The duchess read the few lines to her husband over breakfast and said with a smile, "What do you think Duff will say about this?"

"Since he was the one who suggested that we all go to the

races next week, I venture he won't care. Obviously he's not worrying about what people say apropos his liaison with Miss Foster. Nor am I, as you well know," the duke added with a wink and went back to reading *The Times*.

Duff found the paper on his breakfast tray, thoughtfully turned to the appropriate page by Eddie. Glancing up after perusing the small paragraph, the marquis cocked one eyebrow. "Are you trying to tell me something?"

"Thought you should know, that's all."

"I doubt it's of huge interest to the world that my family has tea with someone."

"Yer kiddin', right?"

Duff smiled. "The child is not mine. It's not a problem for me."

"Would it be if'n it were yours?"

"Have you become moral of late?" Duff drawled.

"Miss Foster be the one what is going to have to take the stares. Have you thought o' that?"

"Miss Foster is extremely familiar with people staring at her. Don't look at me like that. Since when have you concerned yourself with the welfare of the women in my life?"

"She's right nice—Miss Foster. An' don't say different when you don't mean it."

"Very well. I agree. Miss Foster is very nice indeed. And I shan't use her badly. You may count on that."

"Hmpf."

And so it was left that morning.

The marquis took his batman's censure with good grace and immediately forgot it.

Several hours north of London, a day later when *The Morning Post* reached the small village of Egeleston, a country squire's wife perused the gossip column and openly gasped. "Jeremiah, listen to this!" she exclaimed, shooting a wide-eyed glance toward her husband sitting by the window with his pipe and ale. "That wretched Foster woman has gotten her name in the papers and may very well draw us into her scandalous life!" The squire's wife read the item to her husband with a black scowl on her porcine face.

But instead of taking proper affront, Jeremiah Harrison set down his ale, blew out a puff of smoke, and smiled. "The Duke and Duchess of Westerlands and the Marquis of Darley, you say? I wonder what they might pay to have us take that brat off their hands?"

"You would take that child of that inferior tradesman's daughter?" his wife shrieked, her double chins wobbling in horror. "I forbid it, Jeremiah! My father would turn in his grave if you were to do such a thing!" As the daughter of a solicitor, Millicent Harrison had always considered herself of superior rank.

"If it's a profitable venture, Millicent, it's worth considering. The wench is dead. The child can be farmed out to a foster home and be done with." He smiled. "All we have to do is collect a tidy sum of money. Don't say you wouldn't wish for a new wardrobe or some fancy furnishings for the parlor. And I've had my eye on the property next door for some time now."

"Doing what you suggest would tar us with infamy, Jeremiah." But Mrs. Harrison's indignation had lessened considerably at the thought of a new wardrobe and furnishings.

"Not when it would make us a damn sight richer, by God," her husband declared, slapping his knee. "Have the groom fetch the carriage and send for our son. We have a bit o' business to conduct in London."

Chapter
28

At the same time, the Harrisons were contemplating what they might purchase with their newfound wealth, a poor curate and his housekeeper on the River Thames south of London were staring at a man lying in the curate's bed. He'd been carried ashore from a coal barge several days ago, half dead, his clothes stripped of anything of value by the barge workers who had fished him out of the river.

"I do declare, sir, he looks as though he might be comin' awake." The housekeeper spoke softly as she half-leaned over the recumbent form. "Them coal mongers were right about him mebbe livin' after all."

The curate was one of the bargemen's customers, getting his coal from them in exchange for fresh victuals on their passage to and from Newcastle. When the bargemen had stopped for their foodstuffs, they'd dropped the man on the curate's lawn. "His color seems better and his breathing, too," the curate agreed.

Then both curate and housekeeper jumped back as Walingame opened his eyes and locked his black stare on them.

The curate said afterward that he'd thought he'd seen the devil himself in those eyes. But at the time, he gathered himself together, cleared his throat, and spoke politely, for the man's ravaged clothing had been expensive. "Good day, sir. If I may say, you seem to be much improved."

"Where the hell am I?" Walingame rasped, his voice so cold it sent a shudder down the poor housekeeper's spine.

"Just south of London," the curate answered, debating whether he should call for help or not. The man was large and had a nasty scowl.

"Get me a doctor," the earl growled. "And brandy."

"We have neither, I'm afraid," the curate replied, trying to keep the quaver from his voice.

"I am the Earl of Walingame." Each word was surly and overbearing. "Notify my household immediately of my location. Quickly, dammit!"

The curate and housekeeper jumped back in unison, for he'd half risen on his elbows before falling back on the bed. Not only frightened, but intimidated, they stood frozen in place.

"Go!" he roared.

The curate and housekeeper scrambled from the room and then huddled at the base of the stairs, trying to decide what best to do. The man had been shot several times. Would they be accused of the crime?

"One never knows," the curate said with a worried frown. "The courts are fickle and certainly the man upstairs is not of a benevolent nature.

"Could we just send for his people and disappear when they arrive?"

"Everyone knows who lives here, Mrs. Bennett. I'm afraid we must implement the earl's orders and hope for the best."

"Send young Harry." The housekeeper nodded, as though in affirmation. "The boy knows how to lie with the best of them. He won't say any more than he must."

The curate offered her a perplexed look. "Send him where? We don't know where the man lives."

"You could go ask him."

"I'd rather not," the curate said honestly.

"The coachman at the village inn might have heard o' him—if he is an earl. Harry could go ask like."

Deciding on that course of action, Harry was sent off and quickly returned with the information they needed.

"The coachman heard of Walingame," Harry breathlessly reported. "The man's the devil hisself, old John says."

"Indeed," the curate murmured, his deductions confirmed. "Does John know where the earl resides?"

"He don't. But he says fer me to go to Mayfair and ask someone there. The gentry all live right close by each other, he says."

"Go," the housekeeper ordered without asking for leave from the curate, her wish to rid herself of the frightening man upstairs overcoming decorum. "And come back with his people jes' as fast as you may."

After seeing Harry off, the curate and housekeeper quietly left the house and waited for Harry's return on a bench in the garden. Neither one wished to renew their acquaintance with their temporary boarder.

It was fear, pure and simple.

But then, a poor curate knew better than to incur the wrath of a man like Walingame.

Chapter
29

When Annabelle arrived at Westerlands House the following day, Duff was waiting for her in the entrance hall.

"You're late," he said.

"I apologize for the delay, but Molly decided this was the day the seamstress must be summoned for more baby clothes and Mama thought herself too countrified to deal with a London seamstress." Annabelle omitted saying that she, too, preferred not having her mother spend too much time alone with the woman. Mrs. Partridge was gossipy, like so many tradesmen and women. "We have a goodly supply of infant-wear ordered now and Molly is satisfied," she said instead.

Duff had watched Annabelle closely as she explained her delay, and the moment she finished, as though having sufficiently conformed to the courtesies, he took her hand and nodded toward the door. "I thought we might go for a short drive."

"I saw the carriage out front."

"It's a lovely day."

She smiled. "I noticed. You seem to be in a rush."

"I've been inside the house long enough. Come." He moved toward the door, drawing her with him. "I have something to show you."

He wouldn't explain, no matter how much she questioned him as they drove past Hyde Park, then Green Park and thence to St. James.

He would only say, "If I told you, it wouldn't be a surprise."

When the carriage came to rest before his town house, Annabelle turned to him with a smile. "Are you sure you're up to this, Duff?"

"I bought something you might like to see."

He hadn't answered her. Perhaps she was mistaken in her conjecture. Or perhaps not. But he was already opening the door before the groom could put down the step, and after exiting the carriage, he turned to offer her his hand.

"We needn't stay longer than it takes for you to look at it."

"I'm not worried." She placed her hand in his. "I can very well walk home from here."

"As you wish, of course."

But his drawl had a familiar assurance, she thought, and she wondered if he'd ever been turned down by a woman.

Having instructed his driver to wait, the marquis ushered Annabelle up a short bank of steps. A door was immediately thrown open by a young footman, and Duff was greeted by his majordomo with great warmth. "We hadn't heard you were well enough to travel yet, my lord. What a pleasant surprise to see you in such good health."

"Thank you. I trust all is well here?"

"Indeed, sir. We only wait for your return."

"We won't be staying long today, Byrne. But I expect to be back soon. Has the item I ordered arrived?"

"It's in your study, sir. Put up as you instructed."

"Send in a bottle of champagne." Duff glanced at Annabelle. "Would you like cakes?"

She should have refused, and had she not been rushed through her breakfast by the commotion over the seamstress, it would have been easier to do so. "Cakes would please me vastly."

He gave her a quick, searching glance. "Perhaps a small, cold collation as well?"

"Yes, thank you."

"Set out the champagne and food in the dining room then, Byrne. I find myself hungry, too."

"Yes, sir—right away, sir." The tall butler bestowed a sunny smile on his employer. "May I say—and I know I speak for the entire household—it's a pleasure to have you with us again, sir."

"Thank you. It's good to be home."

As his majordomo took himself off with alacrity to see to Duff's orders, the marquis turned to Annabelle with a grin. "Allow me to spring my little surprise on you now."

"I confess, my curiosity is aroused."

"You thought you knew, didn't you?" he said with a wink.

She smiled. "I was rather expecting something predictable, my lord. However, you are not the predictable sort, are you?"

He laughed. "In some ways, perhaps I am. But come, my dear, and see what I've had the good fortune to purchase."

They walked down a short hallway to his study. Opening the door, he ushered her in and gestured to his right. "Look over the mantel."

As he shut the door behind them, she turned and beheld a small portrait of her painted by Raeburn. The work was a portrait study of her head in a three-quarters pose. She'd worn a riding habit for the portrait, although only the epaulettes on her shoulders and the high military collar were visible. But a little black shako with a green feather was tipped over one brow and her cheeks were flushed and her curls in disarray as though she'd just come in from riding.

"How did you procure it?" She knew who had it, and the Prince Regent would not relinquish it willingly.

Duff's brows lifted. "The usual way. With a generous offer."

That the Prince Regent was constantly in debt the entire nation knew. On the other hand, she'd heard what the prince had paid Raeburn, and if Duff's offer was more generous than that, she expected he was looking for a quid pro quo. Perhaps her first estimate of the reason for this stop in St. James had been correct. "I don't know what to say. I do like the portrait, however," she declared neutrally, although her emotions were in flux. She wanted Duff, of course. What woman wouldn't? But she disliked the overly familiar circumstances—a pettish cavil, perhaps, but real nonetheless. "Raeburn has a way of making one look natural," she added in a conversational tone, her years on the stage coming to the fore.

"That's why I liked this particular portrait."

"You have good taste. It's one of my favorite ones." She'd posed for several. She met his gaze squarely and asked in an equally direct tone, "Do you have further expectations?"

"No . . . honestly—very well, perhaps—but not for anything to do with the painting." He blew out a small breath. "I find myself like your former employer—the one when you were a governess."

"You're not like him at all." Had he been her first employer, she may have fallen in love on the spot and then what might have happened?

"In some ways, I am." He inhaled deeply, turned, walked to the window that overlooked the square, gazed out for a flashing moment before swiveling around. "There's no subtle way to approach this. God knows, I wish there were."

She took pity on him, or perhaps allowed her feelings to rule—too often the case with Duff. "You needn't be subtle."

"Good," he said with naked relief. "The truth is—I've been thinking about this since you left Shoreham"—he pursed his lips—"whatever number of days ago that was . . . I've lost count. And I am, at the moment," he muttered, holding out his hand for her, "nearly mad for wanting you."

"Are you strong enough?" Blind desire aside, she felt compelled to ask.

"I think so," he said, glancing down at his rising erection, clearly visible under his buckskin breeches. "And if I start bleeding too much"—he grinned—"we'll slow down."

As she moved toward him, she smiled. "Clearly you are mad."

"Clearly."

"And I surmise you knew I wouldn't do . . . this . . . in your parents' house."

He nodded as her fingers touched his, and curling his fist around her hand, he pulled her close. "I confess to the artifice, although if you prefer to simply eat and leave, I will accede to your wishes."

"Are you sure?" Her voice was teasing.

He hesitated fractionally. "I could do it." A taut, strained reply.

"On the other hand, your lordship, I've just recently come down from the country," Annabelle said brightly in a broad, north-country dialect, swinging away and posing for him with a smile, "and have never seen such a glorious sight as this fine house and you."

He laughed. "As I live and breathe—it's Nelly Primrose."

"In the flesh, my lord." She made him a proper bow, looking very much the innocent in her white muslin gown trimmed with silk bows, a matching yellow ribbon in her hair. "Do you think you might help a poor country girl make her way in the city? I'm quite without sponsors in the fashionable world."

He'd first seen Annabelle in the role of Nelly Primrose and remembered even now how she'd turned every male head in London in her debut role. "If we play this game, my dear Miss Primrose, you may learn more of city ways than you anticipate," he drawled.

She gazed at him from under the fringe of her lashes. "I am told I am a very quick study, my lord."

The play was not so risqué as Annabelle's current pose, but Duff found her playfulness enchanting. "I may have a position open in my household. I need a personal secretary. Do you read?"

"Oh, yes, my lord. I read very well indeed. Our curate took special care to teach me"—she paused for effect—"reading, my lord."

"And other things as well, I surmise," he noted drily, not certain whether he should take issue with her comment about her curate. His jealousy extended to her imaginary past as well. "Perhaps you should tell me exactly what he taught you before I decide whether you will be suitable for my household."

"Oh, you misunderstand, my lord. He taught me my numbers and such was what I meant to say." As would any woman wishing to please the handsome Lord Darley when he was known far and wide for the lavish sexual pleasures he offered. And she wondered for a jealous moment of her own whether his maidservants were used by him for more than household duties.

His gaze narrowed, the line between reality and play unclear in his mind, ambiguity in both his words and thoughts. "You must not lie to me, my dear. I will not tolerate it."

"Now, why would I lie when I wish to please you? If you are concerned with my chastity, Lord Darley, I swear I am chaste."

As if he hadn't already been primed for fucking, his cock swelled even larger at her feigned innocence. "I may have to see for myself," he murmured. "I wouldn't want to be deceived."

"I understand. A woman should be virtuous," she said, even while the sight of his burgeoning erection was inciting her body to a glowing receptivity. "Does not society demand it, my lord?"

Her intonation had turned breathy, a flush was warming her cheeks. "City ways may be different from those in the country, my dear," Duff said with a knowing smile. "You will find that virtue is flexible in the *Ton*."

"Does that mean I may be flexible as well?" Annabelle murmured.

The double entendre in her words, the sweet guile in her eyes, was doubly provocative. "We will see, Miss Primrose. I can't promise anything," he said with mock sternness. "Your advancement will depend on your ability to please."

"You, my lord?"

"Yes."

"Oh, good—your housekeeper scowled at me something fierce when she let me in." She nibbled on her bottom lip in an affecting show of unease. "I'm not certain I could ever please *her*."

"You needn't fear, my dear," he replied in reassuring accents. "Your duties would be confined to serving me."

"I would like that enormously—I suspect," she murmured with another little curtsy, her gaze on his crotch where the buckskin was stretched taut over his flagrant arousal.

"I would require my paper brought to me in the morning. You would read to me from time to time, answer my mail, see to the purchase of my books. And at night," he said with conspicuous mildness, "I would require your presence close by, should I need a letter scribed."

"I am capable of all those tasks, my lord. You will find I write a fine hand and reading to you would be a pleasure. I would simply adore"—she smiled sweetly—"helping you with anything at all."

He suddenly felt light-headed as all his blood flooded to his cock at her seductive offer of *anything at all*. Dropping into a nearby chair, he gestured his erstwhile Nelly Primrose forward to participate in something more than conversation.

Annabelle moved toward him with a worried frown, questioning whether to continue in their play. "Would you like an elixir, my lord?" she murmured, allowing him to make the decision. "You look pale."

"Perhaps a small cognac. Over there on the table." He shut his eyes for a moment as Annabelle walked across the room and poured him a drink, opening them as he heard her approach. "You needn't look worried. I'm quite well."

He didn't look entirely well, Annabelle thought. But having seen Duff force himself to walk through sheer will when he could barely stand, she rather thought if he was intent on having sex, he would have it. Handing him the drink, she waited for him to drink it, then retrieved the glass and set it aside.

"You are very helpful, Miss Primrose. I rather think you will be a valuable addition to my household."

His deep voice was soft and low, the seductive tenor subtle and familiar, his heavy-lidded gaze lazily proprietary, as though she or any woman he fancied was his for the asking. A dissolving heat drenched her vagina in shocking disregard for her customary aversion to men who looked at her that way. But then, Duff was not like other men. "Are you up to this, my lord?" she murmured, wanting what he wanted with a headstrong urgency that would have been incomprehensible before Duff entered her life.

He was lounging in his chair, his color returned, his dark gaze touched with the willful arrogance that great wealth conferred. "You will find, Nelly, that the first rule in my household is never to question me."

A shameful rush of pleasure streaked through her body at his purposeful declaration. "Yes, sir," she whispered, improbably aroused by his inherent arrogance that assumed all things were available to him.

"Now, come closer and we'll see about your chastity." He used the royal *we*; he was not including her in his statement.

"Do I have the position, my lord?"

"Lift your skirts and we'll see."

"What if someone were to come in?" she inquired nervously. And whether it was Nelly Primrose speaking was not certain.

His gaze idly swept over her. "Do you want the position or not?"

Her profession aside, she was not an exhibitionist at heart. "I don't know if I wish to continue this sport," she said, Annabelle Foster's voice distinct this time.

"Fine. But lift your skirts anyway." Duff smiled. "If you'd be so kind." He, too, was speaking in his own voice—polite, well-mannered, affable.

"The servants," she murmured. "Seriously, Duff, they might come in."

"They won't."

Not a scintilla of equivocation echoed in his words, and for a moment Annabelle didn't know whether to be grateful or cross. But the real Lord Darley was lounging in all his stark and sensual beauty—close enough to touch in his crisp white linen and bottle-green coat, while the sight of his apparently fully recovered and impressive cock stretching the soft buckskin was riveting.

His hands were resting on the gilded crocodile heads at the extremities of the Empire chair arms, his sprawl languid against the red striped silk upholstery, his gaze half-shuttered. "Did I mention how much you mean to me? You do," he went on, answering his own question. He smiled. "I haven't felt this good for a very long time. Humor me, darling—lift your skirt."

"I will humor myself as well. I just want to make that clear."

He chuckled. "I see Nelly Primrose has fled and in her place we have the imperious Miss Foster. I think I like her better, in any event. Submissive women are a bore."

"Pray, abstain from mentioning your previous amours." Annabelle quirked her brow. "Unless you wish a quid pro quo."

"God, no," he said with a grin. "It might curb my ardor."

"Somehow I doubt that," she noted sardonically, dipping her head toward his blatant erection. "He looks in excellent form." Then she gracefully lifted her skirts and petticoat and held them out as a frothy frame to her lower body. "Do you like what you see, my lord?"

She stood before him, nude from the waist down, save for white silk stockings, pretty slippers in Pomona green kidskin and ruffled garters that matched the yellow ribbon in her hair. "One would have to be dead not to like what I see, darling." He drew in a soft breath. "Indeed, it's been much too long. Might I entice you to take off your gown as well? I would help you if I could; I apologize for my disabilities. I will make it up to you very soon."

Aware that his chest wounds were still only partially healed, Annabelle didn't question his asking her to disrobe herself so much as she took issue with the venue. She shot a quick glance at the door.

"Would you be more comfortable if the door was locked? Please, feel free to do so."

His casual assumption that his privacy wouldn't be breached annoyed her. Was his staff so accustomed to him having women in these rooms that none dared enter? "I gather your staff won't come in," she said, unable to dragoon her jealousy into submission. "Why is that?"

He lifted his gaze, a half smile on his lips. "They know I like my privacy."

She abruptly dropped her skirts. "For activities like this, no doubt."

"No. I never bring women here. You are the exception," he said, and not waiting for the surprise in her eyes to be given voice, he added, "Now gladden the heart of an invalid"—he waggled his fingers—"and lift up your skirts again. Leave your gown on if you're more comfortable that way, though." He smiled. "After years on the stage one would think you would have exhibitionist tendencies in abundance."

"Disregard for the censure of the world comes with wealth and privilege, darling." She was appeased, or rather her jealousy was appeased, and she could smile as sweetly as he.

"I stand corrected, or rather, I sit corrected," he replied pleasantly. "Let me see you now."

"How far is Dr. Stewart from here?"

Following Annabelle's gaze, Duff glanced down. A small bloodstain the size of a thumbprint had appeared on his cream-colored waistcoat. "It's hardly bleeding. Don't be concerned."

"Duff, be sensible. You've moved much too much already with the drive over here. You could hurt yourself."

"Byrne knows where Stewart lives. But we're not going to need him. What I do need is you. And don't say you don't feel the same because I can smell your arousal from here." A faint smile lifted his mouth. "Come now, you can't always be sensible. We are not bookkeepers with balance sheets. I want to feel you close around me. I want to fill you and cram you full and make you scream like you do when you lose yourself to passion. So, tell me," he said with a grin. "Have you practiced your usual prudence? Is your sponge in place?"

"Of course."

"Of course," he echoed. He'd known the answer before he'd asked the question; Annabelle never took chances. He crooked his finger. "Let me see."

After spreading his legs, he indicated he wanted her between them and she complied because she could no more curtail her lust than he. Her promiscuous indifference to reason unnerved her, but in the chaos of lust and desire overwhelming her senses, scruple was cavalierly dismissed.

When she stopped at the edge of his chair, he said quietly, "Spread your thighs."

She obeyed. She could not have resisted no matter the cataclysmic consequences. Every beat of her heart echoed in the throbbing center of her body, every breath she took was one of longing for this man who was a byword for profligacy and vice.

"More," he said, and as she complied, he leaned forward and slipped two fingers up her sleek, pulsing vagina. "There," he whispered a moment later, his fingertips brushing the sponge. "I see you are impregnable, indeed. It almost makes one want to breach such an unassailable citadel. What do you think, Miss Primrose. Would you like your master's child?"

A defenseless yearning, avaricious and improbable, swept through her senses like a flood tide. "Don't say that," Annabelle breathed.

It wasn't an answer. It was a nonanswer. It was consent and permission from a woman who valued her independence above all else.

But then she suddenly said, "No," in a strong, firm voice and tried to move away.

He held her in place, his fingers anchored in her heated cunt. "I won't," he murmured.

"Promise," she said, vehement and emphatic, holding his gaze.

He could have said no. He could have done to her what he wished. Even now, in his invalid state. For a fleeting moment, he struggled with his volatile impulse to father a child on her. But ingrained habit prevailed in him as much as it had in her, and as quickly as she, he opted for reason. "I promise."

"Now let me go"—she wiggled her bottom around his fingers—"and I'll service you. You're not strong enough yet for more."

He didn't remove his fingers, nor did his indolent gaze look as though he might. "If I wanted that," he said, softly abrupt, "I'd call in a chambermaid."

"That's what I thought." He was what he was and she'd do well not to forget it.

"So, then," he murmured lazily, as though he'd not heard the temper in her voice, "would you like to come first—like this"—he moved his fingers delicately inside her—"say as a first course in the event I don't last too long? I wouldn't want you deprived of the multiple orgasms you favor."

"You're being foolish, Duff." Her voice had turned gentle, her gaze on a second spot of blood that had blossomed on his waistcoat. "I can wait until you're stronger."

Having glanced down, he ignored what he saw. "If you

choose to be selfless, I cannot." He grinned as he slid his fingers free. "You may blame my aristocratic privilege or male selfishness or any of those faults you assign to men like me, but I must feel you"—his voice went soft—"everywhere. Come," he whispered. "Come sit on me. I promise to barely move."

He helped her unbutton his breeches, helped her climb onto his lap, his breath in abeyance after waiting for this so long.

She braced her hands on the chair arms to lower herself over his penis he held lightly in place beneath her. Careful not to brush against his shoulders or chest, she slowly lowered herself down his hard, rigid length until she rested gently on his thighs, his erection buried deep in her succulent flesh.

There was a moment of utter silence.

They were holding their breath, absorbing the full measure of sumptuous pleasure for a shimmering millisecond before galvanic delirium finally reached their brains.

She whimpered when the rush of ecstasy struck.

He grunted, as though punched in the gut.

A moment later, when he found the breath to speak, he whispered, audacious and heedless, "You cannot leave me."

"No, never," she whispered back, as rash as he.

They came quickly the first time, she moving more than he so his pain was kept to a minimum. But after that, anesthetized as he was by glowing rapture, he ignored health issues and proceeded to take a more active role, smiling with satisfaction as her orgasmic scream filled the room at their next climax.

"We should wait now," she said afterward. "Until you're better."

In answer, he gripped her hips and drove her back down.

His virility was undiminished despite his orgasms, and she experienced a fleeting resentment at the thought of how many other women had been beneficiaries of his unflagging vigor. But Duff happened to flex his hips just then, ramming upward with a particular precision that resonated in every quivering nerve in her body, and after that, she disregarded the vexing question in lieu of more immediate sensation.

He was finally bleeding so much, she said emphatically, "If you don't stop, I'll shout for Byrne despite the circumstances. I mean it, Duff," she added tersely. "I won't have you bleeding to death for this."

There was something in her tone that curtailed his lust, and glancing downward, he took note of a wide swath of blood that had soaked through his bandages, shirt, and waistcoat. "Oh, Christ," he muttered.

"Don't move," she murmured, scrambling off him and shaking down her skirts. "Don't move a muscle. I'll find some towels and have someone go for the doctor." After quickly making herself presentable, she arranged Duff's clothing into some semblance of order and left to find Byrne.

While they waited for the doctor, Annabelle brought Duff another cognac and nervously eyed his pallor. "I blame myself," she lamented, gently placing another clean towel on his chest. "I should have said no and meant it."

"It's not your fault," he said softly as he rested his head against the chair back. "Honestly," he said, smiling, "I've never felt so damned good. Stop worrying. I've bled more than this many times. If Eddie were here, he'd tell you as much."

Hopefully, he was right, Annabelle thought. She'd never seen a man with so many old wounds. Perhaps she was unnecessarily alarmed.

Dr. Stewart said as much when he arrived. "A little too much activity, I see," he noted casually, tactful enough not to allude to the pungent aroma of sex in the air. "We'll have you bandaged up again in a thrice," he added briskly.

"Tell Annabelle wounds bleed at times. I've had enough to know. She's overly concerned."

Annabelle had chosen to sit behind Duff's desk, since her muslin gown was wrinkled beyond redress at the moment.

"Duff is right, Miss Foster. He will have occasions like this

before he's fully recovered. There's nothing to worry about."
James Stewart was a worldly man, and knowing Duff as well as
he did, he expected he might be called to minister to him
once or twice again before his wounds had healed. Particularly
if Miss Foster continued in residence.

As the bandages were being replaced, James Stewart and
Duff conversed as though they were meeting under normal
circumstances, the men remarking on some recent events in
Edinburgh as well as an upcoming sale at Tattersalls. Once his
task was complete, the doctor left with only a bland admon-
ishment to rest for the remainder of the day.

"I'm not coming anywhere near you," Annabelle asserted
as the door closed on the doctor.

"I will oblige James." Duff grinned. "I'll give you my
pledge in writing, if you come sit by me."

He was content when she did as he asked.

He didn't think beyond that simple joy.

Annabelle was less prone to *carpe diem* conceits, but in the
snug comfort of Duff's affection, she allowed herself to relish
her happiness.

At least for now.

Chapter
30

Giles burst into his father's library as the duke was conversing with his steward. "Sorry, sir," he muttered, standing in the doorway for a moment before striding into the room. "Do you mind, Galworth?" He dipped his head toward the steward. "I won't be long."

"I gather this is of some import," the duke said, leaning back in his chair as the door shut on his steward.

"It's of considerable import!" Giles shifted his stance as he stood before his father's desk. "Walingame is alive!" he blurted out. "They brought him home this morning!"

"So I understand." Nothing moved in the duke's placid pose save for a deadly gleam in his eyes.

Giles didn't question his father's sources nor the look in his eyes. "Good." With an exhalation of relief, he dropped into the chair Galworth had vacated. "You're going to do something, then."

"Naturally." Julius steepled his fingers under his chin and smiled faintly. "I have a vested interest in my children living long and productive lives. And men like Walingame who frustrate my plans must be dealt with."

"Let me go with you." His father wasn't the kind to let others fight his battles.

"If you promise not to do anything hasty. One son shot by Walingame is quite enough."

He shrugged. "I promise. What do you propose to do?"

Julius glanced at the small clock on his desk. "Your brother has gone out with Miss Foster. I'm only waiting for your maman and sisters to set out for their daily perusal of the shops on Oxford Street before calling on Walingame."

"He might not let us in."

The duke's lashes fell slightly. "I don't anticipate that happening. However, I suggest you arm yourself."

"There's no doubt the world would be a better place without Walingame," Giles said bluntly.

Julius sighed. "Much as I agree with you, his cousin seems to be cut from the same cloth. I'm not sure sending Walingame to Hades will solve our problem."

"Get rid of them both." Blunt, gruff words.

"So bloodthirsty, my dear Giles. Recall the legalities, if you please."

"I'm not sure Walingame understands such niceties."

"He will, you can be sure," the duke said, his voice hard as nails. "I intend to make my position uncompromisingly clear."

Forty minutes later, the Duke of Westerlands' carriage drew up before Lord Walingame's house. Julius and Giles exited the carriage, two men jumped down from the driver's seat, a groom was left to tend the horses, and the small group proceeded to knock on Walingame's front door.

The footman who answered the knock opened the door without comment, as did a second servant who merely indicated the floor above with a raised hand. Without further communication, the duke and his entourage raced up the wide staircase lined with portraits of Walingame ancestors. Striding down the corridor, Julius counted doors as though he knew exactly where he was going, and having reached the fourth door on his right, he pushed it open and entered Walingame's bedroom.

His sources were excellent.

Walingame sat upright in his bed as they strode in, shock writ large on his face.

"You should pay your servants better," Julius said suavely.

"Get out!" Walingame shouted. "Get the fuck out of my house!"

"You may shout, but I fear no one will hear you. Or at least the men at your front door." Who were even now on their way to Westerlands House to enter the duke's employ.

Julius nodded at his two henchmen, and as though responding to previous orders, one man shut the door and stood guard while the second walked to the windows overlooking the street and took up watch.

"This won't take long," the duke murmured—whether to himself, his partners, or Walingame was unclear.

"I'll have you dragged into court for this!" Walingame blustered. "I'll have you sued for assault! For breaking and entering!"

"Let's be done with him," Giles muttered, pointing his pistol at Walingame's head.

"Perhaps later, Giles." Julius's voice was bland as he moved toward Walingame's bed, his booted footsteps on the carpet whisper-soft. Coming to a halt at the end of the bed, the duke surveyed the earl for a fleeting moment, his mouth set, his dark gaze malevolent. "I should kill you now for what you did to my son," he said softly. "No one would fault me for it. But I'll allow you to live under certain conditions. And you'd do well to pay attention to what I say, for I'll say it but once."

Walingame heard the suppressed violence in Julius's voice, saw the enmity in his eyes, and shrank back against his pillows. Julius had a dark side, rumor had it, the death of the duchess's first husband having always been open to speculation. Lord Grafton had been in the midst of a very public divorce case against his wife when he'd suddenly died of an apoplexy—at the same moment Julius had returned to London with Lord Grafton's wife.

The timing had been suspect to those who thrived on tittle-tattle, talk of foul play rampant. Then, with the rushed nature of the widow's new marriage—Elspeth and Julius had been wed within hours of Grafton's death—there were those who said Julius D'Abernon, then Lord Darley, had done in his rival.

"If you so much as look askance at anyone in my family," the duke began, disrupting Walingame's fearful musing, "I will have you killed. And I won't take the time to go through any of the formalities. You will be shot, or drowned or thrown down a cliff. Do you understand? The means of your death makes no difference to me. You put yourself beyond the bounds of protocol when you shot my son. Will or Morgan, here,"—he gestured at his men guarding the room—"will take your life without a qualm. Or I will, or Giles, or any one of my many friends who will be apprised of my warning to you. In fact, England will not be to your liking. I suggest you take yourself abroad forthwith. Tomorrow morning at the latest."

"You can't make me go," Walingame challenged heatedly.

"It's your choice, of course," the duke said, his voice silken. "Go or die."

Walingame blanched before the ruthlessness in Westerlands's gaze.

"I believe we're done here." Julius stepped back from the bed and said in parting, "You will be watched until you leave England. If you return I will know it the moment you set foot on English soil; you won't reach London alive." Turning without another word, Julius signaled his men, and taking the lead, walked out of Walingame's room.

"Do you think he'll leave?" Giles asked as they strode down the corridor.

"He has a choice, but my guess is he'll find the Continent more salubrious," the duke murmured. "Men like Walingame are cowards at heart. Until the earl has departed England, however, there's no need to mention any of this to Duff. I don't want him calling out Walingame."

"He might have heard already that Walingame still lives."

The duke smiled and shook his head. "Byrne sent word that Duff and Miss Foster are enjoying some solitude in St. James. I doubt we'll hear from him anytime soon. And Walingame will be gone by morning. Either willingly or not."

Before the carriage drove away, Julius spoke quietly to Morgan and Will, who stayed behind.

As he entered the carriage a few moments later and took his seat across from Giles, he said, "In the interests of safety, I'd appreciate it if you'd not go much abroad tonight. Stay at your clubs or with the ladies you favor, but don't go out alone into the night. I don't trust Walingame. Once he sails tomorrow"— the duke waved his hand negligently—"life will return to normal."

Chapter
31

The duke was right about Duff and Annabelle. They stayed in St. James until evening, when Duff accompanied Annabelle home. On the pretext of fatigue, he spent the night there playing cards with Miss and Mrs. Foster, entertaining both the ladies with exceptional charm. Unfortunately, he slept alone in Annabelle's guest chamber in the interests of propriety, but after his very enjoyable afternoon, he accepted his solitary bed with equanimity.

The duke, however, was not correct about his life returning to normal. Shortly after breakfast, he'd no more than received news that Walingame was being driven south to Dover, than a footman entered his study to inform him that a Mr. and Mrs. Harrison were at the door asking to speak with him.

Since he had no knowledge of such persons, he sent them on their way.

The Harrisons refused to take their congé, telling the footman with a great deal of belligerence that they had no intention of leaving until they met with the duke on a matter concerning Miss Foster and a child.

The butler was called to the entrance hall to deal with the recalcitrant couple.

Mr. Harrison threatened to strike old Bamford, while Mrs.

Harrison told the duke's butler in no uncertain terms that she was the daughter of a solicitor and she would be given the courtesy due her station in life or know the reason why.

As the dispute escalated and the shouting became audible in the duke's study, Julius put his fingers to his brow, sighed in frustration, then rang for a servant. "Show them in," he ordered grudgingly.

He was grateful that Elspeth was busier than usual in the city and was out with their daughters. He wouldn't have wanted her involved in what looked to be an irksome incident.

A rotund man and woman, squeezed into their country best, appeared in his study a short time later, red-faced from their skirmish in the entrance hall. Looking up from his desk, Julius bid them enter with civility if not warmth.

Neither moved for a moment, as though suddenly struck dumb in the presence of such distinctive rank.

Understanding two such persons weren't often—if ever—in the presence of nobility, Julius did his best to put them at their ease. "I understand you have some matter you wish to discuss with me."

An act of courtesy he regretted a moment later when the corpulent Mr. Harrison, apparently shaken from his stupor, strode up to his desk and said, "I've come here to do you a favor, Your Grace. And you are going to thank me for doing it."

Knowing full well he required no favors from men such as Mr. Harrison, the duke sighed silently and said, much against his will, "Is that so?"

He didn't ask them to sit, but the man's wife came up nonetheless and sat, plopping down in a chair before his desk as though she had the right. Julius winced slightly, but otherwise gave no indication of his displeasure.

"It is indeed so, Your Grace. You see, my wife called my attention to a piece in the paper a few days back that mentioned a Miss Foster and a child. I would be willing to take that child off your hands"—the man smiled greasily—"for a price, you might say."

"I'm not altogether sure I require any child taken off my hands," Julius replied. But intrigued with learning the identity of his visitors, he asked, "Are you related to this child?"

The woman sniffed. "In a manner of speaking, I suppose."

"And how is that?" The duke raised his brows.

"Our son made a very deplorable marriage," the woman said with another sniff. "His wife was quite beneath his station. Fortunately, she died in childbirth, but the child did not," she noted with pursed lips.

"And yet you do not have this child, if you think it here?"

"That actress"—another sniff of disapproval—"Miss Foster has the child."

The picture was suddenly clear. The duke had heard the story from Duff; the Harrisons were the ones who had incarcerated Annabelle's sister. "What makes you think Miss Foster's connection is of interest to me?" he asked, a new coolness in his voice.

The man smirked. "You know as well as I that the piece in the paper gave everyone to suspect the child is your son's. We'd be happy to acknowledge the babe as our son Thomas's, take the child away, and be done with it. For a price, of course."

"You wish to raise the child?"

"Not in the least!" Mrs. Harrison retorted contemptuously. "It could be sent to some foster home."

"They don't last long there, if you know what I mean, my lord," Mr. Harrison said with a wink. "So you see, if you'd like to pay us a reasonable sum, we could allay any further hint of scandal, and your son, Lord Darley, would be completely exonerated."

"What sum did you have in mind?" the duke inquired, whisper-soft.

"I was thinking perhaps ten thousand pounds."

"A tidy sum."

"We didn't think it would be an overlarge sum for Your Grace—if we cleaned up the scandal, as it were."

"Unfortunately," Julius murmured, "our family is immune to scandal." He nodded in dismissal. "I wish you a pleasant journey home."

"Just a minute," Mr. Harrison protested. "Do you realize we could make a deal of trouble for you? Accuse you of abducting our child or worse?"

"You are delusional if you think you can trouble me. Now, leave or I'll have my servants escort you out." Picking up his pen, the duke went back to his letter-writing.

The Harrisons turned red, then white, with anger, but they didn't move. When the duke finally reached for a bell to summon his servants, they stalked from the room in a rage, threatening any number of dire ramifications.

Had Annabelle and Duff arrived five minutes later, they would have been spared a meeting with the Harrisons. But as bad luck would have it, just as they entered Westerlands House, the Harrisons were stomping out.

"Slut," Millicent Harrison hissed as she passed Annabelle.

"Strumpet," Jeremiah Harrison growled. "You haven't heard the last from us."

Chapter

32

Annabelle turned white.

Taking her hand, Duff drew her close. "No one can hurt you," he whispered, knowing without question who had brushed past them in a huff. "You're safe with me." Then, lifting his gaze, he surveyed the numerous footmen in the entrance hall. "If those people return," he said crisply, "they're not to be admitted. And someone follow them. I want to know where they're lodging."

As one of the footmen dashed for the door, Bamford stepped forward. "The duke just spoke to that common, may I say extremely ill-bred, pair." The butler rolled his eyes, the motion almost imperceptible. "His Grace is in his study, sir, should you wish to speak to him."

"Why don't you go upstairs and lie down, darling," Duff murmured, gently squeezing Annabelle's hand. "I'll handle this."

She shook her head. "If they've come for Cricket, I must know."

But her voice had quavered at the last, and Duff understood the magnitude of her anxiety. The Harrisons had killed her sister. They were not the sort one could cavalierly dismiss. "We'll find out, but in the meantime, why don't we have your family brought here for safekeeping. Don't look at me like that. It's the simplest solution—the most sensible, and, without question, the most secure."

"I don't know, Duff," she equivocated, all the strictures of rank and society aligned against such a proposal. "Think of your family—they might not approve."

"Of course they will," he disputed—unlike her, without equivocation. "My family adores you. You single-handedly brought me back into this world, and for that, they are more than happy to give you carte blanche in all things. Now, sit for a minute," he added, easing her into a nearby gilded chair, one of several that had graced the splendid entrance hall since the structure had been built a century ago. "And once I've given Bamford instructions for delivering your family to us, we'll go and see my father."

He spoke quietly to the butler, who nodded once or twice but spoke not at all, eminently capable of carrying out any task assigned him. "With all haste, now, Bamford," Duff added as he turned back to Annabelle.

"Yes, your lordship." Without looking either left or right, the tall, elderly man snapped his fingers and two young footmen ran forward.

Moments later, as Duff and Annabelle entered the duke's study, Julius looked up and immediately took note of Annabelle's pallor. "I surmise you had the misfortune to see the Harrisons. Do not be alarmed, Miss Foster. They can be dealt with easily enough."

"What did they want?" Duff asked, handing Annabelle into a chair near his father's desk.

"Money. What else?"

"They didn't want Cricket?" Annabelle burst out.

There was no point in adding to her dismay. "As I understood it, they were primarily interested in blackmail," Julius remarked evasively. "But there's no need for concern—people like the Harrisons are easily subdued."

"They are ruthless, Father." Duff gave his father a significant glance.

"I understand. But we have considerable power that Miss Foster's family—excuse me, my dear, I don't mean to be discourteous—but clearly the situation is quite different."

"Annabelle is worried for her family, particularly Cricket," Duff interjected. "I gave instructions to bring them here."

"Excellent idea. One can never be too careful with people like"—the duke's mouth twitched into a sneer—"the Harrisons. And all will be well," he hastened to add, conscious of Annabelle's continuing distress. "You needn't give the Harrisons another thought, Miss Foster."

"I am in your debt, Your Grace," Annabelle murmured. Glancing up at Duff, who stood beside her chair, she gave him a quick smile.

"To the contrary, my dear," Julius offered. "We are in *your* debt for bringing out son back to sanity." He smiled at Duff. "And a very satisfying sanity, I don't doubt."

"Yes, very." Duff placed his hand on Annabelle's shoulder in a possessive gesture so plain the duke could not but notice.

"Elspeth will be pleased to have guests," Julius said, smiling at Annabelle. "Particularly Cricket, I suspect. My wife is smitten with your niece, Miss Foster. As we all are," he added pleasantly.

That Cricket was a chubby, rosy-cheeked baby with blond curls and big blue eyes gave credence to the maxim, *The world is her oyster*. She was indeed beloved by all.

"Thank you . . . for . . . everything," Annabelle stammered, feeling herself relax for the first time since seeing the Harrisons.

"You are most welcome. Would anyone care for tea or sherry to wash away our distaste with such visitors?"

"A sherry, I think . . . although perhaps . . . it's too early," Annabelle replied tentatively. She wasn't in the habit of drinking in the morning, but then again, she wasn't often so brutally surprised.

"Make it two, Father," Duff said. He didn't drink sherry as a rule, but it was clear Annabelle required a soothing draught.

Over their sherries, both men made a point of turning the conversation to inconsequential issues, and by the time Annabelle had finished her drink, she was relatively composed.

"I think we'll go upstairs and oversee the apartments being readied for Mrs. Foster and ensemble," Duff said, as though he commonly took an interest in housekeeping.

His father's brows lifted slightly, but rather than remark on his son's sudden interest in household matters, he simply said, "Your mother and sisters should be back for luncheon. If Annabelle's family is here by then, why don't we meet in the small dining parlor." The duke, too, rarely involved himself in domestic issues, but he wished to make Annabelle feel comfortable, and to that end, he decided he'd better consult with the chef. There would be several added covers at luncheon today.

As it turned out, it couldn't have been a more delightful family party. Elspeth, Lydia, Georgina, and children returned in good time, and Elspeth took over the menu from her husband, although not without a droll remark about miracles actually happening.

"Very funny, I'm sure," he replied sportively. "At least the wines will be adequate. As for the rest, you may blame François. He overruled me on almost every item."

"With good reason, I suspect. Your preference for plain food is well known."

Between the duke and the chef, however, the luncheon menu needed very little tweaking by the duchess. And the family party, newly enlarged by the addition of Annabelle's family, partook of excellent food and conversation that afternoon in the sunny dining parlor.

The duchess and her daughters had been given an overview of the Harrisons' visit, and they all took great pains to put Annabelle and her family at ease. That the Harrisons would be thwarted in their designs was not in doubt within the duke's family, although, infinitely polite, no one broached the subject.

Annabelle, in turn, had explained to her mother that the Harrisons had made demands, but the duke had sent them away. Mrs. Foster had not only been delighted that they had nothing to fear now that they were under the duke's protection, but she and Molly also shared in some agreeable speculation apropos Annabelle's and the marquis's future. That he was obviously smitten, they both agreed. As for Annabelle, they were optimistic her reservations would be overcome.

Mrs. Foster and Molly's starry-eyed view of the world was illustrative of all those who have kept fairy tales alive over the centuries.

Hope is a powerful and universal impulse.

Chapter

33

Mrs. Foster and Molly were even more encouraged when the duchess suggested they go for a drive in Hyde Park once they finished dessert.

"It's such a lovely, warm day. And Cricket will love being outside, won't she, my dear Julia?" she said with a smile for Annabelle's mother. Without waiting for an answer, she turned to Duff. "Do be a dear and have the barouche brought round."

As Duff rose to do his mother's bidding, Annabelle felt a distinct rush of trepidation. While the duchess was making it clear that Annabelle and her family were under her guardianship, Annabelle found the thought of meeting *all the world* in Hyde Park mildly unnerving. The entire *beau monde* would be out riding or driving in the park, late afternoon the requisite time to see and be seen.

On the other hand, her mother was clearly unconcerned; Cricket wouldn't be aware of the social ramifications, and if anyone could school their expression to one of bland politesse, she certainly could.

So, before long they were in Hyde Park enjoying the summer day, Duff riding alongside the open carriage, Annabelle and her mother in one seat, the duchess seated opposite them, holding Cricket. They'd been acknowledged by numerous waves and general greetings by those riding or in carriages when the Regent, being driven in an elegant curricle, waved them to a stop. He spoke to everyone; he was a man known for his charm. He even admired Cricket, a considerable gallantry from a man who generally avoided children, including his only daughter. And in a particular mark of favor, he invited Duff and Annabelle to dinner at Carleton House.

Duff accepted with good grace, although the prince was of his father's generation, not his. But Prinny had an eye for beautiful women and Duff suspected Annabelle was the reason for their invitation.

She said as much once they were returned to Westerlands House.

"Must we go?" she said, wrinkling her nose. She and Duff were in his sitting room after the rest of the family had gone off to play with Cricket. "I've been avoiding the Regent for years."

"You needn't worry. I'll be with you, and prince or not, I don't allow poachers."

Annabelle's gaze narrowed. "I'm not your property." She was already out of patience with a dinner at Carleton House in the offing. She didn't need any further instances of male prerogatives.

"Let me reword that. If you need assistance keeping Prinny at bay, please allow me to be of help."

She laughed. "You are a disarming rogue."

"I know," he drawled, his brows flickering in mockery. "For your information, I am also universally adored."

He might be teasing, but she rather thought not.

"And speaking of adorable, did you notice even Prinny commented on Cricket's beauty?" he said like a proud father.

His remark warmed Annabelle's heart. "Cricket always commands attention, there's no doubt," she agreed. "Although," she added, coloring faintly, "you know what gossip will imply."

"About what?"

"Please. You know full well what I mean."

"That Cricket is yours and mine? Let them talk. It makes no difference."

"Disregard for gossip is much easier for you than for me. Not that I'm not familiar with censure, but this?" She made a moue. "I have purposefully avoided the plight of unwed mother. Good God, Duff, don't panic," she said with a smile. "You are not expected to do anything—nor am I alluding to marriage."

He was courteous enough not to say, *Thank God*, although a moment later, he took issue with the fact that she had no wish to marry him. For a man who had been pursued by every female on the marriage mart for a great number of years, her indifference was disconcerting. "Do you mean you don't wish to marry me?"

"Of course I don't. It's impossible, anyway, as you well know."

"Impossible? Why?"

"For a thousand reasons, all of which you and I are cognizant of—and the world is as well. As for rumors about Cricket, don't give them another thought. It's no concern of yours. I will deal with them."

"Hmm," he said, sliding lower in his chair, gazing at her from under his lashes, his expression restive. "It wouldn't necessarily be out of the question for us to marry."

"For heaven's sake, Duff, you're acting like a child who has been told he can't have something. I am more than content with things as they are. Gossip about Cricket is not the first time I have had to stare down the public. Rest easy—this is none of your concern."

"What if I make it mine?"

"You can't. Cricket has nothing to do with you."

"I could claim her."

She smiled. "You are vastly spoiled, Duff. You cannot have your way in all things."

"But I always have." He conveniently overlooked the misery of the year past, but then, he wasn't currently arguing with either reason or dispassion.

"Then perhaps it's time you don't."

He slid upright in his chair. "Are you saying you can keep me from doing what I want?"

"That depends, I suppose, on what you want," she said with a wink.

"Dammit." He grinned. "I'm serious."

"And I'm not. Come, we'll talk of more pleasant things."

He glanced at the clock. "Or not talk at all. We don't have to go down for dinner for at least—"

"Please, Duff, consider. You bled all over yesterday."

"But not since then"—he opened his arms wide—"as you see. And Stewart said these things will happen. You heard he wasn't concerned. Why don't I lock the door," he murmured, coming to his feet.

"I can't, Duff. Not here."

She didn't say she *wouldn't*, which was encouraging. As was the slight tremor in her voice. "Next door, then. In my room."

He had made it clear earlier that no one entered his bedroom unbidden, Annabelle found herself thinking when she shouldn't be thinking anything of the kind. When she should be wary of hurting Duff or having family members knock on the door and be told to go away. When it wasn't *imperative* she have several orgasms before dinner.

"There's plenty of time," Duff whispered as though reading her mind.

She made the mistake of glancing at the clock.

Duff was attuned to subtleties of female behavior; there had always been husbands eyeing him warily in the presence of their wives. He could interpret the smallest gesture with ease. "Why don't I promise not to move at all. I'll show you how it works," he added, covering the small distance that separated them and taking her hand.

"I don't know, Duff . . ."

"I'll be sure for both of us. How would that be?" Lifting her hand to his lips, he kissed her fingertips lightly and smiled his most seductive smile—the one that promised wild pleasures and unforgettable memories.

She had meant to resist. Had she done so, she would have been the first to withstand that lazy smile. "I shouldn't," she said.

Which didn't mean *shouldn't*, as he very well knew. "It sounds as though you need convincing," he murmured diplomatically, drawing her toward the connecting door to his bedroom.

"If you must know," she said pettishly, struggling with the altered dynamic in terms of amour, tugging at his hand in a fit of pique, "I dislike feeling this way. As though I'm at your mercy."

He stopped abruptly and turned to her. "We could argue about who is most in thrall," he said pointedly, a certain moodiness in his tone. "If I had my way, I would keep you under lock and key and never let you out of my bed. It is not my usual way."

"Oh," she said softly.

"Indeed, so don't talk to me about who yields to whom."

"I see," she murmured.

"Indeed," he said, somewhat snappishly this time.

"We are both not used to these unrestrained feelings," Annabelle said gently.

He seemed to visibly bring himself under control, and a moment later a small smile appeared on his lips. "On the other hand," he murmured, "why not enjoy them?"

"While the sun shines," she said with an answering smile, understanding perfectly. "How much time do we have?"

"Not enough," he said, moving toward his bedroom once again.

A short time later, flushed and panting after her second orgasm, her hands braced on his shoulders, she whispered, "How do you do it?"

They were ensconced in Duff's bed, he lying immobile beneath her, she straddling his hips, impaled on his erection. And so they had been—his lean, rangy form utterly still except for relevant blood flow, while she had climaxed twice and he once and counting.

He didn't explain that he'd learned the practice from a mystic in Morocco. Nor did he mention that it took him a month in the mountains with the mystic, some very good hashish, and a number of accommodating young women. But he'd mastered the capacity to control his arousal and ejaculation for lengthy periods of time.

Never say he couldn't apply himself if he wished.

"It's all in the breathing," he said, in lieu of more controversial and complex answers. Then consciously directing his thoughts, some portion of his anatomy stirred infinitesimally and Annabelle didn't ask any further questions.

She was too busy.

Although the frenzy of their passions was in accord and they both gave themselves up to every degree of pleasure in the interval before dinner.

And when they appeared in the dining room—slightly late—no one mentioned their hastily combed hair, nor their heightened color.

They were merely greeted with bland smiles and piquant interest.

Chapter
34

The next morning at breakfast, there was no other word for it but pandemonium. With everyone at the table, including children, the combined families numbered twelve. The noise levels were considerable, the conversation skipping from subject to subject as Lydia's and Georgina's children asked about one activity or another they wished to partake in or harassed their siblings. The duchess, in turn, read aloud various items from the gossip columns that required dissection of one kind or another while the duke looked up from his paper from time to time to offer up some nugget of current interest.

Duff and Annabelle sat side by side, largely silent, quietly exchanging glances and smiles, surreptitiously touching each other under the table and in general basking in the glow of a night devoted to sexual pleasure.

Everyone was cheerful, the family scene both spirited and ripe with contentment.

Bamford came into this agreeable tableau, and walking over to the duke, leaned down and murmured something into his ear.

The duke immediately set down his paper and came to his

feet. "Please go on without me. A small matter of business has arisen."

But Duff recognized an odd note in his father's voice, and pushing his chair back, rose as well. "I'll go with you. There's the Tattersalls auction pamphlet we should look over before noon." He smiled at Annabelle. "I'll be right back."

The duchess glanced at her husband, but said nothing.

Witnessing the look that passed between the duke and duchess, Annabelle felt a shudder of unease race up her spine.

But Cricket knocked over a glass of milk at that precise moment, and as the two men left the room, everyone's attention was centered on the spill.

"Some problem, I gather," Duff murmured a moment later, keeping pace with his father as he moved toward his study.

"A solicitor is asking for me, Bamford said. No doubt the Harrisons have engaged legal help in their blackmail attempt."

"They should be bought off. Then, they'd have no further claim to Cricket."

"I'm not averse to that. However, I dislike being threatened. Nor do I care to deal with people of their stamp. Plunkett can handle the matter for us. And I will say as much to this solicitor of theirs."

But when Duff and his father entered the study, they found one of London's prominent barristers awaiting them. Both men understood that the Harrisons couldn't afford McWilliams, and each, in their own way, braced themselves.

Mr. McWilliams, of McWilliams, Steepleton, and Lowe, came directly to the point. Turning from the window where he'd been surveying the street below, he walked over to Duff.

"Papers for Miss Annabelle Foster, pertaining to a custody action," he said. "If you would be so kind as to give these to her. I understand she is currently in residence. The Earl of Walingame has retained the services of our firm to handle the case for him," he added, dropping his second bombshell with the bland expression of a prosecutor.

"I understood the earl had quitted England," Julius pointed out.

"Prior to his leaving, he spoke with us. He wishes sole rights to a female child in Miss Foster's possession."

Duff's temper showed in the sudden set of his jaw. "What proof do you have that the child is his?" he said, resentful and offended.

"Those facts will be fully disclosed in court," the barrister replied calmly. "I'm sure your barristers will apprise Miss Foster of the relevant position she occupies in regard to this matter. Good day, your lordships." And with a bow he'd perfected after much practice, McWilliams left the study.

As the door closed on him, Duff swore roundly and at length.

"Is the child Walingame's?" Julius finally inquired, his face without expression.

"Fuck if I know," Duff growled. Julius had informed Duff of Walingame's departure after the fact, along with details of his and Giles's visit.

"Then we could have a problem."

"She claims Cricket is her sister's. I could quiz her, I suppose." Duff blew out a breath. "But there's no guarantee I'll hear the truth." That aristocratic women went off to the country or abroad and returned with *nieces* and *nephews* was so common as to affect families high and low. Those outside the aristocracy were no exception.

"There are servants who would know," the duke offered. Servants often testified for or against their masters in court in matters such as this.

"Molly wouldn't. She was hired after Cricket was born. As for Annabelle's staff in London, most have been with her for years. They are loyal."

"Maybe not all."

"God-damn," Duff muttered. "We should have killed Walingame instead of letting him go."

"That's still not out of the question. Although, as you know, I prefer him alive on the Continent to dead with his cousin as heir. With Walingame out of England, we're assured of peace. His cousin is an unknown."

"Call Plunkett," Duff rapped out. "He'll know what we can and cannot do."

Before the order could be issued, however, the duchess appeared.

"I just saw McWilliams in the hall," she remarked. "And from your faces, I gather he did not bring good news."

"I'm not sure you want to know," Julius replied. "Seriously, darling, you might do better to stay out of this."

"Since that isn't likely," she said with a smile, walking to a chair and sitting down. "Do tell me what this is all about."

"It has to do with Annabelle."

"What has to do with me?"

None of them had heard the door open, that fact evident from their surprised expressions.

"Please, dear, go away," Duff said. "We'll take care of this."

But the gruffness in his voice couldn't be denied, nor was Annabelle likely to be willingly sent away like a child. "Tell me or I'll ask McWilliams myself." To Duff's startled look, she added, "One can't overlook his blazing shock of hair, even from a distance." The barrister was one of the most prominent in the city and well known. As was his bright orange hair.

"Come sit down," Duff offered. She hadn't been told of Walingame yet and that news might be better heard sitting down. "Although it's nothing of huge import," he added reassuringly.

From the tone of his voice she knew better, but she did as he wished and sat. "Now, tell me what you will. I'm quite ready."

"First I want to assure you of your safety."

"This sounds rather ominous." Not that she hadn't been expecting problems from the Harrisons.

"Walingame is alive—but he's left England," Duff quickly added as she went pale. "He sailed from Dover and he's gone. Absolutely."

Her eyes were huge. "You're sure?"

"Very sure. We have people following him. He landed in Calais and set off for Paris."

"So this isn't about the Harrisons," Annabelle noted, glancing from person to person as though searching for some clue to the mystery.

"Walingame is suing for custody of Cricket, but don't worry—he won't be successful," Julius said firmly.

"Of course he won't!" Annabelle cried, incensed at such a despicable thought. "He has no right to Cricket! She's Chloe's child!"

Her anger instantly obliterated Duff's skepticism. No matter how skilled an actress, such flushed outrage couldn't be feigned. "We'll tell McWilliams he can go to hell and take Walingame with him," Duff rapped out.

"Perhaps it won't be that simple," the duchess interposed. "If Walingame is after revenge, he may want to drag Annabelle through the courts. You know how the public is captivated by scandal."

"Surely testimony from the midwife who delivered Cricket should be enough to stop this suit," Annabelle offered, knowing better than most how to manage detraction. "Mrs. Malkin has known us for years. She will gladly clear up this matter."

"Why don't we put that question to Plunkett?" the duke suggested. "None of us are knowledgeable about the legal process." But he was relieved that the issue of paternity wasn't in doubt. If Walingame had been the father, even Plunkett may not have been able to solve the dilemma. By law, women generally had no rights to their children.

"Well, it seems, then, as though the problem is solved," the duchess cheerfully announced.

Perhaps it wasn't a day in which the cosmic forces were properly aligned, for the duchess had no more than pronounced an end to their troubles when Bamford entered with another unwanted message.

"I am sorry to inform you that the Harrisons are here with a bailiff and a solicitor," he announced mournfully.

"Little Cricket is in demand," Duff drawled, his gaze amused. No longer disturbed by paternity issues, he was once again in a bantering mood.

"I daresay, I hope there aren't any more litigants who wish to profit by her birth," Elspeth noted derisively. "Although, darling," she went on, smiling at her husband, "at this point Annabelle and I will defer to your masculine powers of persuasion or intimidation, as the case may be. Come, Annabelle, we most certainly do not want to be here when the Harrisons come in."

"I shan't argue," Annabelle replied, yielding to unimpeachable reason. And feeling less anxious about Cricket's future with ducal power and influence on her side, she willingly followed the duchess from the room.

The Harrisons and their solicitor arrived short moments later to find only the duke and the marquis in the study.

Millicent Harrison, frustrated in her hope of seeing Annabelle and giving her a severe set-down, blurted out, red-faced and miffed, "Where is that . . . that . . . doxy of an actress?"

Duff came out of his chair like a bolt.

"Let me take care of this, Duff," the duke murmured.

Duff's heated gaze swivelled to his father.

In contrast, the duke's expression was benign. But he lifted one brow the merest distance in mild reproof.

Duff sat back down.

"Now then, what do we have here?" Julius inquired from behind the vast expanse of his desk. "Please state your business quickly, Mr. . . . . er" He looked directly at the solicitor.

"George . . . Carleton . . . Your Grace," the Harrisons' lawyer stammered, clearly awed, his face turning red as a beet. Nervously twisting the papers he held in his hands, he stumbled over the lines he'd previously rehearsed. "We have . . . come on a matter . . . that my clients—er—Mr. and Mrs. Harrison . . . assure me is . . . will be . . . in Your Grace's best—ah—interests."

"About the money they want, you mean," Julius said coldly.

"Yes . . . well . . . that may be, but you would be relieved of any further—er—implication—or rather, the marquis would be—in terms of—the child." The poor man was visibly wilting under Julius's hard stare.

"I have no intention of haggling over money." If ever the word *arrogance* was represented in the flesh, Julius evinced that attribute in voice and pose and haughty gaze. "However," he went on in the same chill tone, "on one point we can agree. The child is not my son's. So I suggest your clients restrain their greed. My barrister will contact you. Now, you may go." During this conversation the duke never spared so much as a glance for the Harrisons.

"We can take the child! It's ours to take!" Mrs. Harrison threatened loudly, infuriated at being ignored when she'd spent her entire life lording it over country yeomen and servants. "Think about *that* happenstance when you get all high and mighty with us!"

Julius swung around in his chair to direct his scornful gaze her way. "If you so much as consider taking the child," he said, his voice like ice, "I will see that you are sent off to the penal colonies—the whole lot of you—your worthless son included. Now we are done." Coming to his feet, he looked at the solicitor with such rage, the man trembled, then turned and ran from the room.

"Say something, Jeremiah!" Millicent Harrison demanded, her bloated face white with fury.

Her husband opened and shut his mouth like a beached fish. If his wife didn't know the power and influence of a duke, he did. And had he known that only seventeen dukes existed in all of England, he would have been even more frightened.

"Jeremiah! Tell him we have rights!" she shrieked. "Tell him he can't talk to us like this!"

Apparently deciding his current life was far superior to one in a penal colony, Jeremiah Harrison grabbed his wife's arm, muttered something unintelligible to her, and literally dragged her from the room.

Julius softly sighed as the sounds of Millicent Harrison's noisy rancor faded down the hall. "I apologize. I dislike losing my temper."

Duff blew out a soft breath. "It would be difficult not to with a woman like that. Think of Annabelle's poor sister, caught in her clutches."

"A sad situation indeed. Christ—I need a drink. You?" The duke glanced at Duff as he moved to a well-stocked liquor table.

"Yes. How does one live with a woman like that without doing her bodily harm?" Duff murmured, following his father across the room.

"God knows. It makes one grateful for a wife like your mother, though," the duke said, tossing a smile over his shoulder.

"I agree." Having stopped just short of where his father was pouring drinks, Duff leaned one shoulder against a bank of bookshelves. "So, what happens now?"

"I wash my hands of the entire sordid mess. Plunkett will give our blackmailers as little money as possible. We have already discussed the finances; he will deal with this George Carleton person. And that will be that," the duke enunciated with crisp finality. Picking up the brandies, he handed Duff his.

"To peace on earth," the duke murmured, raising his glass to his son. "And the last of the Harrisons in our lives."

"Amen to that."

Both men knocked back the liquor, ringing down the curtain, as it were, on a noxious scene.

"Now that we have—or will have—bought off the Harrisons'

interest in Cricket—and that will be in the nature of a signed document, by the way, Plunkett tells me—what are your plans, if any, with Miss Foster?"

Duff shrugged. "I have no plans."

"You seem quite enamored."

"I am."

"But?"

"But that doesn't require planning."

"Ah."

"Don't say you and Mother think I should be making *plans*—as you so delicately put it?"

"Your mother likes Annabelle a great deal, as do I." Julius dipped his head. "As do you. And Cricket is quite the most adorable child I've seen—in addition to those in our family, of course."

"I'm sorry to have to disappoint you, but even if I were so inclined, which I'm not, Annabelle has already told me she is not interested in marrying me."

The duke looked surprised. "She did?"

"Quite emphatically."

His father smiled. "Are you doing something wrong?"

"I've heard no complaints," Duff drawled. "She is, however, concerned with the conventions—what people will say, that sort of thing."

"What people say is of no consequence."

"And so I told her, but she persists in her beliefs."

"What if she were to leave you? She has a reputation for doing so. What then?"

Duff gazed out the window for a moment, not entirely sure of his answer. And then, reverting to form, he said with a smile, "I expect I'd find something to do."

Chapter
35

And so it was left.

The duke knew better than to press the point. Whether he and his wife liked Annabelle was incidental; it was Duff's life. But neither he nor Elspeth could forget that through Annabelle's good graces, their son had been returned to them.

Dinner that night was *en famille* and lighthearted, the prospect of the Harrisons' control over Cricket at an end, animating the conversation. Plans were made for a boat ride on the Thames, weather permitting, and for another day at the races as well. Several bottles of champagne only added to the gaiety, and a kind of snug pleasure enveloped the gathering.

"I will pay you back," Annabelle said later that night as she lay in Duff's arms. "Let me know what the Harrison settlement is."

"We'll know tomorrow. Plunkett is meeting with them in the morning."

As it transpired, the sum the Harrisons received was considerably less than they'd anticipated. Plunkett informed the Harrisons and George Carleton that the duke was considering bringing manslaughter charges against them in relation to Chloe's death. At that point, Jeremiah Harrison understood whatever leverage they might have had was gone. When

Plunkett offered them a thousand pounds if they signed away their rights to Celia, alias Cricket, despite his wife's protests, Jeremiah quickly signed.

As for the Walingame suit, Plunkett found dealing with McWilliams slightly more difficult.

"The earl is willing to go to any lengths to support his claim," McWilliams began, immediately taking the offensive. "He has the funds to bring this to trial—and the motivation. Miss Foster will not find him amenable on any level."

"I realize keeping this in court would be profitable to your firm," Plunkett noted mildly, never having liked McWilliams's lack of ethics. "And you may do so if you so choose. My client's fortune is considerably more than Walingame's, however. Furthermore, the duke is not concerned with the ultimate cost of this litigation."

"Then we will see how Miss Foster does on the witness stand," McWilliams returned boldly.

"I expect she will do exceedingly well. However, I doubt it will come to that." Plunkett pulled a sheet of paper from a leather portfolio and handed it across the table to McWilliams. "Take note, if you please, of the fact that one Thomas Harrison is named as the father of the child. And here are the documents relating to the marriage between Miss Foster's sister, Chloe, and Thomas Harrison." The papers were duly handed over. "Furthermore, we have testimony from the midwife who attended at the birth of the child, Celia, and two corroborating witnesses to the lying-in and delivery. Let me know when you've seen enough," Plunkett said with a small smile.

McWilliams frowned as he perused the papers, then tossed them aside. "These could all be forgeries and false testimony. My client contends that the child is Miss Annabelle Foster's and he is the father."

"In that case, I'll wish you good day." Plunkett came to his feet and straightened the papers into a neat pile before placing them into his portfolio. "We will be seeing you in court."

He walked to the door, then turned and said, "You might consider your reputation, however. My client has considerable influence. You are bound to lose this case—eventually. And furthermore, occasion the displeasure of my client, the duke. I caution you to weigh the liabilities, particularly with Walingame discredited at every turn. He will not be allowed back in England; the duke has so vowed. I wish you good day." He turned to the door.

"Wait."

Plunkett suppressed a smile and turned back.

"Perhaps we could reach a settlement," McWilliams said, smooth-tongued and bland. "An amiable agreement, as it were."

"Westerlands won't give Walingame a penny."

"I was thinking"—McWilliams let the sentence hang.

"My client would be willing to offer you a fee for services. In lieu of the time you've already spent on this case." Plunkett put up a cautioning hand. "I don't suggest you be greedy. The duke is quite out of humor on this issue."

"Say, five hundred pounds?"

Plunkett had never heard such hesitancy in McWilliams. He was tempted to knock the sum down on principle. But the duke had already given him leave to go as high as five thousand pounds, so he restrained his personal antipathy toward a man like McWilliams with little scruple and less time for the truth. "Five hundred pounds it is," he agreed. "And, may I say, you've made the right choice. Westerlands is in high dudgeon over this."

In short order, McWilliams signed a few documents, relinquishing his interest in the case, and Plunkett left the law offices in Piccadilly to report back to Julius on his successful missions.

Chapter
36

When the news was delivered to Westerlands House, an immediate celebration took place. The duke had his reserve champagne brought up, a fact his family took note of. Only births and marriages had formerly called for the reserve champagne.

The party was replete with good cheer and laughter, toasts were raised to the Harrisons' departure from London, to Plunkett's expertise, to Cricket's future. Annabelle was profuse in her heartfelt appreciation to the Westerlands family for all they'd done for her, particularly in terms of the Harrison settlement. As for Walingame's case, she had thanked them privately, since her mother didn't know of the earl's attempt to claim Cricket.

Sometime later, when the merrymaking and jubilation had moderated and conversation had turned to other, more mundane, subjects like Lady Jersey's upcoming rout, Annabelle made an announcement. "I think it's time our family returns to Shoreham," she said, having purposely chosen the public venue in order to lessen dissent. As shock registered on every face, she brightly added, "Cricket so adores being outside—she would prefer being in the country. As would my mother, I'm sure." Her smile was luminous. "As would I, after the excitement and tumult of the last few weeks."

There was no one at the table who dared to protest, although most would have liked to. The duke and duchess, her mother—even Duff's sisters and brother—had come to cherish Annabelle.

As for Duff, his first reaction was anger. *Excitement and tumult?* Did those bland words refer to his shooting and various lawsuits? What the fuck was she doing? But at base, perhaps, he most resented her walking away. Women didn't, as a rule, leave him. Never, actually, and his father's words came unbidden to his mind. *She has a reputation for leaving men.* In the next flashing moment, he thought about asking her to stay. But as quickly, he discarded the notion. He had never begged for a woman's favor. Nor would he now.

After a transient moment of silence, the duchess stepped into the breach and graciously said, "You and your family must come back and see us whenever you wish."

"Please stop by to see us in Shoreham as well," Annabelle replied politely.

"If you need any help at your cottage, don't hesitate to ask," the duke offered with a smile. "Our staff at Westerlands Park is at your disposal."

"Thank you. Now, if you please, Mother and I will gather our things and set off without delay. The summer evenings are pleasant for travel."

Everyone was well-mannered and urbane, helping with the arrangements, having a carriage brought up to convey the Fosters to Annabelle's town house, making their farewells with polished cordiality.

Duff helped Mrs. Foster into the carriage, then Molly and the baby, before turning last to Annabelle and extending his hand. "I wish you a pleasant journey," he murmured, steeling himself against the touch of her hand.

"Thank you," she said, placing her fingertips lightly on his palm, but not quite meeting his angry gaze. "And thank you as well for—"

"Look at me," he hissed, the taut words for her ears only.

Her gray gaze came up. "Be sensible, Duff." Then slipping her fingers from his, she reached for the handhold alongside the door and stepped up into the carriage.

A footman moved forward to shut the carriage door.

The duke signaled his driver to set off.

And a moment later, Westerlands House was devoid of guests.

Duff turned to his family assembled on the pavement, temper glittering in his eyes. "I'm off to Brooks's," he said brusquely.

"I may see you there later," Giles offered. "I'm going to Jackson's first. Why don't you come? You look as though you could use a little sparring exercise."

"Not in the mood I'm in."

No one in his family pressed him further, Duff's black scowl being explanation enough. They didn't wish anyone at Jackson's boxing saloon to suffer Duff's wrath; he was one of Gentleman Jackson's better protégés.

A short time later, when the marquis walked into Brooks's, he was greeted by one and all like the long-lost friend he was. Immediately plied with welcome-back drinks, he accepted them all, sat down with his compatriots, and proceeded to drown his bitterness in brandy.

After Annabelle and her family returned to her London house, a rushed business of packing took place, her carriage was brought out of the mews, and in extremely short order, the city was left behind.

With Molly and the babies dozing, Mrs. Foster took the first opportunity after the bustling fervor of their leave-taking to question her daughter. "I don't suppose you care to tell me what this is all about. As you know, we were quite welcome to stay at Westerlands House for the rest of the season."

Annabella's gaze turned from the carriage window, where city streets had given way to the green of the country. "Stay to what purpose, Mother?"

"To enjoy ourselves in excellent company, I'd say."

"They are not our kind, Mother. Nor will they ever be."

"You put too much stock in the ways of the *Ton*. Our family, while not of the nobility, was once prosperous and respected. You were educated as well, if not better, than ladies of the nobility—and thank God. That education has given you the opportunity to earn a position of prominence in the world."

"I know, Mama. And I thank you. But having lived"—she paused, her life unconventional by any standard—"in proximity to so many in the *Ton*, I am more aware than most of the conformist nature of society. Despite being taken up by the Westerlands, there are many in the fashionable world who look down on people like us."

"You have a lovely home. You give us a good life. Why should anyone look down on you?"

"Perhaps a man could more easily make his way in the world. Money brings certain favors and titles their way." She chose not to point out the opposite—that a woman, regardless of rank, had little control of her life.

"Don't I know. Squire Hampton was knighted."

"Exactly. But mostly, though, Mama," Annabelle said, hoping she could explain her feelings in such a way that her mother would understand, "I have attained a great deal of independence." She smiled. "And I like it."

"Then you must keep it if it makes you happy." *A shame you couldn't keep it and the marquis, too,* Mrs. Foster thought. But she smiled back at her daughter and said, instead, "I must say I will have fond memories of my time in London with the Westerlands."

"Indeed, Mama, they are very agreeable in every way." Although their heir was singularly more than agreeable. She knew what was expected of her, however. She'd known from the beginning. The time had come finally to leave their little liaison, or infatuation, or whatever folly one wished to call it, behind and set her mind on other things. Without a doubt, Duff would do the same.

"I do admit, though," her mother noted with a smile, "I am looking forward to seeing our snug little cottage again. Lovely as Westerlands House was, one couldn't but feel less than cozy in its vastness."

Annabelle chuckled. "Just so, Mama. *Cozy* is not the word to describe that splendid pile in Portman Square."

After everyone had gone off in various directions, the duke and duchess sat down to tea and tried to unravel what had gone wrong with their eldest son's liaison.

"It's a shame. I like Annabelle immensely and Duff seemed serious about her," Elspeth noted. "He's obviously angry that she left."

"But for how long, is always the question with Duff. If past behavior is any indication," the duke pointed out, "he will soon find someone else."

"No doubt you're right," the duchess said with a small frown. "He's never spent more than a few days with any one woman. I still find it a shame, though," the duchess murmured. "I found Annabelle most charming." She made a small moue. "Unlike so many noble young ladies who are—well, frankly, annoyingly simple."

"Annabelle's intelligence did appeal to Duff, I expect—as well as her beauty, of course," the duke noted. "There's no doubt she can hold her own in any conversation."

"Unlike so many ladies who pride themselves on never reading a book. Lydia and Georgina often lament on the dearth of ladies of their acquaintance who know anything beyond fashion. While our darling Annabelle writes the most delicious and scathingly funny plays."

"Not to mention poetry." The duke smiled. "And as a rule, I'm not overly fond of poetry. But hers is *au courant* and interesting."

"Like our current notable, Lord Byron."

"His poetry is engaging, I admit, but he's rather too fond of his celebrity, if you ask me."

"The poor boy has been, well . . . *poor* for so long—allow him his day in the sun, darling. You have never been poor. You don't understand." The duchess had been left penniless when her father died and her disastrous first marriage had been forced by those circumstances. "As for *our* poor boy," she went on with a smile, "I shall remain optimistic about him coming to his senses. It's time he stopped simply amusing himself with amour—don't lift your brows, sweetheart—everyone doesn't have to wait until they're over thirty to marry."

"I was just waiting for you," the duke said with a smile.

"Well, that's true," the duchess said with an answering smile. "But I for one think Duff couldn't do any better than Miss Foster. And he's very stupid if he doesn't see that for himself."

"Would you like me to talk to him?"

"How sweet of you, darling," the duchess said in a tone of voice one would use to flatter a child. "But I doubt Duff would want us to interest ourselves overmuch in his love affairs."

"Even though you do," the duke noted drolly.

"But never overtly, darling. Although I'm sorely tempted to arrange something with Miss Foster," she said in a bemused tone.

"*Arrange something?*"

Elspeth laughed. "Does that frighten you?"

"Perhaps I'm more curious—about what you could concoct that would bring our Duff to heel."

"There, you see? That's how men look at marriage. For my part, I rather consider this, say, *inchoate* thought process as a means of making our dear boy happy."

While the duchess was considering various ways she could patch up her son's relationship with Annabelle, the marquis, ignorant of his mother's machinations, was trying to drink himself into oblivion.

He wished to rid himself of the reoccurring and beguiling images of Annabelle that were assaulting—nay, *hammering* away at his senses. He was already on his second bottle, yet the incessant impressions were as potent as ever.

He decided to gamble, thinking to force himself to concentrate on other things. But he simply played by rote and instinct, unaware of his surroundings or conversations. Before long, his friends began to wonder if the stories about his problems after Waterloo were true. He didn't answer when spoken to, nor care whether he won or lost, all the time drinking brandy like water.

The worried looks passing back and forth between his friends finally became too obvious to ignore; Duff set his glass down and said with a grimace, "It's Annabelle Foster. We have been"—he paused—"seeing each other." He shrugged. "She just left."

Everyone said, "Ah . . ." and understood. Who didn't know of the celebrated lady in question, of her pattern of disposing of lovers. Not to mention the recent gossip about a child that had the entire town buzzing.

Warr was blunt enough to bring up the subject. "Did she take your child with her?"

"Celia isn't mine. She's Annabelle's sister's child." Even as he spoke, some part of him wished Cricket was his. The sensation was so startling, Duff immediately reached for the brandy bottle, refilled his glass, and tossed down the liquor.

"Walingame is claiming the child is his."

"Not anymore."

"Even with McWilliams handling the case?"

"He's off the case."

"So you are cleared of all gossip with regard to fathering a child on Miss Foster, and Walingame is as well."

Duff looked up from refilling his glass. "True and true."

"And darling Annabelle has left another blighted lover in her wake."

"So it seems," Duff muttered, lifting his glass to the table at large. "To future amours."

"That's the spirit, Darley," Lord Avon pronounced, raising his glass. "Get right back in the saddle."

After which, Duff received a great deal of advice on any number of ladies who could assuage his current black mood. He accepted everyone's recommendations with good grace, and when he quit the game and left Brooks's, he felt markedly improved, perhaps even half reconciled to Annabelle's departure.

After all, he wasn't the first man who had been discarded by the lovely Miss Foster. And no doubt, he wouldn't be the last.

He even found such empty platitudes consoling for another hour or so as he sat in his study in St. James, emptying a bottle, his gaze on the Raeburn portrait over the mantel. Then, struck by an epiphany of sorts, he suddenly came to the conclusion that he didn't actually set much store by platitudes. Putting his glass aside with the kind of slow deliberation typical of someone half in his cups, he called for Byrne. He needed Romulus saddled, he said, a change of clothes packed and a note delivered to Gray's and one to his parents.

As he waited for the man from Gray's to arrive, he surveyed the portrait with a faint smile. Annabelle couldn't have traveled very far yet. It would have taken her some time to close her house, and a carriage couldn't match the speed of prime horseflesh like Romulus.

In the midst of his reflections on his coming journey, he found the thought of seeing Cricket again was of keen interest to him as well.

Who would have thought?

Chapter
37

Duff came upon Annabelle's carriage at the third coaching stop north of London, his swift ride made more manageable in terms of pain thanks to the copious amounts of brandy he'd imbibed. He recognized the yellow primroses painted on her carriage doors, those embellishments familiar to everyone of fashion in the city. And as though to put period to any doubts, Tom was seated beside the driver.

Handing Romulus over to an ostler, the marquis entered the busy inn. Moving directly to the portly man standing at a high counter in the lobby, he said, "Would you please direct me to Miss Foster and company?"

The man who designated himself the proprietor surveyed Duff with a jaundiced gaze. "I'm not right sure she wishes to be interrupted in her dinner."

"I am a friend of hers."

"You be a mite foxed, too."

Duff almost asked if the man was her chaperone, but chose more wisely to hand over a large note. "I'm sure she won't mind the interruption," he murmured, "nor my current state of sobriety."

The man's expression changed at the sight of the banknote. Those exceeding twenty pounds were rare. "Miss Foster and

her party be in the back parlor—last room at the end," he offered, indicating the direction. "Would ye care to be announced, sir?"

Duff smiled. "That won't be necessary. Do you have champagne?"

"Sorry, sir—we don't have nothin' so fine."

"A good hock, then. As soon as may be," Duff said, and
strode away.

A few moments later, he was knocking on the door at the
end of the hall and when Annabelle's voice answered, bidding
him enter, he smiled.

Suddenly all was right with the world.

Pushing the door open, he bent low to keep from knocking
his head on the lintel and stepped into the parlor.

A chorus of gasps greeted him.

"I missed you profoundly," he said, looking directly at
Annabelle. It was the honest truth, and after drinking so long,
he wasn't capable of subtlety. "I hope I'm not imposing."

"Not in the least!" Mrs. Foster exclaimed since her daughter appeared to be speechless. "Do come in and join us, dear
boy!" she cried, jumping up and enthusiastically waving him
in.

Candles had been lit against the approaching night, and in
the flickering light, he found Annabelle more beautiful than
ever—if that were possible, he thought. Her short curls gleamed
pale and golden, her eyes were aglow, her lush mouth half-
open in surprise. And if Duff had had any doubts about what
he felt or wanted in the intervening hours, his uncertainties
instantly vanished.

Mrs. Foster immediately gave up her chair so he could sit
beside Annabelle. "Come, come, sit down, my dear boy," she
murmured, patting the back of the chair. "How very nice to
see you again," she added, since no one else seemed capable
of speech. "Are you hungry?"

It was not a question he could answer without embarrassing

himself; the hunger he felt was sharp-set and lustful. In lieu of the truth, he shook his head.

"Have a glass of wine, then," Mrs. Foster offered, thinking she might have to orchestrate this entire scenario if these two young people didn't soon find their tongues.

"I think I'll take little Cricket for a walk in the twilight," Molly interjected, leaping to her feet with Cricket dozing in her arms.

"I'll take Betty and go with you," Mrs. Foster said with a smile. "One's legs become cramped after riding in a carriage so long. A little walk will do us good."

If either of the principals had had their wits about them, they would have seen the conspiratorial smiles pass between Mrs. Foster and Molly as they exited the parlor.

But momentarily witless as they were, their gazes locked, they neither saw nor cared. Only when the door slammed did they seem to regain their senses.

"I feel as though we are in the midst of a romantic farce," Annabelle murmured, nodding at the door. "Our erstwhile chaperones have run off."

Duff grinned. "Remind me to thank them. And may I say, you look lovely—more lovely than ever, in that shade of rose."

"I gather you missed me," Annabelle noted playfully, feeling in control once again with Duff grinning at her. Feeling happy as well.

"I'm afraid I did."

"How brusquely unromantic," she teased. "You sound displeased."

"I was at first. You shouldn't have left."

"Why shouldn't I?" She could speak as plainly as he.

He frowned a little. "Because I didn't want you to."

"I don't recall you saying so at the time."

"It might have had something to do with the very public venue in which you made your announcement." He gazed at her from under his lashes. "And the surprise of it."

"Let's just say, I didn't want any problems."

"Such as?"

"Such as you asking me to stay, if you must know," she said with a twitch of her lovely nose.

"Arrogant puss."

"Duff, darling," she said with a small sigh, "we are neither of us neophytes. You and I know exactly how the game is played. And this *is* a game, whether of short duration or long."

"What if I'm interested in changing the rules?" he drawled. "What do you think of that?"

"It's still a game, darling, and frankly, I don't choose to play."

"Then marry me and we will make our own amusements in our own way, with or without rules."

"You're drunk." The scent of brandy on his breath was strong.

He shrugged. "That may be, but I'm well aware of what I'm doing."

She gave him a dubious look. "Come morning, you may not think so."

"Do you want me to beg? Is that what you want? I'm more than willing." It was curious-strange how love could turn the world upside down.

She smiled. "Please don't."

He laughed. "Good. I'm not altogether sure I could."

"Because you've never had to," she said coolly. And perhaps that was the rub—that great divide of wealth and privilege that separated them.

"Nor have *you* ever begged for love, so don't look at me so critically. Look, I brought you something," he added, deftly reverting to familiar habit when under the squinty-eyed gaze of a woman who was speaking to him in that cool tone. Fumbling in his coat pocket, he pulled out a small red leather box. "See, I am dead serious about this." Flipping open the lid, he pulled out an enormous pink diamond ring, reached for her hand, and slid the ring on her finger. "It fits. Obviously, it's meant to be as in kismet, fate, whatever you want to call it. Now, let's get married. We should be able to find a minister around here somewhere."

She was trying very hard to resist his blandishments, casual as they were. She was telling herself he was drunk and would surely regret this in the morning. She was reminding herself of her long-held reservations about marriage between unequal classes and all the misery associated with such unions. "We can't," she said, keeping her voice deliberately temperate. "Have you forgotten? You need a license."

"No, I have not forgotten," he cheerfully replied, pulling a rumpled sheet of paper from his other coat pocket. "*Voila*! And, darling, I've only drunk two bottles at the most, so I am quite rational. I'm never foxed until at least the fourth."

She didn't know if she should be relieved or not by his casual disclaimer. "Think of your parents," she added further, feeling at least one of them should be responsible. "They certainly won't approve of what you're doing."

"My God, you are difficult to convince," Duff grumbled. "Here—my parents have sent you their most obliging felicitations." Digging in his pockets once again, he came up with a scented note that he handed to her. "Now, then," he muttered when she'd finished reading his parents' good wishes, "do you require the approval of the Regent as well, because I will damned well get it for you if need be!"

"I accept."

"Maybe you require the mad king's signature as well, or the queen's, who fortunately can still write her own hand. Give the word and you shall have their approval as well," he proposed heatedly.

"I said yes."

"I hope you realize that I've never so much as *thought* about asking anyone to marry me and now when I have, all I hear is a great deal of—"He suddenly met her gaze. "You said *what*?"

"I would be happy to marry you, Lord Darley."

"Finally," he growled, although his mouth twitched into a

smile. "You are a most vexing woman. Although I say that with the highest regard and affection." His smile widened. "Actually, if you must know, I find not only your vexatiousness, but everything about you, vastly agreeable."

She laughed. "Nevertheless, I give you one last chance to change your mind, for I bring a good deal of vexation in my wake. I come with an entourage, you know."

"At the risk of offending you, darling," he teased, "Cricket figured rather largely in my decision to propose to you."

She hit him.

Or tried. Even half drunk, his reactions were superb; he caught her hand just short of his face. Then, swinging her onto his lap, he pulled her close. "You could come with an army and I'd have you," he whispered. "Satisfied?"

She nodded, tears welling in her eyes.

He gently kissed her; then, framing her face between his large hands, he smiled. "We will be happy, you and I. My word on it."

He had no idea how much his offer of happiness meant to her. But she'd lived too long in the fashionable world to naively accept such a premise. "Everyone will talk. The gossip will be brutal. You know that."

He held her gaze. "Let them talk." His smile was benign. "As the Marchioness of Darley, you may give the direct cut to whomever you please."

She shook her head. "I don't wish that."

"Even the Harrisons? Surely you would take pleasure in giving them the cut."

She grinned. "Perhaps you're right."

"You will find I am generally right," he noted roguishly.

"And you will find that I generally dislike men who think they're always right. I am independent in every way."

"Hmm . . . Perhaps we should define some of the perimeters of this marriage. I am a fiercely possessive man."

Her brows rose. "Since when, pray tell?" Darley's habit of flitting from woman to woman was well known.

"Since I met you," he declared crisply.

"Then, for the record, may I state that I am equally possessive."

"But that's not possible," he replied waggishly. "Don't you know this is a man's world?"

"Then you may have your ring back, and your proposal. My answer is rescinded."

"Perhaps we can come to some agreement," he interposed smoothly.

"An agreement on fidelity."

"Yes, on that. I fully concur. Is that better?"

"Very well, then."

"Very well, what?"

"I will marry you."

"I'm finding a minister before you change your mind again," he said briskly, lifting her from his lap and setting her on her feet.

"And find Mama, Molly, Tom, and the babies, too." She felt as though she was alight from within, she was so happy.

He was partway to the door when he turned back. "We're going to have to be married again," he said, temperate and measured. "My mother will be distrait if she can't marry off her eldest son with full pomp and ceremony."

"Why don't we talk about it?"

Half drunk or not, his skill at reading women was unimpaired. He understood this was not the time to press the issue. He smiled. "Whatever you say, darling."

Epilogue

The Marquis of Darley, long thought inexorably opposed to marriage, wed Miss Annabelle Foster, the most beautiful woman in England, in the back parlor of the White Horse Inn with her family in attendance. For a goodly sum, a minister had been found forthwith, the vows read, and before Miss Foster could fully debate all the ramifications of such an unequal union, the ceremony was over.

Which was the point, as far as the marquis was concerned, wanting what he wanted as he did.

In deference to Annabelle's apparent aversion to a fashionable wedding under the scrutiny of the entire *Ton*, a compromise was reached between the duchess's enormous guest list and Annabelle's reservations.

Duff and Annabelle were married again a month later at Westerlands Park with a select number of guests in attendance. The Regent came, making the wedding the preeminent social event of the season, but even without him, the occasion was splendid beyond belief.

And on Duff's second wedding night, when his bride told him she thought she might be with child, the marquis at first blanched. "Are you sure?" he asked, not certain he was entirely ready for fatherhood. "How can it be?"

"Surely, you jest. You have been most assiduous in your attentions of late." Her brows rose an infinitesimal distance. "Is there a problem?"

What could he say? *I just found out I could actually fall in love? Don't rush me.* "No, not at all," he murmured. "It's not a problem."

"You have eight months to get used to the idea," Annabelle said with a benevolent smile.

"Thank God. I mean—wonderful . . . perfect—really . . . absolutely perfect."

She laughed. "Is the pressure too much, Duff?"

He smiled. "Not with you beside me." And if he was uncertain of other things, of that he was not.

"You will be the best of fathers," she whispered. "Just as you are the sweetest of husbands," she added, basking in the warmth of his affectionate smile.

"And you are my own precious wife," he said, knowing he was the most fortunate of men, having found not only love but peace.

Prior to their marriage, no one in the fashionable world would have bet a penny on the Marquis of Darley marrying any time soon. Nor would those in the *Ton* have given any odds on Annabelle Foster finding a man who pleased her.

If not for that village horse fair, who knows if they would have met as they did?

But then, the Darley luck was much intertwined with horses and beautiful women; perhaps the hand of fate had intervened.

Would fate intercede once again with the next Lord Darley?

Years later in the Crimea, in the midst of war, the question is answered.

Don't miss Sylvia Day's
hot new novel
ASK FOR IT.
Available now from Brava!

George looked easily over her head to scrutinize the scene. "I say. It appears Lord Westfield is heading this way."

"Are you quite certain, Mr. Stanton?"

"Yes, my lady. Westfield is staring directly at me as we speak."

Tension coiled in the pit of her stomach. Marcus had literally frozen in place when their eyes had first met and the second glance had been even more disturbing. He was coming for her and she had no time to prepare. George looked down at her as she resumed fanning herself furiously.

Damn Marcus for coming tonight! Her first social event after three years of mourning and he unerringly sought her out within hours of her reemergence, as if he'd been impatiently waiting these last years for exactly this moment. She was well aware that that had not been the case at all. While she had been crepe-clad and sequestered in mourning, Marcus had been firmly establishing his scandalous reputation in many a lady's bedroom.

After the callous way he'd broken her heart, Elizabeth would have discounted him regardless of the circumstances but tonight especially. Enjoyment of the festivities was not her aim. She had a man she was waiting for, a man she had arranged covertly to meet. Tonight she would dedicate herself to the memory of her husband. She would find justice for Hawthorne and see it served.

The crowd parted reluctantly before Marcus and then regrouped in his wake, the movements heralding his progress toward her. And then Westfield was there, directly before her. He smiled and her pulse raced. The temptation to retreat, to flee, was great, but the moment when she could reasonably have done so passed far too swiftly.

Squaring her shoulders, Elizabeth took a deep breath. The glass in her hand began to tremble and she quickly swallowed the whole of its contents to avoid spilling it on her dress. She passed the empty vessel to George without looking. Marcus caught her hand before she could retrieve it.

Bowing low with a charming smile, his gaze never broke contact with hers. "Lady Hawthorne. Ravishing, as ever." His voice was rich and warm, reminding her of crushed velvet. "Would it be folly to hope you still have a dance available, and that you would be willing to dance it with me?"

Elizabeth's mind scrambled, attempting to discover a way to refuse. His wickedly virile energy, potent even across the room, was overwhelming in close proximity.

"I am not in attendance to dance, Lord Westfield. Ask any of the gentlemen around us."

"I've no wish to dance with them," he said drily, "so their thoughts on the matter are of no consequence to me."

She began to object when she perceived the challenge in his eyes. He smiled with devilish amusement, visibly daring her to proceed, and Elizabeth paused. She would not give him the satisfaction of thinking she was afraid to dance with him. "You may claim this next set, Lord Westfield, if you insist."

He bowed gracefully, his gaze approving. He offered his arm and led her toward the dance floor. As the musicians began to play and music rose in joyous swell through the room, the beautiful strains of the minuet began.

Turning, Marcus extended his arm toward her. She placed

her hand atop the back of his, grateful for the gloves that separated their skin. The ballroom was ablaze with candles, which cast him in a golden light and brought to her attention the strength of his shoulder as it flexed. Lashes lowered, she appraised him for signs of change.

Marcus had always been an intensely physical man, engaging in a variety of sports and activities. Impossibly, it appeared he had grown stronger, more formidable. He was power personified and Elizabeth marveled at her past naiveté in believing she could tame him. Thank God, she was no longer so foolish.

His one softness was his luxuriously rich brown hair. It shone like sable and was tied at the nape with a simple black ribbon. Even his emerald gaze was sharp, piercing with a fierce intelligence. He had a clever mind to which deceit was naught but a simple game, as she had learned at great cost to her heart and pride.

She had half expected to find the signs of dissipation so common to the indulgent life, and yet his handsome face bore no such witness. Instead, he wore the sun-kissed appearance of a man who spent much of his time outdoors. His nose was straight and aquiline over lips that were full and sensuous. At the moment those lips were turned up on one side in a half smile that was at once boyish and alluring. He remained perfectly gorgeous from the top of his head to the soles of his feet. He was watching her studying him, fully aware that she could not help but admire his handsomeness. She lowered her eyes and stared resolutely at his jabot.

The scent that clung to him enveloped her senses. It was a wonderfully manly scent of sandalwood, citrus, and Marcus's own unique essence. The flush of her skin seeped into her insides, mingling with her apprehension.

Reading her thoughts, Marcus tilted his head toward her. His voice, when it came, was low and husky. "Elizabeth. It is a long-awaited pleasure to be in your company again."

"The pleasure, Lord Westfield, is entirely yours."

"You once called me Marcus."

"It would no longer be appropriate for me to address you so informally, my lord."

His mouth tilted into a sinful grin. "I give you leave to be inappropriate with me at any time you choose. In fact, I have always relished your moments of inappropriateness."

"You have had a number of willing women who suited you just as well."

"Never, my love. You have always been separate and apart from every other female."

Elizabeth had met her share of scoundrels and rogues but always their slick confidence and overtly intimate manners left her unmoved. Marcus was so skilled at seducing women, he managed the appearance of utter sincerity. She'd once believed every declaration of adoration and devotion that had fallen from his lips. Even now, the way he looked at her with such fierce longing seemed so genuine she almost believed it.

He made her want to forget what kind of man he was—a heartless seducer. But her body would not let her forget. She felt feverish and faintly dizzy.

Take a look at "Player's Club" in
HelenKay Dimon's
hot new anthology
VIVA LAS BAD BOYS.
Available now from Brava!

"Nothing to see. The lights are off. I don't hear the air-conditioning, so I'm guessing we blew a circuit breaker or something."

"You're trying to say your kisses were so good that we blew a fuse? Try again, stud."

Zach's chuckle rumbled against her chest. He flicked back the edge of the curtain and let the light from the Strip stream into the room. "Probably from the construction. Though think how impressive the kiss thing would be."

Dumb didn't begin to describe how Jenna felt at the moment. She'd made every professional misstep imaginable. Lose control? Check. Let her desires overwhelm her good sense? Check. Let her consulting client go one step too far on the floor of her office? That was new, but still a check.

Damn hormones.

What she needed was a little decorum. Getting off the floor and out from under him would be a good start. "Okay, fun time is over."

"Most people would look at the lights being out as a message."

He felt so right there with her body curved into his. "Right. The message being to get up."

He frowned at her and managed to look adorable doing it. "I was thinking more like the opposite conclusion."

She tried to concentrate on his argument, lame as it was, but his firm body kept dragging her attention away. From the impressive bulge pressing against her thigh to his hard-as-granite everything else, she wanted him.

His pretty-boy face and easy charm had attracted her from the beginning. With every day that passed she wanted him more.

"Shouldn't you get back to your kitchen?" she asked.

"Sam has it under control. He's my second in command. He could run his own kitchen and is totally qualified to take over in my absence."

Common sense didn't seem to be working, but she tried again. "Yeah, well, we should be out there checking on the guests."

"Unless you plan to hand out flashlights, I'm not sure what you could do."

"I could . . ." Something.

"We can't do any work. We're all alone. It's dark. I'm on top of you."

"I notice you're not getting up," she muttered under her breath.

"Think of the darkness as the universe's sign we should keep on doing what we're doing." His hand rested on her breast and showed no sign of moving, so it wasn't hard to figure out what the "what" was.

"We need to go," she insisted.

"Most people wouldn't view the lights going out as a reason to stop having fun."

Then it hit her. She was having sex with Zach. On her floor. In her office. She'd even touched his ass. So much for professionalism. Nothing prepared her for Zach.

"Zach, I'm serious." More like embarrassed, but he didn't need to know that.

He lowered his head until his forehead touched her breasts.

The move sent an ache spinning from her chest to the damp space between her thighs.

"You're actually going to do it," he mumbled into the thin material separating them.

Her breath caught in her throat. "Do what?"

He skimmed his finger under the edge of her camisole and flimsy bra and outlined her nipple until it puckered. "Call a halt. Go right to the edge and pull back."

"I didn't—" She gasped when he slipped the two layers of silk down, exposing her breast.

Then he palmed her, his hand warm against her chilled skin. "Man, you're beautiful."

She couldn't speak.

"I wanted time to do this." He licked her nipple, flicking his tongue across the tight bud.

She tried to remember her name. Bartholomew something . . .

"And this." He placed his hot mouth over the tip and suckled her. Twirling his tongue over her, wetting her skin.

Someone moaned. She feared it came from deep inside of her.

"So pretty." His reverent whisper tickled against her breast.

Two more seconds and her skirt would be over her head. "Stop!"

"You still want that clipboard?"

"Yeah, so I can beat you with it."

"Well, honey, I'm not usually into that, but I'm game."

And finally, take a peek
at Diane Whiteside's
THE SOUTHERN DEVIL.
Coming next month from Brava . . .

The mantel clock began to chime.

Jessamyn's head flashed around to stare at it before she looked back at Morgan.

She forced back her body's awareness of him. "I needed him as my husband, you fool! For two hours, starting now."

"Husband?" Jealousy swept over his face.

"In a lawyer's office," she snarled back. "I have to be there with a husband in fifteen minutes, or all is lost. Damn you, let me go!"

The clock chimed again.

His eyes narrowed for a moment, then he pulled her up to him. His grip was less painful but just as inescapable as before. "A bargain then, Jessamyn. I'll play your husband for a few hours, if you'll join me in a private parlor for the same span of time afterward."

She gasped. A devil's bargain, indeed.

"Nine years ago, before you married Cyrus, I promised you revenge for what you did, and you agreed my claim was just. Two hours won't see that accomplished but it's a start," he purred, his drawl knife-edged and laced with carnal promise.

Her flight or fight instincts stirred, honed by seven years as an Army wife on the bloody Kansas prairies. She reined them in sternly: No matter how angry he'd been, surely Morgan would never harm a woman, no matter what preposterous demands he'd hurled nine years ago when she'd held him captive.

Her fingers bit into his arms, as she tried to think of another option. But if she didn't appear with a husband, she'd lose her only chance of regaining Somerset Hall, her family's old home . . .

The mantel clock sounded the third, and last, note.

She agreed to his bargain, the words like ashes in her throat. "Very well, Morgan. Now will you take me across the street to the lawyer's?"

Morgan escorted Jessamyn across the street with all the haughtiness his father would have shown escorting his mother aboard a riverboat. It was a bit of manners ingrained in him so early that he didn't need to think about it, something he'd first practiced with Jessamyn when she was five and their parents first openly hoped for a wedding between them. Such an ingrained habit was very useful when his brain seemed to have dived somewhere south of his belt buckle as soon as she'd agreed she owed him revenge.

What was he going to do first? There were so many activities he'd learned in consortium houses, of how to drive a woman insane with desire. How to leave her sated and panting, willing to do anything to repeat the experience. More than anything else, he needed to see Jessamyn aching to be touched by him again and again.

A black curl stroked her cheek in just the way he planned to later. He smiled, planning, and reached for the office door.

Ebenezer Abercrombie & Sons, Attys. At Law announced the sturdy letters on its surface.

Morgan stiffened. Her lawyer was that Abercrombie? Halpern's friend and Millicent's godfather, who Morgan had dined with last night? Who'd beamed approval as Halpern and his wife had shoved Morgan at their daughter and he'd made no mention of a wife?

Damn, damn, damn.

Jessamyn, who'd never been a fool, caught his momentary hesitation and glanced up at him.

He shook his head slightly at her and put his hand on the doorknob. Suddenly it turned under his fingers and swung open to frame Abercrombie's well-fed bulk. The man's eyes widened briefly as he took in both of his visitors.

Jessamyn leaned closer to Morgan and squeezed his arm, with all the assurance of a long-married woman. God knows he'd seen her do it with Cyrus before.

Morgan shifted himself so she could fit comfortably, as he'd seen his cousin do. She settled easily within a hand's-breadth of him and tilted her head at Abercrombie expectantly. The entire byplay took only a few seconds.

The lawyer's eyes narrowed and his mouth tightened before a polite professional mask covered his face. "Good afternoon, Evans. What an unexpected pleasure to see you here today."

Morgan smiled with all the smooth charm he'd polished as one of Bedford Forrest's spies. "The pleasure is entirely mine, Abercrombie. I've the honor of escorting my wife. Jessamyn, my dear, have you met Mr. Abercrombie?" He could have kicked himself. His Mississippi drawl was slightly heavier than usual, a telltale sign of nervousness.

Jessamyn took Abercrombie's hand, with all the charm of her aristocratic Memphis upbringing. "Yes, Mr. Abercrombie was my uncle's lawyer for years. I've known him since I was a child. Hello, sir."

Abercrombie kissed her cheek. "My dear lady, I'm so glad you were able to bring your husband." His eyes flickered to Morgan but his countenance was impassive. "Your cousin Charles and his wife are seated in my office, waiting for the reading of the will to begin. Please come with me."

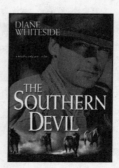